"Until the planet's magnetic field flips again," the Dr. noted, kneeling down next to another tuft and only half paying attention to him as she clipped off a tiny sample of the needle-like leaf. "I find the name appropriate...besides, Davis said I could name any new species I found, so the name sticks whether you like it or not."

"Seems unscientific if you ask me," he commented, walking around behind her as he did a quick scan of the area. Nothing but flat, barren terrain save for this odd little patch of sprinkled green.

"I didn't," Kimberly pointed out, moving onto a thicker cluster of the Santa grass further inside the perimeter. "There's no reason for you to be here. I can handle myself in the field, so feel free to head back to base whenever you like."

"Believe me, I wish I didn't have to keep babysitting your cranky ass, but it's Pegasus procedure that all scientists in the field..."

"...be escorted by region specific personnel," she finished for him. "I'm familiar with protocol. If you want to head on back early I won't say anything."

Eric smiled humorlessly. "Not happening, Doctor. Wouldn't look good on my record if you got lost out here...or worse."

"This isn't my first trip to the Antarctic," she reminded him, moving on to yet another tuft of grass and adding more clippings to her collection vial.

"Then you should be more wary of..." Eric said, suddenly stumbling forward. He caught his balance in a few awkward steps, the last of which landed squarely in the middle of a large cluster of grass.

"Are you really that clumsy!" she yelled, pitting him with another razor-sharp glare.

Frowning, he ignored her and walked back over to where he'd stumbled. There was a two inch depression where his boot had sunk into the 'hard' ground.

"That's not right," the guide said, pressing the toe of his boot next to the mark experimentally. The ground gave way as well, soft to the touch. "The ground should be frozen."

"Step aside," Kimberly urged, suddenly curious. She pulled off her thin glove and touched the light brown soil with her fingertips. She pulled back, brushed off the dirt on her pant-leg, and put her glove back on. "I'd hesitate to say it's warm, but there's definitely a heat source underneath. The ground is moist beneath the surface."

"Wait a second," Eric said, gently nudging her aside. "I tripped on something hard."

The guide kicked the tip of his boot into the imprint, resulting with a hard 'thud' on impact. He repeated twice more, then dragged his toe sideways, revealing some type of rock beneath.

"Stop!" she said, eyes gleaming. "Step back."

Eric pulled his boot away as Kimberly knelt down next to the sloppy excavation. She brushed aside the top layer of dirt with her hands, ignoring the mess it made on her gloves. Within a moment she had the edge of the stone visible...a perfect 90 degree angle running laterally.

Eric knelt down beside her. "That's manmade."

"Thank you for pointing out the obvious," she snipped, but her attention was on the artifact. This didn't make any sense.

"I don't recognize the material," Eric said, ignoring the banter, "and it's perfectly smooth. Must be something recent. Let me see if I can dig it out...unless you have any objections?"

"Go ahead," she said, standing up and taking a step back.

Eric pulled a small shovel out of his pack and went to work on the stone. The dirt pulled away easily, as it was all soft beneath the half inch of snow that covered the otherwise frozen ground. Below the surface the stone

STAR FORCE

Origin Series

1 – Inception

2 – Integration

3 – Nemesis

4 – Trailblazer

Inception

1

December 27, 2022

"Watch where you're stepping!" Dr. Travis yelped as he crunched a delicate green stalk beneath his boot.

"Whoops," her escort said, stepping back into the thin Antarctic snowpack.

She knelt down next to the tiny plant he'd smashed into the hard, frozen ground and glared up at him. "I don't believe you!"

"*Sorry*..." Eric said, overemphasizing the word. "It's not like it's the only one here."

"There shouldn't be anything here," Kimberly reminded him. "So would you please try and avoid killing anything else?"

"It's grass," he argued. "Stepping on it doesn't kill it."

"Santa grass," she corrected him, standing up and looking around. There were small tufts of the hardy green plants spread around the windswept area that only four weeks ago had revealed itself to Pegasus's orbital satellites...a tiny point of green in the center of Antarctica's bone white mass.

"I can't believe you're calling it that," the Antarctic guide, also an employee of the multi-national Pegasus Corporation, reiterated from an earlier discussion. "We're at the *South* Pole."

extended down more than a foot, and continued laterally for more than a meter.

"Stop," Dr. Travis said after several minutes of watching him dig. "It's too big."

"You think?" he said sarcastically, brushing off the half meter wide top that he'd cleared. The stone was a dark green, almost black, and clashed violently with naturalistic motif of snow, dirt, and Santa grass.

Kimberly's face went blank as Eric shuffled his feet and accidentally kicked a bit of snow onto the stone...where the tiny flakes disappeared as they melted.

"What?" Eric asked, glancing down at his feet where her eye line indicated.

The Dr. pulled off her dirty glove and touched the stone surface with her bare hand, then glanced up at Eric. "It's warm."

The guide frowned and pulled off his own glove, placing his hand next to hers on the smooth, dirty surface. His eyes widened in confirmation.

"We have to call this in," he said firmly.

"You think?" she said mockingly.

"Do you know what it is?" he asked in all seriousness.

"No, I don't," she admitted. "But I know it shouldn't be in the Antarctic."

Eric stood up and pulled off his pack, digging out a small locator beacon and attaching it to an expandable tripod which he planted firmly into the soft ground next to the stone. He activated the navigational beacon and checked it against his Pegasus issue GPS wristband.

"Alright, let's go," he said, offering his hand and pulling Dr. Travis to her feet. "We should be able to get an initial excavation team back here tomorrow morning."

"Hold on a second," she said, digging out a small camera. Kimberly took several shots of the 'rock' up close, then stepped back and added more from a wider perspective.

"Step next to it," she urged Eric. "I need a size comparison."

The guide walked over to the stone and knelt down beside where he had been digging.

"Alright," she said after adding another two shots. "Now we can go."

2

5 months later...

Sean Davis cinched his belt tighter as the helicopter lifted off from Pegasus's main Antarctic base and began its 150 kilometer journey out to the dig site. The winds buffeted them around a bit, the first prelude to a storm front rolling in, but the pilot had little difficulty getting them into the air and on their way. The CEO and owner of Pegasus Corporation glanced out the window of the cramped chopper as the icy, barren landscape passed beneath them, his mind elsewhere.

Sitting across from him Eric Shoball touched his earpiece as an incoming transmission gave him an update on the dig site, which he'd been tasked with overseeing since the discovery. He glanced over at Davis.

"They've finished the widening."

"Half a meter?"

Eric nodded. "Just before they ran out of drill bits."

"Impressive," Davis mewed.

"You don't know the half of it," Eric understated.

"Your team knows to wait, I presume?"

"No one's going in before we arrive," Eric assured him.

"How long?"

Eric glanced outside unnecessarily as he thought. "Given the tailwind, I'd say an hour at most."

Davis nodded and returned his gaze to the snow covered landscape passing by outside the window. One more hour...then Human history would make an abrupt change in direction. For the better, he hoped.

The Pegasus helicopter landed on a small, makeshift pad next to a cluster of tents, ostensibly a makeshift camp and research site...but that was just cover for the real project that lay beneath the white camouflaged dome that covered the dig site half a kilometer to the east. Eric led the CEO out of the chopper and onto the back of a small four wheeler that had been extended as a three-seater.

After strapping his boss on Eric drove them across the barren landscape, swerving sideways microscopically to hit a small tuft of Santa grass that lay just outside the dome. A few meters later he slowed to a creep and drove underneath the white fabric of the largely flat dome that was hiding their excavation from satellite surveillance. Thus far the ruse had worked, and they'd been allowed to work on the recovery project with anonymity.

Underneath the canopy lay several piles of dirt, the nearest of which had a large chunk eaten out of it. Pegasus personnel had slowly been hauling the dirt away, one backpack full at a time, back to base where it could be disposed of discretely. With the blanket white snow cover, any local spreading measures would be easily visible.

In the center of the six mounds stood the top of a metallic catwalk disappearing below ground. As Davis followed Eric to the entry railing he caught his first glimpse of the top of the subsurface structure.

"Amazing," he said under his breath as he paused to look over the smooth green/black stone. One corner of it had been excavated, but it clearly stretched much farther out than the acre-wide area that they'd uncovered. Less than a meter away from the catwalk, the top of the structure seemed to draw his hand towards it. Kneeling down and reaching through the railing bars, Davis brushed his fingertips along the edge.

"It is warm," he commented, studying the strange material.

"A lot more so below," Eric said, waiting patiently. "You'll want to leave your parka here."

Davis pried his eyes away from the artifact and stood up, noticing that Eric had already shed his winter weather gear. He did likewise, handing his hat to a nearby worker. His parka he reluctantly unzipped and discarded as well, but a few steps down the catwalk stairs and a wall of warm air hit him.

"Are you sure there are no geothermal vents?"

"Not that we can find," Eric answered as they descended down into the hole they'd painstakingly excavated around the edge of the massive artifact. "The heat appears to be originating solely from the stone."

"Have you determined a size or shape?"

"I can give you a ball park estimate...the stone continues to defy conventional scans. All our equipment says it's not there, even the seismogram. However, we have been able to get some hits on the rocks around the structure. It's sketchy, but I'd have to guess this thing is bigger than any structure on Earth."

Davis reached ahead and grabbed his shoulder, prompting him to stop. "Say again?"

Eric frowned. "We can't say for sure, and I hate to speculate, but it appears to be a massive pyramid, extending well below the bedrock. If you look down you can see it jut out..."

Davis looked over the edge of the railing and saw what he meant. Three flights down and the catwalk extended laterally before disappearing into the sidewall of dirt. Beneath the metallic grate he could clearly see another flat top of green/black stone.

"Best guess..." Davis reiterated.

"At least a mile wide, maybe a lot more. We really can't tell without digging the whole thing out."

"Unfortunately that's not an option," the Pegasus CEO said as the pair continued walking down. "We can't let anyone else know of this, so we have to work with as small a team as possible. Looks like you've found your assignment for the next decade."

"Hey, as long as the pay is good," Eric offered sarcastically.

"Doubled, as of now."

The other man's eyes narrowed. "You are serious about this..."

"Very," Davis confirmed as they reached the bottom of the stairs. A long tunnel into the dirt wall lay before them, running on top of the second level of the pyramid. "If this gets out, we'll lose all access and possibly start World War III in the process. We *have* to keep this a secret."

"What exactly do you think we've got?" Eric asked as they entered the tunnel.

"Two possibilities as I see it. One...this is evidence of technology far exceeding ours possessed by our ancestors. Why we lost it, who knows? We've had evidence of technological dark ages before, though nothing ever on this level recorded."

"What's option two?"

"Evidence of technology far exceeding ours possessed by someone else," he answered ominously as the end of the tunnel came into sight.

Eric's face flickered with light as they passed under staggered flood lamps attached to the ceiling at regular intervals. "You're talking about aliens?"

"Do you have any other possibilities to offer?" Davis asked, half serious.

"Elves," Eric answered deadpan.

Davis raised an eyebrow.

"You're asking the wrong person," the guide explained. "I deal with the here and now. History is a mystery to me."

"It has a special interest to me..."

Eric studied his face as they took to a second set of stairs going down even further. "I get the feeling this isn't the first...*unusual* thing you've found."

Davis glanced at him approvingly. "There have been a few unexplained archeological discoveries that have come to my attention, and I'll admit, I've been actively searching for others...but nothing even remotely comparable with this."

"What about this stone?"

"I've never heard of anything like this. All of the unusual things were cultural, not technological, but I always suspected there was something more behind it all."

When they reached the bottom of the stairs they emerged into a much larger cavern. The top of the pyramid had been cleared off for about the size of a football field with support struts and panels covering the two story high ceiling.

Davis stepped off the catwalk and onto the surface of the pyramid. Strangely it felt almost soft beneath his feet.

"It's an illusion," Eric informed him. He'd felt the same thing when he'd first walked across the mysterious stone. "Trust me, it's the hardest stuff I've ever come across. Case in point," he said, gesturing to a heap of damaged drill bits to their left.

"The laser had no effect?"

"Damn stuff soaks up energy like a sponge. We couldn't even make it hot to the touch. Two seconds after the laser shuts off, it's the same temperature as the rest...78.2 degrees Fahrenheit."

"You said none of the scanners worked?"

"Completely useless. I have a feeling the stone is absorbing the signal."

"How did you find the door?"

"Look down."

Davis frowned and looked at the surface of the pyramid beneath him. It was dirty, with many footprints crisscrossing in multiple directions, but underneath the grime were faint grooves.

"Led us right to it," Eric explained, "though we didn't know for sure until we did a thorough examination of the surface. The door seams are nearly invisible, thinner than a sheet of paper."

The pair followed the intricate scrollwork across the pyramid surface until it intersected with four other 'lines' which combined into a single, short river of markings that dead ended against the wall...a wall that now sported a narrow hole in the center that led to a dark interior.

Off to the side the expedition team was standing by, six men in all, one of which handed Eric an equipment pack and sidearm. Davis noticed that the rest of the team was equally armed.

The guide noticed his boss's glance. "I've watched far too many movies to even think about going in there unarmed. Could be all manner of creepy things."

"Where's my pack?"

"We'll carry everything we need. You don't have to worry about it," Liam said, standing a full head taller than Davis and twice his mass.

"I may have recently hit the half century mark, but I'm not an invalid," he argued. "Get me a duplicate pack."

Liam nodded, offering no argument, and retreated to an equipment bench filled with all sorts of gear set up against the far wall.

"And a sidearm," he added, turning to look at Eric. "If we're going to run into a hoard of zombies I want to be prepared."

"Sam, get the man a weapon."

A blonde-headed man in full gear smiled and detached his own hip holster and tossed it to Eric, then went to grab a second for himself.

Eric graciously handed it to Davis. "Remember to shoot for the head."

Davis accepted it with a rueful smile and attached the belt around his narrow waist. "I presume no one has gone in yet?"

Eric glanced to the others.

"None yet, as per your orders, sir," Liam said, returning with a generic pack of equipment. "Spare mags in the left pouch."

"Thank you," the CEO said, accepting the pack and snugging the straps to match his dimensions.

Sam returned with a new sidearm and several two meter long glowrods, one of which he tossed to Eric.

The lead guide thumbed on the activation switch and the entire length of the rod lit up with a bright orange glow. "With your permission?"

"Proceed," Davis allowed, motioning to the man with the pre-requested camera gear. "Make sure you get every second from entry to exit."

"Alright fellas, who wants to go first?" Eric said lightheartedly, already heading there himself.

"That would be me," Liam said, placing a hand in front of him.

"Be my guest," he relented as Liam squeezed his linebacker-sized frame through the tiny gap.

3

Eric stepped up and over the bottom edge of the hole in the foot-thick door and emerged into a hallway lit only by his and Liam's glowrods. It was ovoid, with the floor the only flat exception to the elegant curve, which extended upwards a good 10 meters. He stepped aside to make room for the others, guestimating the width of the hallway at the base at four meters, then widening up above head height to maybe five or six. The video recorder that Adam was carrying had a distance finder that would record all dimensions for later analysis, but regardless of the exact measurements it was the largest hallway he'd ever seen.

Davis came through fifth in line, and took everything in with a discerning glance. At the far edge of their visual range the hallway ended in a junction, but before that were two doorways, one on each wall. Both were sealed shut, with no visible opening mechanisms.

Eric noticed his line of interest and walked over to the tall doorway on the left and gave it a closer look under the direct light of his glowrod. It wasn't ovoid, rather it was a straight rectangle, beveled to match the curve of the hallway. There was a narrow slit down the middle that wavered slightly at chest height.

Taking a step closer and holding up his light bar, Eric ran the fingers of his other hand over the warm material of the door and felt a slight depression where the line wavered. It was minute, but visible now that he knew what to look for.

A moment after his hand touched the slightly recessed surface the entire block of rock-like material pushed out towards him, prompting an involuntary jump backwards that nearly sent Eric to the floor as he stubbed over his own booted feet.

"Steady," Davis calmed as the curved door panel slid out into the hallway then split in two, sliding laterally to open the doorway. He waited until the smoothly gliding panels came to a halt then walked up alongside Eric, who was holding his ground while peering inside.

"Liam..." the guide urged.

The taller man nodded, barely visible in the shadows cast by the orange lights, and walked inside, his glowrod held in front of him, both defensively and to provide maximum light. All the expedition team members were jittery...only Davis seemed to have a steady hand, though whether that was out of ignorance or experience was unclear. The others had had days to observe, wonder, and worry about the mysterious structure...while Davis had just arrived and perhaps was a bit too eager for his own good.

Or so Eric wondered as the CEO followed Liam inside without hesitation. He went in just behind his boss, noticing more smooth lines to the geometry of the large room which clashed with the blocky outside of the pyramid. But what drew their immediate attention were the racks of egg-like pods spread out in concentric rings, three high and what looked like four deep. Eric guessed at more than 100 total as they walked to the center of the formation where there was a low pit.

Two stair steps depressed into the floor was a reflective circle a little over a meter wide. Around it were three curved, low seated benches with gaps in between. Liam crossed the center circle enroute to the other side and began to step over the far bench when the room suddenly lit up with a non-orange glow.

Above the reflective circle a holographic icon appeared, glowing deep red. It was a symbol of some kind, similar in script to Chinese, but unlike any language that

Davis had ever seen...and given that he spoke five he was something of an expert on linguistics.

"It has power," Eric noted, bypassing the obvious 'holographic technology shouldn't exist' issue. "Don't suppose there's a light switch anywhere?"

Sam didn't feel so generous. "How is this possible?" he asked, looking at Davis who was studying the floating and slowly rotating symbol intently.

"I don't know," he said slowly, carefully cataloging his thoughts as they flew through various permutations. "But I have a feeling that the answer to that question is going to rewrite our history books."

"No shit," Sam echoed, ignoring the hologram as he walked over to one of the pod racks. The top of the 'egg' was open, with a curved depression inside yet well above the bottom. He poked the end of his glowrod into the depression and it sank into the smooth material a few inches deep.

"I think these are bunks," he offered as the material reformed when he withdrew the rod.

"Heated too," Kevin added as he felt another one on the opposite side of the hologram.

"Bunks for who?" Eric asked. "Who used to live in Antarctica?"

"Some say the legend of Atlantis originated here," Davis offered, reaching a hand out to touch the symbol. To his surprise the hologram resisted the pressure and wouldn't allow his hand to pass through. "Interesting."

"Another chamber," Liam's voice called out from behind the far rows of bunks. He was out of sight, but the ambient glow from his rod marked his location.

"Alright, everyone spread out and give me a check of the room," Eric ordered. "Liam stay put."

"Got an alcove," Sam's voice announced as Davis and Eric remained at the central hologram.

"Another here," Kevin reported.

Eric waited for the others to conduct their search, but nothing else was found aside from more bunks.

"Sir?" the guide prodded.

Reluctantly Davis stepped back from the hologram and followed Eric across the room, taking a closer look at the pods as he passed them by enroute to Sam's position.

"Storage, by the look of it," the man surmised as they walked up. "Don't know how to open the doors though."

Davis frowned as he saw the problem. The alcove was the equivalent of a huge walk-in closet, with clearly visible containers protruding up from the floor, coming out from the walls, and hanging down from the ceiling. None of the curved structures had ornamentation of any kind...no edges, symbols, ridges, bumps, or hairline gaps to indicate their function.

On impulse Davis reached out and touched one of the wall mounted pods...nothing happened.

"Hold on," Eric said as an idea struck him. He reached out his hand and pressed his fingertips on the top of the smooth, almost soft material, finding himself flinching backward again when the material seemed to melt as the pod morphed into a flat workbench taking up a third of the space in the alcove.

Gleaming like forgotten treasures were five objects neatly aligned in small niches. Each held jewel-like components in metallic sheaths.

"What the hell?" Eric asked, not wanting to touch anything again.

"Gloves," Davis commented, pulling his thin hand protection off. He reached to the right and touched another wall mounted pod. It extended as well, revealing three larger objects, also gleaming with jeweled insets.

"What do you think they are?" Sam asked, taking a closer look but knowing better than to get grabby...though the objects did seem to invite curiosity.

"As much as I want to know," Davis said wisely, "there's too much here to investigate in one trip. Let's focus on a general inventory for now."

He touched the pod again and it retracted back to its storage position, once again hiding and protecting the items it contained.

Eric touched the other and hefted his rod in front of him, motioning toward the next point of interest.

"Large room, multiple alcoves," Liam reported, standing in the archway.

"Go ahead," Eric indicated.

With his glowrod moving inside, the adjunct to the 'barracks' revealed several individual compartments set within the walls, bracketed by hourglass-shaped columns in the center, six in total.

"Lavatory," Davis guessed, more on instinct than deduction. The architecture was altogether unfamiliar.

Eric approached one of the columns and circled it, noting that the center had three deep depressions. Not wanting to risk his fingers, he pointed the tip of his glowrod into the hole...where it was met with the crackle of what looked like a forcefield, at least according to Star Wars standards. He'd never seen anything in real life remotely similar.

Liam managed to open one of the chambers, noting an entirely empty interior of the roughly cylindrical chamber. "Shower maybe?"

Davis glanced around, noting that there were no other exits. "Let's move on."

Investigation of the other alcove resulted with similar, but not exactly duplicate containers. He really had no idea what they were, but the feel of the location suggested residential support facilities...but which was the restroom or kitchen he couldn't tell for sure, perhaps neither, and he had the feeling he could spend the next 24 hours in the room and still not find out. He had to squelch his curiosity for the moment and keep the team moving.

Remembering the size estimate Eric had quoted him, he chose to bypass the other door and directed the team forward toward the end of the hall, which split in a curvy T-junction. They took the left branch, dropping a small glow stick on the floor to mark their passage. If the pyramid was as big as suggested, they didn't want to get lost inside.

They bypassed more doors enroute to an even larger spherical atrium that sprouted two additional hallways. Attempting to proceed towards the center of the pyramid, Davis headed the team to the right, bypassing yet more doors until they reached a series of ramps heading up and down.

Upon closer inspection the ramps resolved into stairs, with random block-like protrusions providing footholds.

"Sam, Kevin, Adam...head up one level and report. Liam, Henry, Cam...down one."

He received confirmation nods, then his team silently split and disappeared with their diminishing glows never completely fading from view.

"We're going to need a much larger team," he whispered to Davis.

"I know," the CEO agreed. "But we can't bring in too many people without risking a security breach."

"Humans or aliens?" Eric asked lightly.

"60/40...our hands opened the locks."

"Point," Eric conceded.

"It'll take some time, but I can assemble a 50 man team of experts from Pegasus personnel...maybe a month."

"My people can map out the place in the interim," Eric offered. "But I have a feeling that 50 isn't going to cut it."

"We need to take this slow," Davis warned. "The most important thing right now is to keep this secret. We can and will take our time. I don't want to squander this opportunity."

"I hear that," Eric agreed, "but we're still going to need more men."

"We'll get them, one way or another," Davis promised as Sam ran back up the ramp and into view.

"Boss, you've got to see this," he said, slightly panting and eyes wide in awe.

"What is it?"

"I don't know, but it's big."

"Go ahead," Eric said, "I'll wait here."

Davis nodded and followed Sam down the ramp, taking care to watch his steps. The blocks were uneven, so he had to dance around a bit, but the descent wasn't overly difficult. They emerged into another hallway with a distinctive orange glow coming from an offset atrium. He followed Sam inside and found the other two men standing on the edge of some type of hip-high bench.

"Look down," Sam gestured as Davis joined the others, suddenly realizing that it wasn't a bench, but a railing of some sort. The glow of their rods didn't extend to wherever the far wall was, but it did outline the ceiling just a few meters above their heads. He looked down, but saw nothing.

"What am I looking for?"

"Step back," Sam told the others as he took Davis's glowrod from him. "Look again."

As their illumination sticks moved back from the edge and lessened their glow, Davis was able to spot a tiny dot in the blackness below them, but couldn't make out what it was. He had to squint to confirm that he wasn't seeing things.

"That dot?" he asked.

"It's my glowrod," Adam said.

Davis did a double take, then the sheer size of the chamber struck him. It had to be at least 100 meters down, if not more.

"Big is right," he agreed.

4

It took them more than an hour to navigate their way down the ramp system to the main floor where Adam's glowrod lay, during which they realized that the large scale of the hallways and rooms on the upper levels expanded drastically below. The ramps broadened to the size of a freeway, with the individual blocks looking more like basketball courts than steps. Along both sides the smaller steps remained, allowing the Humans access, otherwise they would have had quite a bit of climbing to do.

The 'main floor' wasn't the bottom of the pyramid, the ramps continued on lower, but Davis and the expedition team didn't want to press their luck just yet, so they exited into the great chamber and headed towards the tiny glow in front of them.

"Is it just me, or are we too low?" Eric asked after walking several hundred meters from the entrance. Their small light sources didn't extend far into the room, and it felt as if they were walking in a dark mist without sign of ceiling or walls.

"I was thinking the same thing," Davis said walking on his right. "Perhaps the floor here isn't entirely flat."

"Hold up!" Liam's booming voice announced.

"What?" Eric asked, taking two steps towards him on the left.

"Something over there I think," he said, pointing off into the darkness. There was some sort of object, barely visible, picking up a small reflection from the glowrods.

Eric pulled out another small glow stick, snap-activating it and dropping it on the floor to mark their position. In the distance behind them was another marking the location of the ramp, though it was now too far away to be seen without turning off their glowrods for contrast.

They'd been following a straight line trajectory from the entrance towards the distant light source, and Eric knew better than to start wandering around in the dark. With their waypoint marked, they deviated from their route and headed for the object Liam had spotted.

"Bones," Sam pronounced when they came closer.

Eric wasn't sure until he got a closer look, but as he knelt down next to the pieces of skeleton he nodded his agreement. In the orange light they looked odd, but bones they were, and large at that. "Not Human."

Davis stooped down next to him and began studying the skeleton intently. Eric watched the older man quizzically until his eyes widened with surprise or alarm, Eric wasn't sure which.

"What is it?" he asked, glancing around.

"I've seen one of these before," Davis admitted. "In a museum."

Eric frowned. He couldn't make out what the tangled mess was.

"Holy shit," Kevin said as he suddenly made the connection.

"What is it?" Eric demanded.

"It's a dinosaur," Liam said slowly as his mind sorted out the skeleton. "Raptor I'd guess."

Eric turned to Davis's orange-lit face. "Seriously?"

"I believe so," he answered as Cam walked a long circle around the skeleton, recording all angles.

"Hey, there's something else," he noted when he got to the opposite side. He pointed with his foot.

Eric and Davis circled around to get a better look.

Loosely shackled to the wrist bone was some type of object, similarly jeweled to the items found in the 'storage closet' but definitely different in shape.

"Is it wearing that?" Adam asked.

"Some kind of tracking device," Sam offered. "This place is big enough to be a zoo."

Davis reached out and touched the glittering device. "I have no idea."

Eric pulled out another glow stick and snapped it on. "Mark and move on. We've got a lot to see."

Reluctantly Davis agreed and stood up. He followed Eric and the others back to the waypoint marker, then they headed on towards the glowrod which, ironically, should have been near the 'edge' of the room rather than the center based on where it had been dropped from. He was beginning to wonder just how massive this pyramid really was.

They passed three more small skeletons that popped up within glow-range, two Raptors by the look of it plus another slightly larger one that none of them could guess at. Each of them also wore some sort of device on their wrist bones.

"It keeps getting higher," Eric noted of the glowrod's position.

"So far this room has been entirely flat," Davis commented. "I'm interested in seeing what it's laying on. This room must have some purpose."

"Holding pens, maybe?" Kevin guessed.

"That'd explain the size," Eric agreed.

"I doubt it," Davis said, his eyes focused on the ever rising position of the glowrod in front of them. "There were no gates."

"Not to mention the size of those ramps," Liam added.

"So what, you're saying the dinos built this place?" Kevin asked, half laughing.

"Or giant aliens," Eric responded. "We don't know what we're dealing with here, so let's have less guessing and a little more shut the hell up."

"Agreed," Liam said, mildly frustrated. The lack of visible objects was beginning to wear on him.

"Here's something new," Adam pointed out, bringing the butt of his glowrod over a small depression in the floor. "Looks like it was melted."

Eric knelt down next to the thumb-sized mark on the otherwise perfectly smooth floor. Given how hard it had been to cut through the outer wall, whatever had damaged the stone-like material here must have been intense. He looked up, unable to see anything, wondering if they were in some kind of smelting factory. Adam was right, the mark in the floor had been melted.

"Watch your step," he warned, getting back to his feet and moving on. "There could be more."

Liam paused when he crossed over the mark, letting the others get a few steps ahead of him. He knelt down and rubbed his massive index finger through the groove. "Weaponsfire, maybe," he whispered to himself, then walked off to rejoin the group.

Adam's glowrod was still a ways off, but the dot of light was beginning to elongate back into a line so Eric knew they were getting closer. It was still several meters up off the floor, at least, though guessing into the darkness was almost pointless. All the orange glows from the team's rods showed was a wide expanse of flat, featureless floor...along with another skeleton off to the far right just at the edge of the shadows.

"Now there's something," Sam pointed out ahead of them. The floor suddenly ended and a ridge appeared.

"Spread out," Eric ordered. "Let's make better use of our light."

Liam and Sam veered off to the left while Kevin and Henry went right, leaving rod-less Adam with Cam, Davis, and Eric in the center.

"Take a close look," Cam said, tossing his rod to Adam while he adjusted his shoulder-mounted camera for a more panoramic view.

"Thanks," he said, catching the rod midair before walking up to the ridge. It stood about two meters tall with a smooth edge on top and, thanks to the light from the others, appeared to be vaguely curved, like the outside edge of a giant circle.

"Adam, stay put," Eric yelled eerily...there wasn't even a trace of echo in the place, "Liam, Henry, scout the perimeter of that thing. See if it circles around to the other side."

The two pairs and their glowrods headed off, eventually disappearing around the curve of the ridge. Eric walked up beside Adam and set his glowrod against the wall, then cupped his hands together to create a makeshift step. "Up you go."

Adam slid his glowrod up over the edge of the ridge so the top would be lighted then stepped into Eric's hands with his right foot while steadying himself against the ridge with his left hand. One solid heave on the guide's part and his friend was chest-high up on the wall.

Adam bent forward at the waist and crawled onto the top, feeling his arms sink in a bit on the soft material. He grabbed the glowrod and stood up, looking back down at Eric. "I don't see anything, but the top is padded. Feels like a wrestling mat."

Eric poked the side of the ridge experimentally, feeling the slight give there as well.

Suddenly his radio crackled to life. "We found another skeleton," Liam's voice reported. "This one is huge and its tail is hanging off the rise."

Eric pressed the call button.

"Have you made it all the way around?"

"No, not yet, but it does...hold on. Sam just found a set of stairs. Some sort of workstation on top too."

"Stay put, we're coming to you." He turned to face Davis who was standing a few meters behind him. "Did you get all that?"

"Yes."

"Let's go," Eric said, leading the trio off to the left. Adam followed on top.

Just before they got to the stairs, the giant skeleton came into view, partially blocking out the light from Liam's glowrod on the other side.

"Holy shit that's huge," Adam said, seeing a bit more from his vantage point than the others. He paused when he reached the bones, then cautiously wiggled his way through the tail spines to get to the other side. The men on the floor had it easier and walked through the small opening underneath next to the wall. Not far after they saw the short staircase, with Liam waiting for them at the top, his glowrod illuminating the misplaced stepping stones beneath him.

"Looks like this place was designed for both them and us," Davis commented as he climbed up. Sam meanwhile had already activated another of the holograms...this time with a different, yet similar symbol. It was floating above another reflective circle on the ground, bracketed by several workbenches with beveled tops...at least that's what they looked like. Their actual function was mere conjecture at this point.

Davis recalled how the other hologram had been solid and reached out to confirm the fact on this one as well. As soon as his ungloved hand touched the burnt yellow symbol the workbenches lit up with glowing symbols and an array of floating holographic icons in a multitude of colors.

"Alien computer station inside a dinosaur pen," Sam said despite the harsh glare that Eric was giving him. "What the hell is this place...sir," he added, looking at Davis.

"For the first time in my life," Davis had to admit, "I truly do not have a clue. It seems you are right, Mr. Shoball," he added, still looking at the entrancing workstation icons. "We are going to need more men. A lot more."

5

18 months later…

Sean Davis stepped out of the elevator on the 45th floor of Pegasus Corporate headquarters in Phoenix, Arizona nervous but hiding that fact extremely well. His outward demeanor was tight and formal, as was usual, but the meeting he was about to step into was going to be the most important of his life to date…and would decide the course of events for both himself and his company for the next decade.

He walked across the small foyer at the elevator hub and opened one of two massive doors a crack and slid through into the main conference room.

"Thank you for coming," he said casually as he closed, locked, and privacy sealed the door.

"Thank *you*," Mark Neville, CEO of Dynamics Corp and a longtime associate of Davis's responded pithily. "You've been out of the country for more than a year now. Some of us were wondering if you'd retired and forgotten to inform your secretary."

Davis smiled. "My apologies. A high priority Pegasus project has been consuming my full attention, and will continue to do so in the near future. However, I felt it was time to make you all aware of a very lucrative business proposal I'm floating in concert with the project."

"You need investment capital," Richard Blark guessed.

"Indeed...though the word 'need' is variable. I've already devoted a third of Pegasus's operating budget to the project, along with half of my own assets. That is sufficient to sustain the endeavor, but will not allow for fast implementation. The more capital investment outside of Pegasus I can acquire, the quicker the timetable will proceed."

"Alright, I'm curious," Sarah Draken said with a knowing smile. "What have you got cooking this time?"

"Something grand...and something not yet in the public's eye, which fortunately leaves us with a window of opportunity to exploit. Thus I am coming to you for financial assistance to make sure we utilize that window as much as possible. As you all know, space technology is in its infancy and aside from a couple of moon bases and a handful of tourist facilities in orbit, the only commercial viability of such technology is tied to the launching, maintenance, and recovery of the growing satellite network in orbit. I am here to tell you that there is a much more lucrative angle."

Davis reached down to the tabletop that spread the length of the 33 seated potential investors and activated the wall mounted display screen.

"I give you Star Force...a splinter company from Pegasus. Startup costs will be astronomically high, but the tradeoff is a virtual monopoly on the space industry that does not yet exist. Unlike other commercial endeavors, space is the hardest, because infrastructure is required. If you want to build a shoe factory in Ohio, you purchase the land, contract a builder, and get the ball rolling. In space, you have to build not only the facility, but the land as well, in the form of orbital habitats."

Davis adjusted the display to show several proposed schematics.

"Not only that, you have to build the transportation infrastructure necessary to reach orbit...and the housing for the workers...entertainment facilities...waste disposal...education, and so on. Space is empty, and in order to work in it you must build EVERYTHING. This is why the market for space technology and exploration is limited, and the market for space colonization is nil. Until now."

"Star Force, thanks to several new technologies that my aforementioned project is already beginning to provide, will make it economically viable to take commerce, industry, and habitation to orbit and beyond. As I said, the startup costs are high, which will discourage competition. Once we get up and running it will be far more economical for a nation, company, or individual to buy services or facilities from us rather than devote the time, personnel, and research necessary to build their own space program...thus giving us a monopoly until such a time that another organization can make the transition and close the technological gap."

Davis switched the prototype designs to a map of the Earth and its orbital tracks.

"Now, many of you are probably thinking 'what's the point, there's nothing in space of value beyond vacation potential.' Some of you are also probably conceding that there are military concerns given the reliance on satellites for communication and navigation, but beyond that you don't see any value. The rest of the planet agrees with you...and they are equally wrong. Space is more valuable, and potentially more lucrative, than all of the surface economies *combined*."

"How you say? Well, I'll bottom line this for you. It's new LAND."

Several of the assembled members laughed, but Davis waved off their amusement.

"Consider this...what would happen if, by tomorrow morning, a new continent the size of the United States, or even half the Unites States, just appeared in the middle of the Pacific Ocean? Would anybody care?"

He let that thought hang for a moment.

"You're damn right they would. And the fight to possess it could very well start World War III. Now, if someone were to ask you what was the point of possessing that land, what would you tell them? There's nothing there at the moment. No markets to invest in, no new discoveries to exploit, just empty land."

No one was laughing now. In fact they all seemed to be in 'think' mode, so Davis pressed on.

"Look back to history for what happened when new land was discovered. Columbus came to North America by accident, and no one cared. He came back again, four times in total, and died thinking he was a failure, but his discovery sparked a landgrab of never before seen proportions in which nation was pitted against nation to cross the Atlantic and claim lands, resources, and gold for themselves as well as to keep their rivals from attaining the same and gaining an advantage over them."

"In the beginning nobody cared...until somebody figured out there were riches and glory to be had in the empty nothingness across the ocean. Then everybody wanted in and it became a madhouse. Wars were fought, colonies were established only to wither and die. Native populations were looted and enslaved, if not totally eradicated. It was anarchy, with so much lost in the beginning years because nobody knew what they were doing...but everyone agreed that there was something of value to be had."

"This country in which we now stand didn't exist, and wouldn't have existed if Europe had said there's nothing to be gained across the ocean. Could Columbus have foreseen all of this," Davis said, spreading his arms wide as if to encompass the entire continent, "let alone have explained it to the Kings and Queens that subsidized the New World expeditions?"

"Well, space dwarfs the landgrab that started in 1492. Space is everything. We are in space right now, though you don't realize it. The Americans and Chinese outposts on the moon. The men there…are they in space? Many of you would say yes. If they are in space, then so are we. If the Earth were to suddenly become transparent, you could look down at your feet and see stars and distant galaxies beneath you, because we, on this planet, are *in space*."

"It's the equivalent of some 90 year old guy living on an island in the Bahamas saying that the land under his feet is all that matters. The ocean around him is trivial. It's just water and everything out there doesn't matter. His home is all that there is of consequence."

"We would call that a delusional mindset, because the man is in the ocean. His home is a tiny part of the ocean, far from the coast of the real land that is the continents. But from his point of view he's not in the ocean, it's what is around him. Just the same is space. It's not what is around us, it's what we are in and to deny that point is folly."

"Another example from history is the prominence of naval warfare. The oceans were seen as meaningless. Very early on everything happened on the land, aside from some shoreline fishing. But over time power was seized by those who controlled the waterways, for they held in their grasp the bulk of transportation and resupply. Even today, most cargo shipping occurs through ships, not trucks or planes. Some of you know this…and you know that if a hostile nation developed a navy superior to that of the United States, then worldwide commerce could be held hostage. The same is true for space, only a hundred fold."

Davis paused a moment, bringing his hands together and touching his lips as if in thought. "We are at the point in history where everything changes. When the Wright brothers first developed their prototype airplane, it flew a few hundred meters at best. No one at the time could conceive of the future value in the technology. It took decades of improvements and a number of visionaries to see the potential. And yet, no one could have foreseen the types of airliners we have flying through our skies now back then."

"I can see the potential of space...enough at least to know it is more valuable than anything that has come before. And where there is value there is the potential to make money. The kicker is, space is an expensive startup. This isn't like setting up a lemonade stand on the side of the street to begin your business empire. A huge amount of capital must be invested, with little or no gains to be had in the first few years. This is a 20 year+ investment, but potentially the most important endeavor you will ever have the privilege to come across."

"The purpose of Star Force is this...to provide the technology and infrastructure necessary to create and maintain an orbital economy, as well as provide a stabilizing rod for when the landgrab madness sweeps this planet. If we get there first, and establish ourselves and procedures by which to divvy up the 'land' that will become available, we can avert World War III and secure a virtual monopoly simultaneously. So you might say this endeavor is part capitalist, part philanthropist. Regardless, we only have a small window of opportunity before Columbus reports back and the wheels of history are set in motion. I am going to seize that opportunity. How well or fast I am able to do that depends on your cooperation."

Davis crossed his arms over his chest defiantly, but also to steady his hands that were microscopically beginning to shake with adrenaline and nerves.

"I don't expect you to understand the full implications instantly. Nor do I expect all of you will agree with me, but I *am* doing this, and you know from my history that I'm not one to take excessive risk in my investments. I foresee no risk in this endeavor...only the question of whether or not I'm able to pull it off in time. The market will emerge sooner or later. The quicker we can get Star Force up and running the more lucrative our slice of the pie in the sky will be."

"To all of you I'm offering non-controlling partnership. I and my people will run Star Force, with the philanthropic angle weighing heavily on our choices. But in order to accomplish those goals, we must have the resources to do so, thus our business approach will be aggressive. I mean to be the first and foremost provider of space technologies and to develop the transportation infrastructure needed to create an orbital economy...and that infrastructure will be toll roads, if you take the metaphor."

"The question before you today is whether you are willing to devote capital to a long term investment, which, in coming years could provide the most lucrative returns in recorded history."

With that, Davis finished his pitch and scanned the assembled faces for their reactions, belatedly realizing that he'd remained standing the entire time.

The cream of the corporate world remained silent, exchanging a few glances here and there, but none of them wanted to be the first to speak. In truth, they couldn't determine if Davis' Star Force proposal was for real or a gigantic joke.

Mark Neville finally leaned forward over the long, shiny black table and rested his elbows as he cradled his chin in his hands and looked to his left at Davis.

"I want to hear more."

6

17 years later...

Paul had a little over a lap to go with barely a 5 meter lead on Northridge when he launched into a half sprint, intent on keeping his team's lead in the Distance Medley. As he crossed the finish line the 1-lap to go bell sounded and he dug his spikes into the track a bit more as his momentum swung him out slightly as he rounded the curve. He could now hear the footsteps of Northridge's anchorman behind him, closing with every step.

With 300 meters to go Paul still had the lead and accelerated a bit more, past what he thought his body could maintain. His quads began to protest halfway down the backstretch but his lead held into the final turn. If Northridge was going to pass him before the final straight, they were going to have to swing out into lane 2 to do it now.

That didn't seem to matter to the opposing runner, for when they hit the apex of the curve his lithe frame glided up next to Paul's shoulder and inched by him. Paul responded with his full speed...an all out kick using what energy he had left.

He resurged into the lead momentarily, but Northridge had another gear left in him as well, and sailed on past Paul when they hit the final straightaway. He finished less than a half second behind as they crossed the finish line, but the other runner had made up 13 seconds on him during the last leg of the race.

Paul handed the baton to the Assistant Coach and collapsed onto the infield grass, waiting for his breathing to slow. He heard the coach's voice telling him his split...4:36.8 for his four laps of the relay. His teammates had given him a monster lead, but he hadn't been able to maintain it.

"Way to go, Paul," Barry said, knocking him in the shoulder.

"Hey, we lost by half a second," Frank argued. "If you'd run your 1200 a bit faster we would have won too."

"I doubt it," Brad said in disgust. "Carter had his number the whole way. I don't think a 20 second lead would have been enough. The guy is the State Champ in the mile, you know."

"I wouldn't have been outkicked," Barry muttered.

"Feel like swapping legs next time?" Paul asked their 400 runner as he finally sat up.

"Easy boys," the Head Coach said, walking up behind them. "We may have lost the race, but the 8 points you earned just clenched the team title. Congratulations."

"We beat Carmel?" Frank asked. "We've still got two events left."

"Mathematically they can't catch us," the Coach said confidently. "Grab yourself a bottle of Gatorade and get your sweats on. We've got a victory lap coming in a little bit."

He clapped Paul on the shoulder and walked off to oversee the next event on the track.

"Up you go," Frank said, offering Paul his hand and pulling him to his feet. They walked back over to their tent camp slowly and grabbed their sweats, then joined the rest of their teammates along the fence circling the track and watched their 4x400 team run the final event of the meet, after which they all met on the infield for the awards presentation and gave the Championship trophy an escort around the track before heading back to the bus.

Paul caught up to the Head Coach as he was leaving the press box with the results on his way to the parking lot.

"You need something, Paul?"

"Is it alright if I do my workout in the afternoon tomorrow on my own?"

"What's wrong? You have a date at 8am Saturday morning?" he asked sarcastically.

"No, Coach, but I do have a test at 9:00."

"What sort of test?" he asked, frowning.

"At the Star Force recruitment center in Indy."

"Really?" he asked. "What branch?"

"It's a new category, an A-7."

"What's the job description?"

"Not much with this one. It just says they're looking for the best of the best…and you have to be able to run sub 5:00 in the mile to even try."

"I thought most of their positions were tech-related."

"No, they've got some pilot and security slots too. Don't know what this one is about, but what have I got to lose? At least I pass the preliminary requirement."

The Coach thought for a moment. "25 minute run, 4 strides, double stretching."

Paul smiled. "Thanks, Coach."

"Just don't make a habit of finding ways to skip practice. We've still got half the season left and I want you as sharp as can be come Sectional."

"Will do, Coach," he said, running off back to the bus.

The next morning he drove himself down to the recruitment center in Indy, the only one in the state of Indiana. He arrived early, then spent nearly forty minutes trying to find parking, leaving him barely 6 minutes to spare when he jogged up to the wide double revolving doors that marked the entrance to the 12 story tall recruitment center, on top of which he noted was one of Star Force's trademark transports, sitting quietly on the rooftop landing pad.

When Paul got inside he found himself at the back of a short line of people leading up to the attendant's pod-like station. The woman inside was congenial and soft spoken, and was eating up Paul's six minutes as she patiently worked her way through the people in front of him in line.

Two men in front of him left the building altogether, while another three were directed to the elevator station…the only other visible item in the main lobby. It was incredible Spartan, but had the trademark spacey feel about it none the less. The whole place felt…sterilized.

"How can I help you?" the attendant asked, flashing Paul a small smile.

"I have a test scheduled. A-7. 9am."

She glanced up at what must have been a clock inside her booth. "Better get going. Floor 6, room 3," she said, thumbing him towards the elevators.

"Thanks," Paul said, rushing off.

"Mr. Taylor, I presume," a man wearing a dark blue Star Force uniform said when Paul finally arrived at the door to room 3. He was waiting for him outside.

"Yes," Paul answered pithily.

"You're right on time. Please step inside." The middle aged man pulled open the door for him.

Paul walked through, greatly relieved that he had made it on time, but to his surprise there was no one else inside.

"The test you will be taking will be auditory, meaning that the computer will ask you questions and you will respond as if you were talking to a person. Hit the blue button when you're ready to begin your answer. When you're finished answering hit the green button. Take as long as you need, this isn't a timed test," the man said, opening one of seven small booths in the room. Paul could see a chair and screen inside.

"What kind of a test is it?"

"A mix of things. Don't worry about your score like a normal test, just answer each question as honestly as you can. It won't be like anything you had in school."

"Good," Paul muttered, half laughing. "Do I start now?"

"Whenever you're ready. It will auto-start when I shut the door."

Paul took a couple of quick breaths. "Let's do this," he said, more to himself than the man. He ducked inside the 5 foot tall door and sat down.

"Good luck," the man said, pulling the hatch-like door closed behind him.

All was dark for a moment, then the screen lit up with the Star Force symbol bracketed by illumination strips attached to the wall.

"State your name," a female voice requested.

Paul looked around for the blue button. He found it and two others just in front of his knees.

"Paul Michael Taylor," he said, then pressed the green button.

"What is two squared?"she asked, along with the numbers appearing on screen.

"Four."

"In what year did the first moon landing occur?"

"1969."

"What was the most recent book you have read, if any?"

"Halo: Fall of Reach...or, well, reread actually," he clarified, realizing that every word he was saying was being recorded. He bit his tongue and pressed the green button again.

"What is your favorite color?"

"What?" he gasped, half laughing. He wasn't sure he'd heard that right so he hit the white 'repeat' button.

"What is your favorite color?" the voice said again.

"Are you serious?" he asked. "Ok, well, I don't really have one so let's just go with," he hit the blue button, "clear."

"If a woodchuck could chuck wood, how far could he throw it?"

"Is that supposed to be a riddle?" Paul asked, not understanding what this had to do with anything. When he couldn't figure anything intelligent to say he figured he might as well have some fun with it.

"Depends if his last name is Norris."

"What is the magic number of Star Wars?"

Ha! That one he did know.

"327."

"What is the second element in the periodic table."

"Helium."

"Blonde, brunette, or redhead?"

"Whichever one is the hottest."

The mix of academic, cultural, and nonsense questions got more bizarre the longer the test went. By the end of it all Paul had completely lost track of time and in some ways his sanity. He had no idea what the point had been, nor any idea of how he did.

The testing chamber opened on its own when the questioning was complete and Paul staggered out, stiff from sitting so long. He glanced down at his watch and did a double take.

He'd been in there 4 hours.

"You look a little rough," the same man said. No one else was in the room, but Paul did notice that three of the other chambers were closed, which conceivably meant that others were going through the same insane test at the moment.

"What was that all about?"

"I get the same general question from everyone who takes it," he explained, motioning Paul to the door. "And I tell them all the same thing...I'm not allowed to take the test,

I don't know what the questions are, and I'm not told anything about what it's for, so your guess is probably better than mine."

"Results?"

"Will be posted when available. They'll contact you when they have them. For now, head back down to the main lobby via the elevator, go get something to eat, take a nap, and thank you for taking the Star Force recruitment test."

"It'll be a long nap," Paul commented as he left the test proctor and walked awkwardly back to the elevators.

As he left the building he looked back, wondering what the hell had just happened, then shrugged it off. Whatever score he got was a done deal now. It was time to get back home and get his track workout in.

What he didn't realize was the blue button had been a placebo. His entire four hour testing session had been recorded, and the point of the test had not been in soliciting answers, but in analyzing his reaction to the questions.

7

Three weeks later Paul was contacted about a follow-up test. He went back down to Indy where he was met by the same man as before.

"Welcome back, Mr. Taylor," the man said, greeting him in the lobby this time. "This way."

Without saying anything further Paul followed the man into the elevator and up to the 10th floor where he was put into a very large room filled with what looked like children's games. Again, he was the only person present.

"What you see," the man began to explain as he shut the door behind them, "is a series of puzzles, 15 in total. Solve as many as you can."

"Is there a time limit?"

"You can stay as long as you like, but you only get one chance, so make it count."

"Are you going to explain these or do I have to guess?"

"I will remain for the duration, but other than explaining what lies before you, I can offer no assistance."

"Bet that's boring...ok, what's this one?"

"The irregularly shaped blocks you see before you can be arranged into a cube 12 units wide. Assemble them correctly and you pass the challenge."

"What about those?" Paul asked, pointing to a series of levers, pullies, chutes, and other assorted gizmos.

"Mousetrap. Use the available components to get the ball from the red tray into the blue tray to pass the challenge."

"And that one?" Paul asked, beginning to like this.

"Unlock the door."

"And that?"

"Deduce which unit is powering the light."

Paul went on and got the basics on each of the challenges before diving in head first. He had 12 of them solved within three hours, then got hung up on a brain teaser that took him an hour and a half to crack. The remaining two challenges took him another hour, but he had no real trouble with them, finishing the set in the middle of the afternoon.

"Impressive," the man said, abandoning his silent post against the far wall. "No one at this facility has passed more than 7."

"What now?" Paul said, beaming.

"Well, I would have you scheduled for a third test on another day, but since we've still got daylight left we can proceed now if you like? Or are you too brain fried?"

"I'm game."

The man smiled. "Good. Follow me."

Paul was led out of the 'play area' and back to the elevator, which took them down to level 4 and a specialized gaming terminal with a large screen, wide keyboard, and an attached chair with ample cushioning.

"Have a seat..."

Paul slid into the chair as the man activated the system. "Are you familiar with RTS games?"

"A few."

"What you have before you is one, and only one, scenario to pass. You can try as many times as you like, on as many days as you like, which is why I wanted you to start now."

The screen activated and a large simulated landscape appeared with various locations marked.

"You and five computer players are assaulting one heavily fortified base in a capture the flag scenario. Get the flag, win the game. Simple as that."

"Sounds a bit too easy," Paul said warily.

"I didn't say it was easy," the man warned. "It may take you a while to get acquainted with the controls and balance. Take your time."

"How many people have beaten the game?"

"Can't tell you that unless you pass."

"Fair enough," Paul said, flipping through the control menu as the game began. The man disappeared and left him to the intense time-warping mind lock that was video gaming.

Paul's first attempt was a trial and error venture, which he quickly lost. He and the other computer players didn't have the firepower necessary to breach and hold the base's perimeter defenses. As soon as they had a foothold inside the base, reinforcements would overwhelm and destroy what was left of their attacking force.

Conventional gaming strategy held that if a direct attack was impossible, try for a roundabout approach. Paul's next line of attack, after the base defenders had counterattacked and wiped out his own encampment, was to probe around the base perimeter for weaknesses using long ranged attacks. He learned a great deal about the position and distribution patterns the enemy was employing, but whatever long range damage he incurred required too many units, leaving him without sufficient assault units to actually invade the base.

His third attempt was a try at misdirection, using a number of faints to reposition the enemy away from his true objective. He partially succeeded, which prompted him to try several more times. It wasn't until his 8th run-through of the game that he realized he was missing the whole point...and stupidly so.

It was his computer allies. He had to coordinate attacks to break the base defenses...but how?

He highlighted one of his allies' main bases and smiled as he found a menu prompt. When he opened it he found four preset strategies that he could order them to employ, though he still had no control over their individual units.

With that revelation he compiled a basic strategy, assigning his own troops the most sensitive challenge...that of long range bombardment. He tasked his factories to spew out the siege tanks and set them up at appropriate range, creating a few guard units from the remaining unit slots available to him to protect the valuable assets.

Able to reach the wall while remaining just clear of return fire, Paul's tanks beat down the outer defenses closest to his position while two of his computer allies assaulted the perimeter uselessly with infantry and conventional tanks. As he took down some of the base's wall turrets, the survival rate of his allies' troops in that area increased, allowing them to do yet more damage to the perimeter.

The enemy then counterattacked with air assets, slaughtering most of the assault force as well as coming after Paul's siege tanks, but some anti-air assets he'd built thinned their numbers enough that he only lost two tanks to the assault before a large mass of allied air units flew into the fray using a pre-requested rush tactic, taking out the enemy air assets and assaulting the wall defenses of their own accord as more infantry and tank reinforcements began trickling in underneath their protective swarm...which was even now thinning from combat attrition.

Now was the key, Paul knew. While his allies assaulted the base...an assault that wouldn't prove effective in the long run...he repositioned his tanks closer to the wall, in territory that originally would have put them within the range of the base's defense turrets. Those turrets were currently out of operation and, thanks to his allies' diversion, the base defense units couldn't counterattack during his moment of transitional weakness. He set his tanks and arrayed his defenses, then proceeded on pounding additional base defense turrets and units that had previously been beyond his reach.

Paul repeated the advance numerous times, locking down the territory around his tightly packed and defended tank group and leap-frogging forward when his allies collected enough forces to temporarily punch their way forward. It was time consuming, but easy enough that Paul was certain that he'd discerned the purpose of the test.

"Teamwork," he whispered as computer player number 4 broke through the final defenses and arrived at the target, capturing the flag and winning the scenario for the team while not a single one of Paul's units had so much as even entered the enemy base.

He smiled, then squinted as his vision left the computer screen. How long had it been anyway?

He glanced down at his watch, then turned to look out the windows behind him, seeing that the sun was just going down. He'd been playing for another 5 hours...but it had been time well spent.

"When do you graduate?" the man asked, reappearing beside him and tossing a small card into his lap.

"Next Thursday," Paul said, looking at the card. It had a swipe strip and a Star Force logo on it. "What's this?"

"Fifty bucks...go get yourself something to eat. You've got to be starving."

"I hadn't noticed," Paul said, pocketing the corporate debit card. "How many others passed?" he asked as he pulled himself out of the chair, finding his legs a bit wobbly. The man was right, he was hurting for food right now, and his mouth was dry as a bone. He walked over to the nearby water fountain and took care of his thirst, stretching out euphorically as he did so.

"Sixteen," the man told him. "On this continent."

Paul blanched. "Really?"

"Do you want in?"

"To Star Force?" Paul asked, wanting clarification. He didn't believe this was happening.

"Into the A-7 program, yes."

"What is that, exactly?"

"The best of the best...beyond that, I don't know. You have to enter orientation on a blind contract."

"What does that mean?"

"It means that whatever they want you for, it's a corporate secret. I can tell you that the base pay starts out at $110,000."

"Where do I sign up?" he asked enthusiastically.

"Downstairs...but you can sign the papers later. Report back to the recruitment center on December 15th and don't expect to see home again anytime soon. Where exactly you're going I'm not allowed to know, but you have to leave everything behind. No phone, bag, clothes...nothing. From the time you ship out from here Star Force becomes your life."

"Wow," was all Paul could think to say.

"If you want in, that is. Think it over long and hard. If you decide that's too much for you, just don't show up the 15th and nothing further will be said. If you want in, show up, sign the contract, and ship out on the adventure of your life."

"Oh, I'll be here," Paul said, grinning from ear to ear.

8

True to his word, Paul showed up at the Indy recruiting center on the 15th with his parents and sister, who watched him sign the paperwork and said their final goodbyes. A bit misty eyed, but eager to get underway with the promised adventure, Paul left his family in the lobby and entered the elevator...not realizing it would be the last time he'd ever see them face to face.

"You ready for this?" his handler asked. This was the third time he'd met the man, who had yet to give his name.

"Not sure what *this* is," Paul noted, "but yeah, I'm ready."

"Good," he commented as the elevator doors opened. "First things first though. I need you to take a shower and get into a recruit's uniform. Your clothes, shoes, watch and anything else on your person stay here. Do you have any piercings?"

"No."

"In there," the man pointed to a side room. "Various sizes of clothing have been laid out. Make sure it all fits before you leave."

"Clean break...I get it," Paul said, going inside the pristine locker room. Again, he was the only person present.

There were six booths, lined up two by three with a long bench in between the rows, on top of which his clothing options were laid out, along with a towel. He looked inside one of the booths and saw it was a mini-bathroom, including a shower. He grabbed the towel behind him and went inside.

A long ten minutes later he emerged from the booth clean as a whistle wearing nothing but the towel. The shower had a massage setting and he'd been tempted to stay in longer and soak up the warm water, but he didn't want to keep his ride waiting. Paul sorted through the various sizes and styles of underwear, socks, and pants, grabbing what he thought would fit best and retreated into the booth to get dressed.

He came back out with pants on, but the socks had been too big. He changed them out for a tiny pair that looked far too small to fit him, but the material was stretchy enough that they ended up fitting just right.

The pants he wore were white with a blue stripe down the sides, and there were a number of matching jackets laid out, along with blue T-shirts made of some type of synthetic material that form fitted to his body as Paul wiggled one on. He tried on three of the jackets before again picking one that looked smaller than it fit, then went about trying on shoes.

Smooth covered with no laces, the shoes felt like his running shoes but had different size numbers than he was used to. Normally he wore a 9, but the ones labeled 3.2 fit him best. There was no way to tie or fasten the shoes, which felt odd, but the material also flexed enough to lightly grip his feet. While he would have classified the shoes as slip-ons, they didn't wear like them and actually fit with the body-forming motif of the entire ensemble.

He took a few seconds to check his reflection in the wall length mirror then walked back over to the booth he'd used and grabbed his old clothing, which he deposited in an empty bin sitting on the table labeled as such.

Paul glanced around, taking in the moment.

"Here we go," he whispered before heading back out the door.

"Looking better already," the man commented, pointing him back towards the elevator. "You're going to be flown down to Phoenix, then transferred to another flight that will take you to your final destination. And no, I don't know where that is. From here on out you and the other A-7 recruits become ghosts as far as the rest of us are concerned."

"Others?" Paul asked, entering the now familiar elevators.

"Everyone is being shipped out together, though you're the only one from here. You'll probably meet up with a few others at Phoenix, then the rest at your destination."

"How many are there?"

"First recruiting class contains 100 slots," the man said as the elevator opened onto the rooftop landing platform. "There's your ride."

Paul couldn't help but smile as he saw the blocky VTOL Star Force transport sitting on the pad with its massive fan blade engines whining softly in preparation for launch. The design reminded him of the Pelican dropships from Halo, though this one looked a bit more robust. In fact, it looked too heavy altogether to leave the ground, but Paul had seen footage of the aircraft before and knew they were much more nimble than their fattish appearance allowed.

"Thanks," Paul offered, leaving the man at the elevator hub and crossing the wide snowy rooftop pad to where another Star Force member was waiting for him at the aft boarding ramp.

"Welcome to the party," she said jovially, motioning him inside. "Guess you're the only customer today."

"Looks like it," Paul said, walking up the ramp and into the *Mantis*-class transport. There was an equipment/cargo bay directly aft, looking like the bottom half of a metallic box, but in front of that were a pair of rows of high backed seats underneath an overhead storage compartment.

"You need to strap in for takeoff, but after we get underway just relax, take a nap, or do some reading," she said, handing him a small computer pad with internet access.

"Sweet," Paul said, accepting the anti-boredom device as he sat down. There were no windows in the aft section of the Mantis, and the two rows of seats were facing each other over a small open section with the pilot's compartment to his right, from which there was a steady stream of outside light in addition to that coming from the boarding ramp.

When the co-pilot closed it, the interior illumination panels lit up and kept the inside amicably cheery despite the Spartan design of the Star Force workhorse. Virtually all personnel and cargo transfers were accomplished via a fleet of these small aircraft, giving the space-focused corporation the 5th largest airborne cargo fleet on the planet.

After checking to make sure Paul's straps were secure, the co-pilot retreated to the forward compartment and strapped herself in for takeoff. Though he couldn't see it, he could both feel and hear the six fan blade engine pods on the Mantis's exterior ramp up and shoot the transport into the sky.

It gained vertical altitude quickly, then extended four recessed wing blades and tipped the engine pods to begin lateral thrust. Within 10 seconds they were gaining speed and headed out of Indiana's capitol city towards the southwest.

Paul quickly realized the necessity of the restraints, having dropped his pad during the abrupt takeoff. Once the flight settled out he unstrapped and retrieved the device from the floor, glad to see that it hadn't broken. When he turned it on he realized it wasn't just for internet access...it was also a link-in to Star Force's own data network.

His attention immediately caught, he perused through historical records, schematics, data files, and even found the tracking program that showed his Mantis's exact position and projected flight path along with hundreds of others currently in the air, as well as the ground to orbit traffic coming out of four Star Force spaceports at or near the equator.

The otherwise long flight passed quickly for Paul, who was devouring the newly accessible information as fast as he could retrieve it. Star Force had been in existence for nearly 15 years, and in that time they'd established quite an extensive database.

Paul had barely scratched the surface when the co-pilot stuck her head back into the passenger compartment.

"Hi. Need to strap in again, we're about to land."

"Got it," Paul confirmed, grabbing the couplers and cinching himself back in. The co-pilot waited to make sure he was snug then disappeared back into the cockpit. A few moments later he heard the wing blades retract and the engine pods ramp up their thrust as their speed slowed and Paul's head tilted right, his shoulders testing the strength of the restraints, but the violent acceleration that he'd felt on liftoff never manifested itself and the landing went much smoother than he'd anticipated.

The co-pilot reappeared and watched him unstrap. "I'll need that back."

"Thanks," Paul said, handing it back to her.

"These trips can get pretty boring if you don't have something to focus your mind on," she said as the aft boarding ramp began to lower.

"Sweet ride though," Paul offered.

"That it is," she agreed with a smile as the ramp hit the ground. "Off you go."

Paul nodded to her and walked down to meet another Star Force member, this one wearing a uniform much like his own, only without the blue stripes.

"You're Paul?" he asked.

"I am."

"Follow me," the man said, heading off what Paul soon realized was an insanely large airfield, with dozens of Mantises parked on individual pads sprinkled throughout a sea of empty ones, along with some larger transports that he'd never seen before.

"What is this place?" he asked, catching up to the man and falling in step side by side with him.

"It'll be our 5th spaceport when it's completed next year. For our purposes it's a staging area to assemble the trainees."

"Our?"

"I've been assigned to the A-7 project as one of your handlers. Name's Jenkins," he said, extending his hand.

"Paul Taylor," he said, accepting the gesture. "Can you tell me what A-7 actually is?"

"Not yet. It'll be explained to all of you simultaneously once we reach the training site."

"And where's that?"

"Classified," Jenkins said almost apologetically. "Don't worry, you'll get all the answers you want soon enough."

9

Paul was led inside a commons area that was partially operational and got a bite to eat while he waited for the rest of the trainees to arrive, which took another two hours. Then he and five others boarded another Mantis and took off for locations unknown. Jenkins sat on one end of the twin rows of seats, next to the cargo section on Paul's side while the trainees were seated three facing three with ample room to spare between them. The seating compartment was designed to hold a dozen.

Across from him sat three guys, each looking to be about 20 or so. Seated to Paul's right was another guy that he guessed was his age, while on his left was, to his surprise, a girl that was probably older than them all, though he couldn't be sure. All of them could easily have been college students, which was where Paul had been headed in a few months had he not tested out for Star Force.

None of them spoke much, and the first half hour of their trip was sat in silence with them seeming to size each other up then interest themselves in the computer pads they'd been given to pass the time, but after a while Paul couldn't help himself and leaned over his shoulder and whispered to the girl.

"Did you really run sub 5:00?"

She looked back at him. "4:39 converted from a 1500."

"College then?" Paul guessed, impressed.

"Duke, last year. You?"

"4:29 converted from a 1600," he said, happy to have still been faster than her.

"Relay split?"

"Regional, actually."

"High school?" she asked, frowning. "What state runs 1600?"

"Indiana."

"Really?" she asked. Most states ran 1500 as their 'mile.' Colleges and pros too.

"Four laps makes more sense than three and three quarters," he argued, sticking up a bit for his state. "And we don't have the stupid classes either. Our state meet is a real state meet."

"Relax, kid. I just didn't realize anyone ran 1600."

"Kid?" Paul asked disappointed, overacting the part. "Guess that means dating is out of the question."

She laughed. "If I wanted a love life I'd already have one."

"Hard to get, huh?"

"No, I just get tired of guys seeing a girl and thinking we have nothing better to do than fall in love," she said with a mix of sarcasm and levity.

Paul smiled. "Fair enough."

"I'm Sara, by the way," she offered.

"Paul," he answered her, then turned to the others. "We're all A-7, right?"

He received four nods of agreement.

"Am I the youngest here?" he asked, glancing around. "I'm 17, just graduated from high school. She's out of college," he said, pointing at Sara, "and you guys?"

"22…name's Scott," the guy directly across from Paul said.

"18," the guy on his right said. "I just graduated too. I'm Ryan."

"Yori…21…and I was a sophomore at UNC before getting this gig."

"How old are you?" the last guy, seated to Paul's cattycorner left, asked Sara.

"23," she answered.

"Guess that makes me the old man at 24. I'm Greg Statburn."

"*The* Greg Statburn..." Ryan asked, doing a double take. "...from the Denver Broncos?"

"The same."

"Actually," Jenkins interrupted, "you're Greg 073 now. Your last names got left behind along with all your other possessions. You're Sara 012," the handler continued. "Paul 024. Ryan 096. Scott 055. Yori 007."

"Awesome," Yori exclaimed at getting James Bond's number.

"How many of us are there?" Sara asked.

"A hundred."

"So does somebody have number 100 or 000?"

"All of your group start with numeral 0. Number 100 will be the first member of the second class," Jenkins explained.

"Why not start everyone with number 1?" Paul asked. "That way it matches the group number."

"No..." Yori muttered in protest.

"Not my decision," Jenkins deferred. "But the identifiers are going to stick. Like it or not, that's your name from now on."

"Anything else we need to know?" Greg asked Jenkins.

"Not at the moment."

"Well then," Greg continued. "My background is obviously football, what about you?"

"Track," Sara answered.

"Same here," Paul chimed in.

"Soccer," Ryan said, tossing a warning glance at Paul.

"Soccer?" he echoed dramatically. "Can't believe I'm sitting next to you."

"Same here," Ryan said tongue in cheek. The two sports in high school didn't mesh well.

Sara elbowed Paul in the ribs, but he could see she was cracking a smile.

"What's wrong with soccer?" Scott asked.

"You too?" Paul accused.

"No, I'm Canadian...or was," he said, glancing at Jenkins.

"Hockey?" Ryan asked.

"What else?"

"What about you 007?" Greg asked.

"Gymnastics," he answered deadpan.

Paul glanced at Ryan, then back at Yori. "That's even worse."

"Na," he said, laughing, "I'm just kidding...Triathlon."

Paul had to laugh at that. Gymnasts' builds were so ill suited to running that he doubted any of them could have run a sub 5:00 mile. In fact, he should have known better. "How fast?"

"4:20," Yori answered.

Paul nodded once out of respect. Not quite as fast as Carter, but still well beyond him.

"Do any of you know what we'll actually be doing?" Scott asked. "They wouldn't tell me anything."

"Me neither," Greg echoed. The others all shook their heads no.

"A few more hours and that will all change," Jenkins said calmly, but with a bit of eerie reverence in his voice. "I can promise you that."

The six trainees exchanged glances, catching the odd sound in his voice.

"Guess we wait then," Greg pronounced. "Anyone up for a game," he said, hefting his computer pad.

"Bring it," Paul responded, calling up the games subdirectory.

"I'm game," Sara added.

"Sure, why not," Ryan agreed.

"Jenkins, you want in?" Greg offered.

"I'm good," the man said, leaning back fractionally and crossing his arms.

"I'm in," Scott added.

"Mario Kart?" Yori suggested.

"I call Yoshi," Paul said quickly.

"Mario Kart it is," Greg declared, pulling up the game file. "But I have to warn you, I'm a wicked shot with a turtle shell."

After many hours of gaming, talking, and napping the Mantis finally arrived at their destination with the copilot linking in their computer pads to the external cameras so they could watch their approach.

"What is that?" Sara asked, seeing a grey island in the middle of the ocean.

"It's what will be Atlantis when it's finished," Jenkins said without needing to look at a screen. "It'll be Star Force's primary hub, as well as your new home for the foreseeable future. The training areas are complete, along with about half the interior. The rest will take another two years to complete."

"Is it floating?" Ryan asked, studying his pad intently.

"We're in the middle of the Pacific Ocean, but there are no landmasses in the area. The city is built up from the sea floor."

"How deep?" Paul asked.

"Should be in your data files," Jenkins directed.

The six of them quickly located the 'Atlantis' file and pulled up the city's schematics.

"Six kilometers wide?" Scott said in dismay.

"They started building it over 10 years ago," Jenkins added. "This has been part of the master plan since Star Force's inception."

"Is that master plan in here too?" Greg asked, hefting his computer pad.

"No," Jenkins answered ironically. "But you're going to get the full brief after we land from Director Davis himself. I suggest you save any more questions for him."

The six trainees exchanged glances, then watched their approach to the city intently. Upon closer inspection, only part of the surface of the city was smooth, the rest had patchy holes with support ribs exposed. It actually reminded Paul of the second Death Star, except that it was nearly flat on top, with a slight curve that dropped sharply at the edges.

When the Mantis flew over the edge of the ocean city Paul realized that the surface wasn't uniform at all. There was a smoothness to the design, but with various numbs and flat spots spread out sporadically. Down the center of it all was a system of runways for fixed wing craft, large enough to accommodate even the heaviest of jumbo jets.

Scattered throughout the runway spokes were smaller landing pads for the VTOL craft, one of which they were headed for. As they lowered down towards their mark, the city's size grew exponentially, with Paul and the others realizing that the size had been an optical illusion. The normal sized runways were in fact quads, with neutral zones in between. The pad they were coming down on was also visually deceptive, in that it wasn't one pad, but a cluster of 21 with a number of support structures interspersed between them.

"This place is insane," Ryan commented.

"Wait till you're inside," Jenkins said, holding tight to his restraints as they descended rapidly. A long minute later they touched down.

"I'll show you to your quarters," Jenkins said as they all unstrapped and headed aft. "You have three and a half hours downtime before the assembly. Get something to eat and a fresh change of clothes. You might also want to hit the track for a few laps to shake out of your legs, just don't go wandering off. First time here it's easy to get lost."

10

Paul found himself sitting in a small amphitheatre that was only a 5th full along with the other A-7 recruits as several men onstage conversed with each other. Eventually one of them took the dais as the others retreated down into the seats.

"Welcome," Davis said as he looked out at the 100 candidates clustered together in the front most rows. "I apologize for keeping you in the dark as long as we have, but as you're about to see it was with good reason. My name is Sean Davis, Director of all Star Force operations. You," he said, pointing at the recruits, "are to become my counterparts in the coming days, leading Star Force into an uncertain future. Before we get into that, however, you need to get caught up on recent history."

Davis activated a large display screen behind him, nearly the size of a tennis court.

"18 years ago I held the position of CEO of the Pegasus Corporation, the multi-national entity that spawned Star Force, when an archeological discovery was made in Antarctica."

The screen showed a map of the southern continent and the position of the find.

"It was an accident. A Pegasus biologist was studying a rare find of vegetation amongst the snow and ice. Buried just below the surface was a heat source that supported the Santa grass that she was investigating. The upper edge of that heat source was stumbled upon by the biological expedition and an excavation team was sent to discover exactly what they had found."

Davis altered the screen to show a grid of photos of the dig site.

"What they uncovered was a massive pyramid, buried beneath the surprisingly deep Antarctic soil. It is constructed of a material unknown to us and emits a low amount of heat. It appears as if stone, but it is not. I can tell you that it is the hardest material ever discovered and it absorbs energy directed at it. Our laser mining tools had no effect on the material, and it took many conventional diamond coated drill bits to bore a hole through the outer structure and gain entrance."

The pictures shifted to the interior while the left half of the screen manifested a wireframe diagram of the entire pyramid.

"What we found inside we never revealed to the public, nor any nation, corporate entity, or individual outside of Pegasus. To this day, the site in Antarctica remains a secret, as we continue to study the technology within, which is far more advanced than anything we could have imagined."

Paul squinted at the images, trying to pull it all together. The rest of the trainees were at a similar impasse.

"The pyramid has, among other things, a central computer system that we were eventually able to gain access to. Those who built it used a language different from any known on Earth, and to be honest we haven't completely figured it out yet, but with a limited vocabulary established we were able to retrieve some valuable information about who built it, what happened to them, and what implications it has on the future."

Davis altered the images again, this time showing a number of large skeletons.

"These are images from our first days inside. We counted over 400 skeletons. As you can probably deduce, they are dinosaurs. Some varieties of which have not been found anywhere else on the planet to date."

Davis paused, letting what he had said sink in and preparing to deliver what had been traumatic news to others. Some had refused to accept the truth, others had thought he was joking...he hoped the recruits would take the news better, so he had decided to just tell them straight out.

"The origins of life on this planet have been accounted for by two predominant theories. The first of which is creation by an intelligent, all powerful being or God. The second is the gradual evolution from simple protein chains up through the millennia to current day Humans. What we learned in Antarctica is that neither story is true."

"The skeletons that you see here are the remains of the builders of the pyramid."

Paul stirred in his seat along with the other trainees. *Dinosaurs?*

"They call themselves the V'kit'no'sat," Davis said, continuing on. "There are many races within the greater group, each as intelligent, if not more so than Humans. They are immensely powerful, highly territorial...and not originally from this planet."

Davis altered the display to a star chart with various colored dots and interconnecting lines.

"We were able to retrieve a map of their holdings at the time the pyramid was lost to them, approximately 106,000 years ago. They were, at that time, in possession of at least 2,000 star systems, perhaps more. Detailed records outside of the local region are sketchy, so we don't have an exact accounting, but we do know that our star system is located in what was their frontier region so to speak."

Davis paused again, looking out at the recruits and gauging their reaction. None of them spoke, but he could see in their eyes that they were intently curious. That was a good sign.

"According to the last records, a schism had formed within the V'kit'no'sat in what we've come to call the Raptor Rebellion. It seems they utilize a rigid caste system, which the Rit'ko'sor, what we call Raptors, refuted after more than a million years of collective history. A civil war broke out, during which the frontier colonies were either lost, abandoned, or simply forgotten."

"We don't know exactly what happened on Earth, but there was a battle fought, as evidenced by the remains in the pyramid. Why neither side prevailed or chose to remain is a lingering mystery, but after the battle the pyramid auto-powered down after a period of inactivity and remained in waiting mode until we discovered it and began to figure out how to make things work. To this day, we have nominal control of the pyramid's functions, yet we have barely scratched the surface of their technology."

"What small discoveries we have made have been incorporated into Star Force technology, which as you all know is considerably superior to that from any other corporation or nation. We are slowly revealing what we have learned, so as to not tip our hand, but our current technological assets are considerably greater than what we have made available to the public, which is why we've been able to take on the massive construction project that you are currently sitting in."

"That said, let me emphasize that the technology of the V'kit'no'sat is so far beyond us that we may never understand it all. What we are working with now is essentially sticks and stones compared with their lightsaber. We are completely outclassed...and therein lies the ultimate problem."

Davis sighed. "I'm sure many of you are already thinking ahead to the unspoken questions. Where are they now? What happens if they return? Are they friend or foe?"

He adjusted the display again, going back to the visual records of the skeletons.

"There was one race whose skeletons were not found inside the pyramid, oddly enough. According to the records they were present in the colony world, as well as assigned to duty within the pyramid. We even discovered special living quarters for them at the summit. They are a diminutive race by comparison, with no standing in the V'kit'no'sat. They were a slave race, one of many, but they were the most prominent, the most widely used and, arguably, the most valuable. They were used as soldiers, assassins, cannon fodder for the larger battles, scouts, techs, and any other tasks that their small size and dexterity afforded them."

"You're talking about us," one of the recruits interrupted.

Davis nodded slowly. "Yes. Humans were brought to this planet, this colony of the V'kit'no'sat, as their slaves."

There was silence for a moment before Paul decided to speak.

"Hostile then..." he concluded.

"Very, from what we've been able to glean from their records. I know this is a lot to take in all at once, but the reason why you're here is because you're the best this planet has to offer. You're physically strong, highly intelligent, and moreover you're troubleshooters, adaptive rather than imitative. You learn fast, and seek out the truth by instinct rather than by instruction. Already you are analyzing what I've told you, piecing together the threads, gauging our chances and the difficulties ahead...and realizing why it was imperative that this be kept a secret from the rest of the planet."

Paul flinched as Davis called him out. That's exactly what he had been doing.

He glanced to the side, looking at the others. A guy two seats down looked back and they made eye contact, both realizing that they were more alike than either of them had accounted for.

"I created Star Force with the singular purpose of developing a counterbalance to the threat we face, not just from a potential return of the V'kit'no'sat, but from the other alien races out there, and there are many according to the databanks. We aren't a match for any of them, and the only reason we survive to this day is because of our anonymity. It is our greatest strength, but something that we have absolutely no control over...nor can we assume that it will last forever."

"I don't know how to prepare for this threat...because there is no way we can win if they do return. We are vastly outmatched, which you will learn the finer details about in time. We can't close the technological gap in ten years, a hundred, a thousand, or even ten thousand...and there's no way of knowing how much further they've advanced in the past 106,000 years."

"Bottom line is, if they come back we can't win. So what do we do?"

Davis let that question hang in the air until someone decided to answer it.

"We run," Sara said, two rows down from Paul.

Davis smiled. "We can't even do that, at the moment. We have one planet, limited technology, and no clue what we're really up against. You're here to change that."

He changed the screen to a view of Atlantis.

"While we are training you to become the best that you can be, I'll be attempting to unify the rest of the planet and begin the push for the colonization of space. This city will become an embassy of sorts...neutral ground in the politics that have been choking off any real progress on that front. Star Force will attempt to guide the colonization rush once it begins and seek to avoid the conflicts typical of such events throughout our recent history. This we have already begun, but once Atlantis is complete the push to space will begin in earnest."

"In order to pursue both agendas, Star Force must develop a military of its own, in addition to our corporate angles. This must be done in secret as well, so that we can secure and stabilize our own planet before we begin exploring and expanding to others."

"But do not misunderstand me...we are not attempting to take over the world. Other than Atlantis and our other ground based facilities, we will have no interaction with the surface. All our focus will be on orbit and beyond. We cannot, under any circumstances, allow the move to space to become World War III. To safeguard against that, Star Force must develop a peace keeping force stronger and larger than any nation. Right now there isn't a single nation with military assets in space, which gives us the opportunity to get established there first...before any potential fireworks can break out."

"You will be the first of that peace keeping force. You will be the trailblazers. You will build Star Force's fleet from the ground up. I don't know how to do that, and really no one else does either. You have been selected for your learning skills, and learn you will have to as we go about this endeavor. First in your training, which will be extensive and intense. We will teach you everything we can...but after you graduate from your basic training, you will be the leaders. You will be in charge."

Davis let his gaze sweep over each and every one of the assembled 100.

"I know this is too much to thrust upon your shoulders...but this is the reality of the situation we face. If any or all of you do not want to do this, we'll find you another position within Star Force. Your contract will be honored, and you will still be required to keep the extremely valuable secret I've shared with you, but leadership is not something that can be demanded of someone. It has to be accepted."

"The question before you is this...will you accept the challenge of leading Star Force, and our planet, into a bleak and uncertain future?"

Paul exchanged glances with Greg, who was sitting on his right. The former NFL running back cracked a smile.

"Hell yes."

Integration

1

May 27, 2043

"Get down!" Jason yelled, tackling Paul and knocking him below the barricade just before a three shot salvo from a hidden paintball turret zipped over their heads, splashing blue paint against a short tower three meters away.

"Thanks," Paul muttered as Jason pulled himself and his elbow off of Paul's chest. "Where did that come from?" he asked, getting to his feet but keeping his head low and out of sight.

"Far left, one of the short pillars."

"I've never seen one there before."

"Me neither, must be a sleeper...or they changed up the course without telling us," Jason agreed, pointing two parallel fingers towards the target.

Emily, across an open 'kill zone' and hunkered down behind another barricade, nodded her understanding. She popped her head up and fired off two of her own paintball rounds at the target atop the turret, both missing wide. She ducked back down quickly, successfully drawing return fire.

Jason took advantage of the diversion and took aim on the .4 meter wide sphere atop the dual mounted, remotely-controlled paintball gun turret and quickly nailed it with three green-splattered hits. The turret barrels sank down several inches, indicating that it was temporarily disabled.

"Go," Jason ordered.

Paul and Jack didn't hesitate. Weapons in hand they leapt up over the edge of the low barricade and ran forward to the next. Jason followed a second later and slid in behind cover as another turret tracked and littered the air with paintballs. One of them hit him in the shoulder on his way down, numbing his arm and causing him to drop his weapon.

"Damn it," he swore, tucking his backside up against the barricade as he sat and massaged his arm. The paintballs were laced with stun energy, interfering with the nervous system on contact with the body...and the damn charge even soaked through his clothes where the paint wouldn't.

Paul slid out of cover, grabbed Jason's weapon, and scooted back, drawing some more missed shots from the turret off to the right. "How bad is it?"

"Completely numb," he complained behind his dark safety glasses, the only protection they had from the painful little balls.

Paul laid Jason's weapon next to his leg as his teammate continued to try and work the numbing energy out of his arm. "Stay put and keep watch on our aft. If you see Jenkins or any of the other trainers sneaking up again, give 'em hell."

"Get going," Jason said, taking a one handed grip on his paintball gun then pulling his feet up underneath him in a crouch. His right arm lung limp, with his senseless fingers brushing the floor of the Atlantis training chamber...one of many that their trainers had been kicking their asses in during the past six months.

"Rover incoming!" Paul heard Randy yell. "Left flank."

Paul circled around Jason and put himself in between his wounded friend and the treaded mini-tank that he could now faintly hear coming up the 'street.' He and the other 9 of his teammates were positioned in barricade rows 7, 8, and 9 out of 23 total, with row zero being the guarded bunker with the mission end button sitting atop a chest-high pedestal inside.

The training exercise was a classic 'capture the flag' scenario, with his team entering on the wide end of a 60% cone centered on the flag, meaning barricade row 23 was the widest and least defended, with each subsequent row narrowing down until the far end of the room was barely 15 meters wide where the bunker stood. Four 'streets' were visible, radiating out from the bunker entrance and running in straight lines up through the barricades, leaving wide kill zones for several strategically placed turrets.

In between the streets were a mixture of barricades and pillars. The barricades were a little over a meter high, looking like solid metal fences, each no more than five meters wide, with staggered gaps in between segments that Paul's team had to dart across, hoping the turrets weren't fast enough to catch them in the open...or one of the trainers sitting in the bunker with sniper rifles.

The pillars were wide boxes above head height but narrow enough that only one or a tightly packed two people could take cover behind them. Some of the pillars held hidden turrets, others did not. Some would pop out at knee level, others at face level, and still others would rise up out of the top and fire down on the team from a higher angle, making them skulk down behind the too short barricades even further.

This was the 2's 17th attempt on this course. Each time they ran it they made a bit more progress, learning where the turrets were and beginning to anticipate the trainers' tactics...who always tried to outwit and confuse their charges. Director Davis had said they'd been chosen for their adaptive skills, and he'd ordered the trainers to give them as much havoc as possible to learn from.

That they'd been doing in spades...and seemed to take a perverse pleasure in the task.

Paul's team...those that had been assigned numbers 020-029, otherwise known as the "2s," had gelled well. They were currently the 3rd highest rated team out of 10 and were totally committed to raising that rank to number 1 and keeping it there...but doing that meant passing this capture the flag challenge and catching up with the 7s and 0s who were already several scenarios ahead of them.

Paul waited silently, keeping his two handed grip aimed at the street where he expected the Rover to appear. He, Jason, and Jack were the farthest advanced of the team, thus they would have first crack at the mobile gun turret...as well as being its first targets when it rolled up beside them, bypassing the barricades that they were now cowered behind.

Unlike the permanent turrets, the Rover was treated more like a tank, requiring more hits on its target sphere to deactivate it, leaving the device more than enough time to take out a single attacker. They'd learned early on that they had to combine their firepower to take it out quickly, otherwise it would thin their numbers and deny them any real chance of taking the bunker and the 'flag' within.

Just as the leading edge of the Rover came into view, Megan and Kip popped up from behind cover on row 8, one row further away from the Rover than Paul's group, and fired on it as fast as their triggers would allow. A few of their shots hit the target sphere, but most missed wide or splattered on the front of the small, squarish tank.

The trainers in a nearby chamber swung its remotely controlled quad barrels slightly to the right and peppered the 8th row barricades, forcing them to take cover as Paul and Jack opened fire from the left, blindsiding the Rover. Its quad turret began to swivel towards them when Paul jumped up, his head rising above cover, and ran towards the blasted thing as fast as he could, firing as he went. Jack sidestepped to maintain his line of fire, but Paul was still blocking Jason, who knew better than to risk hitting his teammate in the legs.

Paul put three shots at close range into the target, grateful to see the barrels dip in response, but he knew it'd only be deactivated for a number of seconds, approximately 30 in count, but never the same. The trainers had programmed all the turrets with a randomized downtime to keep the trainees on their toes.

Several turret launched paintballs whizzed by Paul's head from the direction of the bunker, but he ignored them. He had to take out the Rover for good or they'd lose again. Unlike the turrets which, once they advanced past them, would permanently deactivate, the Rover was never permanently out of the fight and would circle around and attack them from the rear when they neared the heavily defended bunker.

It had also, two weeks ago, nailed Paul in the nuts...which was, even with the numbing charge, extremely painful, and now was time for some payback. They were supposed to learn, adapt, and improvise, so that's exactly what he planned to do, even if the trainers would throw a fit afterward.

Paul slid down in front of the Rover, using it as cover from the turrets. A few tiny splatters from rounds impacting the Rover's barrels hit Paul's face, and he lost a bit of feeling on his right cheek and upper lip as a result, but before the barrels directly in front of him could reactivate and cause him a world of hurt, he jabbed the butt of his rifle into the 'neck' of the rover, dislodging the metallic plating. When a small gap formed, he tossed his weapon aside and pried the thin panel back, forcibly bending the metal enough to get at the internal circuitry.

As the whine of the now reactivated barrels rotating to shoot him in the face filled him with a mixture of dread

and haste, he reached inside the Rover and ripped out as many wires as he could get his hand on.

The turret froze in place, having lost either power or its control lines.

Paul smiled, still ducking down behind the dead Rover. Now they had a decent chance at taking the bunker. He reached down and retrieved his weapon from the floor...

The Rover suddenly reversed direction, retreating at maximum speed, its treads apparently still retaining power, leaving Paul completely exposed. Realizing his mistake, he jumped to the side, scrambling for cover.

"Umph..." he uttered as his breath was knocked out of him by a little splash of pain square in the chest. The feeling disappeared almost as fast as it began, but Paul fell to the ground, suddenly finding his chest and upper torso numb. His arms also didn't fully function as his pectoral muscles refused to acknowledge their existence. He fell hard to the ground, his head hitting the slightly soft floor material with a thud.

Next thing he knew, Jack's face was above him as he was pulled behind cover.

"Gutsy, man. Very gutsy," his teammate said, eyes darting about ever alert. "We won't waste it," he said, making additional hand motions to the others, coordinating their advance. A moment later he disappeared from Paul's view of the training chamber's ceiling.

2

With scattered suppression fire from Dan and Brian on the left flank, Jack jumped ahead and skidded behind one of the pillars in between the 4th and 5th row of barricades. This one, as far as they had determined, was a dummy with no turret inside. He took a couple quick breaths then poked his head out for a snapshot look ahead.

A paintball zipped by and hit the barricade behind him where Emily had been crouched…but she was already running cattycorner ahead to another pillar on the other side of the street. Jack circled around to the far side of his and fired two shots towards the bunker as suppression fire.

It didn't work, and Emily got hit in the quad with a paintball from one of the snipers in the bunker. She went down hard, then got pelted with another three shots by one of the turrets. Once she stopped moving the remotely controlled turrets tracked to other targets. The trainers might have been hard on them, but they weren't cruel enough to repeatedly pelt a downed trainee.

Jack winced in sympathy. He hoped she was unconscious, otherwise she was laying there fully awake but unable to do anything more than twitch a few helpless muscles. Her autonomic systems would be unaffected…it took an enormous amount of stun energy to shut them down, and often the body would restart automatically, some sort of resistance bred into the Humans by the V'kit'no'sat. It was possible however, according to the data recovered from the pyramid, to kill a Human with stun blasts, though the

amount required was beyond any weapon that Star Force currently fielded.

The V'kit'no'sat weapons discovered in the temple were another matter. Those designed for Human use would need hundreds of stun shots to potentially kill, but the larger ones that the dinosaurs carried had considerably more kick, and with a square hit had a 50/50 probability of killing the tiny Humans, while merely numbing the larger reptiles.

Both technologies were far beyond Star Force's ability to reproduce, but they'd learned enough to create the 'stingers,' as the trainees had come to call the stun-laced paintballs. They'd been told that direct energy delivery weapons were in the early development stages, but so far no viable prototypes had been constructed, though Star Force security forces had been augmented with recently developed 'stun sticks' that the trainees were scheduled to begin training with in the coming months.

Jack caught Megan's gaze and she gave him the 'leap frog' signal. He nodded and readied himself, ready to spring ahead to the next row of barricades, which would deactivate the turrets in the pillar row he was currently hiding behind. Thanks to the slight arc of the assault course, the other pillars couldn't track him if he was pressed up close behind the back side of one...plus the others had already been deactivated by his teammates, who were even now continually adding shots to their target spheres to keep them inactive.

Back behind her barricade, Megan counted down on her fingers for Jack. When she hit one he heard a salvo of paintballs from his teammates, aimed at both turrets and the bunker with the snipers poking their heads up into gun port slits. With their paintball rifle barrels sticking out in front of their faces they were hard to hit, but thanks to the splatter effect it wasn't impossible to numb their face and hands a bit, so the trainers had to take care not to get too bold in the face of dozens of paintballs firing their way.

Megan's fingers clenched down into a fist pump, prompting Jack to round the side of the pillar and dive headfirst toward the next barricade row 4 meters ahead, tripping an invisible motion sensor a meter prior that shut down the turrets behind him that otherwise would have had a clear shot at his flank and backside.

"Clear!" he yelled.

A moment later Kip and Brian darted forward to barricades on his left while the rest of his teammates advanced halfway to positions behind the now deactivated pillars.

Now was crunch time, he knew. They were being funneled down into the narrow end of the course, giving them less and less maneuvering room. The turrets were now more closely spaced, with the bunker turrets coming into play when they got up to rows 2 and three. The snipers also became more lethal at this range, though that would change if and when they were able to get up to point blank range on the wall. They'd only managed that once before, with Kip and Paul, before they were mowed down by the Rover from behind. With it now out and 8 team members remaining, he felt they had a good chance this time.

Jack knew the position of the turrets just past the barricades and those behind them, which also were in effective range. He steadied himself then popped up and took a shot at one of them, splattering its target sphere with a satisfying green splotch.

He ducked back down behind cover as three blue globs impacted the barricade just below where his head had been and two more sailed over it and hit the bottom of the previous row, which was already looking like a bad art project. He didn't know who they got to clean up the mess afterwards, but he pitied them.

The turret received several more hits and dipped in momentary deactivation, followed by Dan running forward and ducking down next to Jack behind the barricade. He saw

Megan and Kip move forward as well, coming parallel to his position behind other barricades.

Ivan wasn't as lucky when he tried to cross the gap and one of the snipers caught him in the gut. He went down hard, ironically falling behind cover, but the rest of the 2s made it up to the 4th row of barricades without taking any hits. He saw Megan faint, firing off two random shots and ducking back down as a hail of paintballs flew her way while on the opposite side of the course Kip, Randy, and Brian came up and took out the turret on the far right side.

When the snipers and turrets adjusted to cover their mistake, Jack and Dan sprayed the distant bunker with shots, some of them coming close enough to splatter into the gun slots and make the snipers flinch...all the while Megan leapt forward and advanced to the next pillar and slid forward on her chest up to the 3rd row of barricades, deactivating the pillar turrets behind her.

That left two rows and six pillars, three of which were sporting turrets, as well as a fourth that the 2s knew contained a hidden panel at ankle level. The bunker just past the 1st row of barricades contained four trainers and four turrets of its own, one at each corner standing taller than the two meter high walls, able to fire both out on the course and down into the bunker if the 2s got that far.

Jack signaled for Randy, Kip, and Dan to become their own snipers, holding position in the 4th row to take down turrets from afar while the rest of their teammates leapfrogged forward. Given the closing distances, reaction times would be ever more important and even poking up out of cover for a faint could spell a very painful headshot.

When he had confirmation that the others were onboard and in position Jack scurried his way down the barricade row, hopping across the street junctions with paintballs hitting at his heels until he got to the far right side, providing the maximum spacing. The outside street that ran along the wall led directly to one of the bunker's front turrets, but the wall blocked the firing arc of the back turret while the rightmost pillar in the 1st row blocked most of the gun ports. It was the best available cover he had, despite the fact that it put him right in line with the closest turret.

Now he waited. With three of his teammates sniping the remaining pillar turrets, the other two were narrowly advancing up to the third row with Megan under a hail of paintballs, catching a few splatters from the top of the barricades. They couldn't move up much further, but it was imperative that the enemy fire was split and varied, both in firing arc and range. Jack was going to be the rabbit and the key to their advance...but he had to wait for the opportune moment.

When the four pillars directly past Megan and Dan temporarily went down they repositioned exactly behind the center two to block some of the incoming fire and started taking chip shots at the last pair of pillars closest to the bunker. Their three snipers kept the closest pillar row deactivated while adding some distant shots of their own to the mix. Careful to keep their heads down, Megan and Dan slowly started popping off random shots at the bunker, hoping for a lucky hit.

Suddenly a hail of paintballs tracked up high and over the inhabited barricades. Jack wondered what the trainers were doing when Jason slammed down behind the barricade next to him.

"Welcome back," he said, grateful for another man on the field.

"Wouldn't miss this for the world," he said, cradling his right arm precariously.

"Can you use that?"

Jason moved his elbow joint experimentally. "Not much, but I can still fire one handed. At the least I can be a decoy."

"My thoughts exactly," Jack said, flexing his muscles in anticipation.

"You the rabbit?"

"As soon as the turret goes down."

"Good luck."

"No kidding," Jack said as the friendly snipers scattered more and more paint in the direction of the bunker. Most of them missed, and they had to keep putting hits on the deactivated pillar turrets to keep them down...but the stun charge was gradually building up on the four-barreled turret standing guard over the side street Jack was poised to run down.

"Hold onto this," he said, sliding his weapon over to Jason. He couldn't see ahead of him, not only because he wanted to keep from getting hit, but the longer he was out of sight the more likely the turrets and enemy snipers would forget about him or assume he had repositioned, which meant that he had to trust his teammates to signal when it was time for him to make his run.

All of a sudden Dan pumped his fist and forearm up and down three times in a hurry, prompting Jack to jump out of cover and sprint forward, bumping into the wall as he drove hard for maximum speed.

The turret he was now staring at had drooped down, deactivated, but as soon as he had taken three steps he opened himself up to the gun ports and the other two bunker turrets...which at the moment were firing at his teammates on the opposite side of the course.

That didn't last long. As soon as Jack popped up in their peripheral vision they tracked his way, opening an opportunity for Dan to jump out of cover to advance to the next pillar as both distraction and utilizing the opportunity for advancement. Jason also took the cue, standing straight up behind the barricade and started blasting away at the bunker, daring the trainers to shoot at him instead of Jack.

Jack ran past the line of four pillars but didn't bother to stop behind cover. He ran past the 2nd row of barricades and up to the last pillars, diving forward as he got shot in the left shoulder, which spun him around to land on his side.

His momentum tumbled him forward head over heels, coming to a stop with his legs in the air and his feet sticking up over the first and closest barricade to the bunker. His back was to the metal panel and he was staring up at the ceiling as his foot got hit with another paintball.

Jack twisted his body around enough that his legs slid down behind cover, but there was little more that he could do besides that. His entire left arm and most of his left torso was numb, and while his shoes provided a bit more insulation against the numbing effects of the paintballs, he couldn't feel his foot either...meaning he probably wouldn't be able to walk.

The good news was, he'd tripped the sensors for the last two pillar lines, permanently deactivating those turrets...leaving only the four at the bunker active, now that the front right turret had reactivated.

The three snipers abandoned their posts and spread out, moving forward individually as Megan and Dan also advanced up to the 2nd row of barricades. Jason advanced to one of the pillars and took on lookout duty from a standing position.

It wasn't long before the 2s had advanced up to the 2nd row of barricades and taken down the frontmost bunker turrets, with them now beginning to splatter the gun ports with too many shots for the trainers to stand their ground. With only the rearmost turrets firing back the team leapfrogged up to the 1st row of barricades alongside Jack, who was still lying on the ground trying to shake off the stun effect. Thirty seconds later and the back turrets also went down.

Jason walked up alongside the far wall, shooting the front turret sphere again to keep it deactivated. He adjusted his aim to the other and shot it as well. With the gun port snipers out of position he was free to abandon cover to continually suppress the front turrets.

Now came the worst part...

In the center of the bunker was the door, or more actually it was an open slot in the wall with a second inset wall blocking vision and access to the interior, allowing two lateral openings, one right, one left, into the bunker. The trainers had obviously fallen back behind the inner wall and were waiting for them to try and fight their way inside, walking directly into their pointblank fire.

That wasn't the plan though.

Jack wiggled around enough to get his good foot under him and, leaning against the barricade, stood himself up on his opposite knee so he could watch. Dan and Megan ran up to the left side gun ports while Brian and Kip advanced to the right side ones. Carefully they poked their weapons in and fired several rounds against the back wall, but as expected the trainers weren't there. They were cowering behind the inset wall that was blocking their position from the gun ports.

That's exactly what the 2s wanted.

Dan dropped his weapon and, standing between two of the ports, knelt down so Megan could step up on his shoulders with Brian and Kip doing likewise. Randy kept suppression fire on the turrets along with Jason on the flanks, keeping them from pelting their elevated teammates in the face.

From the trainers' perspective two heads popped up over the wall, followed quickly by their torsos and weapons, which fired down atop the foursome as fast as their fingers could pump the triggers.

Three of the trainers went down, but the fourth backed up against the inner wall and out of sight.

Megan stayed on her perch, but Brian let Kip down and as a pair moved into the bunker, splitting as they hit the entrance and circling around from both sides and attacking the last trainer.

Kip got hit immediately, but managed to fire one shot back, hitting the sniper rifle-bearing trainer in the vest just as he was hit from behind by Brian. The man slumped to the ground next to Kip while Brian sidestepped over to the mission end pedestal, keeping his eye on the four downed men as he walked over them.

He reached out and palmed the wide half-sphere, pressing it down more than an inch before it clicked in. The entire training course's lights turned blue, indicating that the challenge had been completed successfully.

With the turrets now permanently offline and a wide smile on his face, Jason walked back to where Paul was now sitting up with his back against the barricade and helped him to his feet as a number of support personnel entered the room. One of them came over to Paul and injected an anti-stun charge into his right arm. It spread throughout his body and took away most of the lingering numbness, though it never quite got it all.

"Me too," Jason said, getting his own injection. The numbness in his arm dissipated almost instantly.

"How many of us went down?" Paul asked.

"Emily, Ivan, Jack, and Kip…not counting me."

"Five and a half," Paul noted. "One better than the 7s."

"That's not an official stat," Brian said, walking up to them.

"What was our time?" Jason wondered.

"Don't know," Paul said, "but it'll up our rating a chunk. What's up next?"

"Showers, Lunch," Megan said as the rest of them joined up to the group, "Math, Tech, Swimming, Obstacle Course, and last but not least, our Halo match with the 4s."

Jack flexed his hand experimentally. "Hope this tingle wears off before then," he said, glancing over at Emily. "How are you doing? You got hit the worst."

"Pins and needles," she said regretfully, then broke into a smile. "But worth it."

Jason clapped her on the shoulder. "Onward and upward."

"Speaking of which, let's get topside," Dan said as he waved tauntingly at the trainers as they walked past the 2s towards the exit, "before the others grab the showers."

"You're right," Emily said, wiping some of the blue paint from her chest onto her hand and swiping it across Dan's clean face. "Terrible 2s," she said, putting her clean left fist into the center of the group, with the others doing likewise, forming a 10-point sunburst.

"2 tough," Paul added.

"2 fast," Jason continued, going through their practiced mantra

"2 smart."

"2 hot."

"2 handle."

"2 bad," Megan finished, with them pulling back their fists and following the trainers out from a distance, careful not to slip on the mass of paint covering the floors. They'd really done a number on the place.

After they'd gone a mixed cleaning crew of Humans and machines got to work on the course, cleaning off every spec of paint for the first afternoon session scheduled a little over two hours later when the 6s would take to the course. Save for nighttime hours, the combat ranges were almost always in use, with one team or another working through their grocery list of challenges necessary to reach graduation which, at present, looked to be at least another two years off.

At the beginning of their basic training, it'd been anticipated to take the best of them no less than five.

3

Three weeks later...

Paul and the rest of the 2s walked out onto the spaceport tarmac atop of Atlantis to one of several dozen small Star Force dropships waiting in a neat row outside the boarding terminal to receive passengers. Usually the two-stage craft would nestle up to a docking port at the terminal and allow direct boarding, much like conventional airports, but at present this particular terminal wasn't yet staffed and wouldn't be open to the public until Atlantis officially came online in a few years.

The Scale-One dropships were the smallest in Star Force's fleet, and used for low end personnel or cargo transport...the equivalent of a private jet to fly around the planet, except that these were used to get into space.

As they walked down the row of craft, toting their personal duffle bags, the pilots lead the trainees to the third in line of the perfectly identical dropships, cutting underneath the massive wings to get to the low boarding ramp sitting in the shade they produced on the otherwise sun-scorched parking grid. Looking up Paul could see three sets of wings on the aerolift cradle, with a smaller set underneath on what looked like an overly aerodynamic dart that was the actual space vehicle, affectionately known as the *Angry Sparrow*.

It had a single jet engine, modified to function at high altitude, that allowed it to fly about as a conventional aircraft, landing and taking off on its own as need be, but it also possessed four variable thrust solid propellant rocket engines that would launch it into space, as well as allow for a decent amount of orbital maneuvering.

Coupled with the aerodynamic design and low cargo weight, the Star Force created polymer/alloy dubbed 'Prometheus' allowed the small dropship to maneuver through and reenter the atmosphere at insane speeds, shrugging off the friction-induced heat that would threaten to destroy any other craft. Upon an exceedingly fast reentry, the hull plating would glow a cherry red for those cameras lucky enough to catch a glimpse of the speedy craft...thus giving it its namesake.

Paul and the others walked up the steep steps that were unfolded on the Sparrow's starboard side and into the white/silver adorned passenger cabin. He and the other 9 trainees stowed their gear in overhead storage compartments and filled in ten of the 16 seats, none of which had any windows, which was typical of all Star Force air/spacecraft. Passengers were afforded outside views via hull cameras, displayed on three large screens at the front of the cabin directly behind the cockpit, which came online as soon as the pilots powered up the ship.

As soon as they were all strapped in, the boarding hatch secured, and their storage bins locked and checked by the copilot, Paul felt a faint hum through his seat's plump cushions as the aerolift cradle's 12 high power jet engines idled into action. A moment later the vibration increased a tick and the dropship began to inch its way out of line with its twins and accelerate across the tarmac towards a service runway that led to the primary.

The cradle's ample landing gear were electrically powered, and could provide movement on their own when required for delicate steering maneuvers, but the dropships were spaced wide enough that the small blowback from the jet engines wouldn't be a problem to either them or the terminal so the pilot gradually cranked up thrust and got them motoring down the service runway without delay.

Paul and the others remained silent, but they all eagerly watched the display screens...one fore, one aft, and the other one split starboard/port. Only Brian had been to space before, on vacation to a resort facility in low orbit, but even he was excited to return. The 2s were scheduled for a week and a half of zero, low, and high gravity training and, according to the 0s and 1s who'd already completed their training stint, it was supposed to be a blast.

In addition to the sheer fun of going into space and diving into new training scenarios, even if they were little more than orientation drills, Paul and the others were eager to add the experience points to their team total that the trip would give them a chance to earn. If they matched the 0s' score, they'd pull within 50 points of second place, with the leading 7s too far ahead to eclipse on this mission, no matter how well they scored. Still, they didn't want to give up any points to them when they went through their own mission several weeks down the road.

Point being, as much as this mission was going to be fun, they had team business to attend to.

As far as individual ranks went, the mission also afforded several challenges on that front. Paul was currently ranked 13th and second within the 2s behind Jason, who was 11th after the last completed training rotation. These challenge scores wouldn't be added to the total until everyone had a chance to go through the space mission, but those scores had already been posted for comparison sake, fueling the ever increasing competition between the trainees.

Unlike other rivalries, this one wasn't detrimental. Each of the trainees sought to become better, and helped each other train to overcome their weaknesses, not only because team scores were figured into individual ranks and vice versa, but because they all knew the stakes and the dire situation the planet faced. Earth needed them to rise to great heights, and the stronger they could make their teammates, the stronger Star Force as a whole would become.

And the stronger Star Force became, the better chance the planet had to survive.

Thus the training staff, along with Director Davis, stoked their competitive fires whenever they had the chance, unnecessary as that was, for the trainees were showing a remarkable amount of self-motivation. Still, any extra goosing of their existing rivalries was considered par for the course, and the trainers took every opportunity to ride those who hadn't performed as well as the others, though sometimes they regretted that choice when they faced off with the trainees during combat challenges.

In addition to a myriad of impressive skills, the trainees had good memories and readily carried grudges against their trainers.

The *Sparrow*-class dropship pulled a slow U-turn at the end of the service runway and taxied onto the end of the number 3 main. Once aligned with the extra-long runway, the dropship's pilots wasted no time and throttled up the cradle's 12 jet engines to half power, with Paul and the others feeling themselves pushed back into their seats.

The small dropship accelerated fast and took to the air before they even reached the midway point on the runway and quickly gained altitude. On the display screens Atlantis disappeared from the forward camera as they tilted up into the sky with the rear view expanding out to give the trainees a good view of their city. The runway shrank rapidly until it was just one of several long spider web-like strands crossing the surface of the man-made island. Before long it disappeared altogether as they passed through a layer of clouds.

After a fairly smooth ascent to about 10 km, Paul felt the engines ramp up again and their speed slowly accelerate over the following minutes, gradually climbing higher and faster using only the cradle's engines to 'slingshot' the Sparrow on the first leg of its climb into space.

When the air really began to thin the pilots switched the engines over into aerospike mode and throttled up to 100%, compressing and accelerating what little air remained above 32 km altitude in an effort to reach a minimum speed of 3,700 kph. As the air pressured decreased so did the drag, increasing thrust efficiency while diminishing the lift property of the cradle's massive wings, but their speed continued to inch upwards as the dropship lightened as it continued to burn off fuel, peaking out at 42.5 kilometers and an airspeed of 4,350 kph.

Once there was no more speed or altitude to be gained by air flight, the Sparrow's pilots disengaged the spacecraft from the underside of the cradle, dropping off of its belly clamps and gliding down below it several hundred meters as the cradle, now lighter without its payload, jetted ahead of the smaller spacecraft, now visible to the pilots as the carrier banked off to the left. The unmanned cradle was now under the remote control of Atlantis, beginning its trip back down to the city.

Once clear of any potential collisions, the Sparrow kicked in its rocket engines at partial thrust and began a hard, but smooth ascent up and out of the atmosphere, accelerating to a minimal orbital speed of 28,000 kph before throttling back, at which point Paul began to feel the first tingle of zero gravity.

He knew it was an illusion, the Earth's gravity hadn't disappeared and was still pulling heavily on his body at this very moment. The thing was, he and the Sparrow were falling towards the planet with nothing to rest his feet on and produce the compression that gravity on the surface afforded. It was the same principle of being at the top of a rollercoaster and feeling 'weightless' for a moment as you roll down the other side.

With no compression, no 'gravity' was felt, but it was ever present and continually accelerating him and the dropship towards the planet...which would have been a very bad thing if they weren't moving so fast sideways. The trick of orbit was that your lateral speed moved you away from the planet as fast as the planet pulled you towards it, and since the tug of war was perpendicular your lateral speed never diminished.

It was a complicated, yet simple concept that Paul and the others had not been taught in school, but had been drilled on in training. Orbits were the foundation of the universe, and if you couldn't understand how gravity redirected your lateral motion into a constant turn, then you could never navigate in space. All movement was dictated or affected by gravity, both that of the Earth, Luna, Sol, and the other planets and even asteroids in the star system. All gave a small gravity pull that had to be accounted for, and potentially used, to navigate in space.

It had been quite an eye opener for Paul when he'd finally got the concept, not to mention the actual names of the Moon and Sun. Why hadn't they taught him that in high school? It made perfect sense now why they lived in the Solar System...because the central star, or 'sun,' was named Sol. And why had the first astronauts landed on the moon in a Lunar lander? Because the Moon's name was Luna.

There were a lot of things like that that bugged Paul. The more he learned from his Star Force training the more he realized that the public was clueless as to what was going on above and beyond pop culture, whether it be cell phone disruption caused by solar flares or magnetic compasses not actually pointing to geographic north.

But not understanding an orbit was akin to thinking the Earth was flat, and that point was made all the more poignant as Paul's body began to tug against his restraints and a wash of vertigo crept over his senses as the dropship entered a coast stage enroute to one of 7 starports orbiting at a lazy altitude of 900 kilometers.

4

The 'Conduit to Space' had been one of Davis's initial selling points to the public, and was the foundation for Star Force's pseudo monopoly on space travel. The basic principle was building transportation infrastructure that passengers and cargo could transit through, rather than designing do-it-all spacecraft akin to the early Apollo program that sent three astronauts to the moon and back on a single rocket.

Functional diversity and specification was the key, Davis knew, and the Conduit to Space formed the base of Star Force's infrastructure, in that it focused solely on getting personnel and cargo up through the atmosphere to orbital speeds, and conversely back down from orbit to the surface.

There were three distinct pieces to the Conduit. The first was a *Spaceport*, the ground roots of space infrastructure and by far the easiest to construct. It was little more than a dedicated airport on the surface that served as a transit hub, whether it used runways, launch pads, accelerator tracks, etc.

The *Dropship* was the second piece of the Conduit, with the design concept being a spaceship that spent as much time in atmosphere as it did in orbit and whose sole purpose was to travel back and forth between the endpoints of the Conduit to Space.

The *Starport* was the third piece and opposite end of the Conduit from the spaceport, and served essentially the same function as its counterpart. It was a transit hub for orbital traffic and commerce, both 'airport' and 'rail station' that served as a waypoint for all Star Force traffic coming up from, or down to, Earth.

As the trainees' Sparrow approached the starport, Paul and the others watched the display screens with growing interest. Far ahead of them was a growing grey dot that was the ugly, yet functional space station...but on their port side a long, train-like ship was pacing them, also enroute to the starport. It had nestled up to less than a kilometer away from the Sparrow and the two Star Force ships were using laser rangefinders to keep their distance steady while approaching the starport in synch.

Traditional wisdom held that spaceships should keep as far away from each other as reasonable, to reduce the chance of collisions, but whether by Star Force tradition or the egos of the pilots that flew the ships for the corporation, Star Force craft had a tendency to group together whenever near, and Paul had to admit that the sight of flying side by side with another spaceship enroute to a space station was just plain cool.

That, and the other ship was many times larger than their Sparrow. It was one of Star Force's *Starships*...the opposite of a Dropship, in that the starship would never land on a planet. It was built in space, flew through space, and would probably end up being decommissioned and disassembled in space. As such, it needed no reentry shielding or aerodynamic design, and its blocky nature stood in stark contrast to the Sparrow's edgeless symmetry.

The two spaceships were visually an odd pair, each designed to accomplish a specific task in lieu of trying to squeeze too much functionality into a single ship. This way, two ships could accomplish the task of one with greater ease, lower cost, and higher efficiency. Thus was the wisdom of the Conduit to Space...it took all the heavy lifting out of the starship designs, leaving them free to ferry about personnel and cargo between the ever growing number of orbital facilities.

As the pair of ships approached the starport Paul could begin to make out the 'TIE bomber' design of the station. It was completely enclosed within an armor plated shell with large bay doors that usually remained open, facing down on the planet. It was towards those doors that the Sparrow flew, depressing its approach slightly to slide underneath.

Now seeing it in person, Paul agreed with previous sentiments that the starport design could also be compared to a pair of binoculars, or even the classic chocolate Ho Hos in twin packaging, but Paul preferred the Star Wars reference. Regardless of which metaphor you used, inside the station were two massive rotating cylinders situated side by side, one spinning clockwise and the other counter clockwise under fine-tuned computer control to null out the rotational list.

In front of the two artificial gravity creating cylinders was a 'crossbar' connecting them to an array of docking pylons alongside pressurized and unpressurized warehouses that partially obscured the view of the cylinders, which were surrounded by a narrow gap of unpressurized space a few dozen meters wide that transitioned to the inner edge of the armored shell that surrounded the station.

The inside of the thick shell was actually several levels of zero gravity compartments connected to the gravity cylinders on the back side, opposite the docking area. All in all, about half of the internal volume of the starport was zero gravity, with the other half seeing multiple variations of artificial gravity ranging from .05 to 1.0 Earth norm, with all residential areas, restrooms, and food courts in the gravity section.

Still strapped into his seat, Paul felt his body tug on the restraints again as the Sparrow decelerated ahead of its pacing starship and begin maneuvering up and under the oversized 'TIE bomber.'

"Busy day," Jason commented to the otherwise silent group as they got their first glimpse of the docking area. There were two dropships, both the midsized *Eagle*-class, and six starships of various sizes attached to the pylons, with one of the small starships just beginning to disengage and drift out from under the protective shell that surrounded both the station and the docking area.

Paul glanced over at another screen and the large starship now trailing behind them, trying to size it up. It was so long that he doubted it could fit inside the docking area with the bay doors closed. He knew that it was standard procedure to shelter the spacebound dropships during a meteor shower or intense solar flare, but apparently that wasn't true of all the starships. He wondered how much armor plating they had...

Their dropship nulled out its momentum and pointed its nose in towards the docking pylons before tapping on the thrusters and nudging closer. With practiced ease the pilots squeezed the wing-like Sparrow underneath the shortest of the pylons as they retracted a dorsal hull plate, exposing their docking port underneath the smooth reentry-hardened hull.

Using an automated docking laser system, four thick but flexible mechanical limbs reached out and grasped the frame around the docking port and killed any remaining list from the dropship before an umbilical extended inside the perimeter of the metal struts and made contact. Seal tests were triple checked and the pressure in the umbilical equalized before the system confirmed a good lock to both docking control and the cockpit of the Sparrow.

The copilot appeared a moment later, floating back into the front of the passenger area just to the left of the display screens and toggled the roof hatch, briefly checking the manual pressure gage, which confirmed 1 atmosphere on the other side, before opening their side of the passageway.

Paul and the others began unstrapping themselves and experienced the free floating wonder of zero gravity for the first time as they clumsily began unlatching the storage compartments and retrieving their duffels.

"This is so cool," Dan said under his breath as he pulled his from what had been the 'overhead' bin. Now that they were in freefall, there was no longer any up or down.

Paul smiled unguardedly the entire time it took him to climb along the shallow handholds in the ceiling to where the copilot was waiting at the base of the open hatch. When he got there she gave him a slight boost upward and floated behind Megan through the short, but well lit tunnel up into a large square room with a low 'ceiling,' making it easier to find handholds to move about with.

Three Star Force attendants were present in the boarding/receiving area and got the 2s moving in an organized fashion. One attendant, dressed in the standard dark blue jumpsuit that designated the personnel relations division, led the group through several customs/tracking stations...all of which they bypassed...and into the starport's zero gravity section where there was a mix of Star Force personnel and tourists milling about as they transferred through a gymnasium sized commons area that looked more like a child's playground at a restaurant.

There were numerous transparent colored tunnels twisting and crisscrossing the area with floating 'tables' intermixed where four people could attach themselves by footholds and straps to work tabletop-mounted computer terminals and entertainment screens, monitoring everything from tv shows to stock market updates.

Paul was so drawn to the amusement park atmosphere on his left that he didn't glance right until several moments later, when he finally noticed the cinematic 'viewport' covering the entire right wall. It was as large as a movie screen and, of course, not a real viewport, but a camera relay from outside the station, letting the patrons watch the docking area, the Earth below, and the ships coming to and from the starport.

The trainees drifted past the screen, barely obscuring even part of the view, as the attendant showed them across the promenade via a slow moving railway that had tiny handholds to grab onto. It carried them in single file to the opposite side where they reentered the working end of another docking pylon.

Again, they bypassed the bureaucracy and moved directly to another airlock...this one leading to one of the smaller starships docked at the starport. When they moved down the umbilical and into a short squarish booth, a line of flashing indicator lights guided them even further into the ship. The attendant led the way and diverted them to the right at a four-way junction where they traveled down a short hall then dropped down a ladder and arrived in a similar passenger cabin to that on the dropship, save for this one was five times as wide and held over 100 seats.

That was, until Paul looked 'up' and noticed another bank above him to the right, suddenly realizing that the floor was curved and that the seats went up and around a central pillar that he'd just dropped out of and mistaken as the ceiling.

Not a single seat was occupied.

"All for us?" Jack asked.

"You and a few Star Force personnel that need to transfer over anyway," the attendant said with a half smile that seemed to be permanently affixed to her face. "Strap yourselves and your bundles into the extra seats until we get underway. The storage areas are in the back, but since this is a dedicated flight you can keep your gear up here with you."

"My name is Kianna and I'll be your flight attendant on this trip. If there's anything you need or have any questions to ask, I'm your go-to person. Please go ahead and get yourselves situated. I believe the captain wishes to get underway in a few minutes."

Using more 'ceiling' handholds, Paul and the others floated over the banks of seats and dropped 'down' into them, belting in their duffels in two neat rows behind where they chose to sit clustered together. A few minutes later four more Star Force personnel entered the pit-like chamber that arced up on either side.

Three dark green-uniformed techs, along with a light green-clad woman, whom Paul knew to be a Star Force software expert, settled down into a different section of seats, leaving the trainees to themselves as the attendant disappeared elsewhere into the ship. Not soon after Paul and the others felt the slight tug on their restraints, indicating that they were pulling away from the starport and beginning their trip out to the D-4 training station in middle planetary orbit.

5

All Star Force orbital stations were designated into three categories. "A" stations were open to the public and could be traveled to as simply as buying a plane ticket and booking a hotel room on one of the habitats. There were various versions, from luxury resorts to sports facilities, training classes, zero gravity romance pods, and even low gravity retirement and medical habitats for people too weak or ill to sustain normal Earth gravity.

Whereas all "A" stations were public domain, "B" stations were private ventures. Star Force built the stations then rented them out to corporations or governments, sometimes in berths or entire facilities, but all were operated by Star Force personnel. These included communications stations, factories, warehouses, research labs and astronomic observatories, all the way up to private resorts and homes, for those wishing for permanent residence in orbit and having the funds to pay for it.

The third category of Star Force orbital installations were for private company use, labeled as "C" and showed the greatest range of functions from hydroponic agriculture to heavy industry, shipyards to build the starships, massive mobile construction 'islands' to build new stations and expand existing ones, warehouses to store the ever increasing amount of cargo transfers, habitats for the Star Force orbital workforce, and a myriad of other functions.

"D" stations officially didn't exist yet, and wouldn't for some time as far as the public knew, but they were internally designated for Star Force's highly secret military branch, of which the trainees were the beginning. Four stations had been built to date...one a clandestine Research and Development facility, another a fuel production factory, the third a small shipyard for the construction of prototypes coming out of the R/D facility, and the fourth a zero gravity training complex , which was the trainees' current destination.

Thanks to another set of video screens, Paul and the others got to watch their departure from the starport, soon followed by a sudden jerk sideways as the passenger compartment of the starship began to rotate ever so slowly.

Paul's recently established inner equilibrium was shattered and his head pounded as the blood started to be pulled towards his feet by the centrifugal force...but that was the norm for Human physiology and his body quickly remembered, settling both his limbs and his stomach, but leaving him with a bit of a headache.

It took several minutes for the rotating cylinder to speed up to 1 gravity of rotation, but once it did the attendant returned, carefully climbing down the ladder in transition from the zero gravity section of the ship, and informed them that they were free to move about for the duration of the trip. She also noted that if a course correction or acceleration was needed, a warning klaxon would sound, meaning they had 30 seconds to grab hold of something or return to their seats before the engines fired.

As if on cue, a mechanical repetitive buzz-like sound blared three times, prompting the attendant to slip into one of the empty seats...but she didn't bother to fasten the restraints, so neither did the trainees.

When the engines did fire, it was a lackluster response. Paul had felt more pull riding in his track team's bus...although this acceleration was constant, lasting for the better part of 20 minutes as the starship accelerated away from Earth, climbing towards middle orbit which, as far as the Star Force definition was concerned, was all orbital tracks between 1 and 50 days in length, meaning geosynch on out past the moon. The training station, however, was over 100,000 kilometers away from the Earth, making it about a fourth of the distance to the moon with an orbital period around 4 days.

Most B-class habitats were parked in geosynchronous orbit, while 70% of the A-class stations were within that boundary or 'low earth orbit,' thanks to the tourists desire to see the planet close up. C-class stations were scattered throughout, with a growing number in middle orbit. Given the increasing volume of space traffic, Star Force had adopted…and heavily encouraged others to follow…its policy of leaving the extreme low orbits empty…those being within an altitude of 600 kilometers or so. Star Force's starports were the closest habitats the company had to the upper atmosphere and were well above that mark.

Not all countries and corporations respected this precedent, and there was a high volume of satellites cluttering the skies, but with Star Force's ever growing number of communication stations, the practice of putting individual telecommunications satellites into space was falling by the wayside. As it was, Star Force had a small fleet of recovery craft clearing the lower orbits of outdated, broken, or abandoned satellites along with other space debris creating potential navigation hazards.

Star Force's competitors operated a small fleet of short range ships…some copying the dropship function, others going their own way with capsule/rocket designs and a few upstarts using acceleration tracks on the surface to slingshot a spaceplane up into the atmosphere in lieu of an aerospace cradle. All their designs were primitive compared to those fielded by Star Force, but they were functional none the less, making a small dent in Davis's monopoly.

Their diminutive orbital stations were, however, all located in extreme low orbit, given that they didn't have the manpower to build them larger or the thrust capacity to launch them farther out. They also liked thumbing their noses at Star Force's edict, and used the 'up close Earth view' talking points in their tourist advertising.

Their main source of income, however, was from military contracts, given that Star Force had a strict policy on what their services could be used for, which excluded weapons placement, service, or research. While Star Force obviously didn't have a problem with such things, they weren't about to help usher in the potential for World War III, nor accelerate the timetable which would run counter to their own militarization efforts. They needed to get armed first…so they kindly declined any military business, which then ran straight to their competitors or the governments' own space divisions.

98% of the orbital economy flowed through Star Force, however, and any legal attempts to diminish that virtual monopoly had been vehemently fought off, based in no small part to the fact that Star Force was an international corporation, with most of its infrastructure in space where no nation had jurisdiction.

The United Nations had been prompted to declare everything in Earth orbit under their legal control, but after Star Force had quietly informed them and their member nations that they wouldn't accept that legal noose, the measure had been dropped and the free and open policy of space travel had been publicly reinforced. What hadn't been publically said was that Star Force promised to cut off all services to any nation voting for the measure, along with the obvious fact that neither the UN, nor any individual nation, had the ability to enforce their laws off planet.

It had been a hopeful bluff on the UN's part, which Star Force had quickly called. Getting their early foothold on space travel had, as Davis predicted, given them the leverage they needed to remain independent.

After the acceleration phase, the Star Force starship began an 18 hour coast stage, traveling out to the D-4 station. Paul and the others were free to walk about the ship, which was part gravity, part zero gravity. The rotating section that the passenger seats were in was connected through the central core to another opposite rotating cylinder directly aft, which gave the ship an elongated design.

Behind it, in a zero gravity section, was the engineering area, which contained most of the ship's machinery, including the engines and fuel reserves, which were ample. Had the captain wished it, the starship could have arrived at the station in less than an hour, but the quicker the transit, the more fuel burned, both in acceleration and deceleration at target.

Star Force designed all its starships with greater cruising ranges than required for their mission assignments, unlike the early days of space travel when the bare minimum was all that was sought for. If the *Cougar*-class starship that they were traveling in wished to flex its engineering muscle, it could travel all the way to Mars and back over the course of two months with a full fuel load at the optimum planetary alignment.

What Davis understood...and the competition was slowly figuring out...was that the key to space travel was not trying to be the first to do something, but to become the first to do that thing on a regular basis and in an efficient way. In an early Star Force edict, Davis had told his development teams that achievement was not the goal, conquest was. They not only had to beat the challenges set before them, they had to beat them in such a way, and with such repetition, that they literally owned them.

Domination was the key to space travel, not pushing the limits...which was why Star Force hadn't yet set foot on the Moon, let alone Mars. The US, China, and Russia all had small outposts on Luna, and the US had even established a temporary settlement on Mars for a few brief months, but what did it gain them other than notoriety? No country had yet begun to claim 'lands' yet, which was good for Star Force, because that monkey was going to drop on their back sooner or later, so what had the Americans' and others' efforts gained them?

Each and every Star Force endeavor advanced the company in some way, whether it be the establishment of another piece of infrastructure, like the construction of a starport, or a field test of new equipment, or even just flight training to raise the experience level of their pilots. As it was, Star Force had by far the most flight hours in space, and that was just racking up kilometers making routine cargo runs.

The *Cougar*-class starship was another good example of Star Force philosophy. It was on the small end of the fleet currently in service, but more massive than any non-Star Force ship. It had been designed with engines and fuel storage above and beyond what was needed for its mission parameters, armor plating more than sufficient to protect it against micrometeorites and radiation, maneuvering thrusters powerful and precise enough to make the ship dance if need be, and above all else artificial gravity, which the competition said was a waste of resources.

Davis knew it was an investment in the health of his people. Humans needed gravity, and going without it for a long period of time would leave a person weak and susceptible to illness. Gravity was like a constant workout for the body that people living on the surface took for granted. Take away that workout and most body functions diminished quickly from atrophy.

And while zero gravity was a big advantage of being in space, both from a tourist and industrial standpoint, Davis knew that the more time his people spent in artificial gravity the stronger and healthier they would be, which is why he decreed that all starships would be so equipped.

The pilots in the forward section of the ship were, however, still in zero gravity, but they spent most of their time in the rear sections keeping up to date with small forearm display screens that doubled as a basic instrument monitor. Aside from docking and course corrections, there wasn't much point in being on the bridge, and had this been one of the larger starship designs, the bridge would actually have been located inside the gravity section, meaning that the crew could operate in full gravity the entire time.

The diameter of the Cougar was too small, however, to allow for a decent gravity bridge. The arc of the cylinder was too sharp and more accustomed to sitting down rather than walking about. The aesthetic designers for the ship interiors had laid down basic guidelines that the bridge should be as secure and stable a place as possible, and the gravity cylinder on the Cougar felt a bit like a carnival ride, thus the bridge had been placed in the forward zero gravity section.

Paul and the others, thanks to their special status, got to tour every inch of the ship's interior during their long trip out to the station, including the bridge compartment. Again, there were no windows, but dozens of display screens imbedded in the walls that made it look as if he was standing inside the cockpit of the Millennium Falcon, affording the pilots a better view of the surrounding space than a window ever could.

In addition to the visuals, they also had radar and laser tracking systems tied into a 3d navigational matrix that served in lieu of a hologram, which Star Force techs still couldn't figure out how to replicate from those in the pyramid in Antarctica. Each of the four bridge seats had its own set of displays and controls, though only two were routinely used. One other thing about Star Force protocol was redundancy, in both volume and function, to deal with unexpected problems if and when they arose.

After thoroughly inspecting both the forward and aft zero gravity sections, Paul eventually landed in the 'lounge' section of the starship, which was the second gravity cylinder. It had sparse, couch-like seating, entertainment screens, a small food station, and most importantly the restrooms. Paul had never liked the idea of using a zero gravity restroom, which the old time astronauts were forced to use and which was still employed on the competition's small stations.

By decree from Davis early on, all Star Force 'facilities' had to be gravity based, a decision which Paul appreciated, and yet another mote of wisdom in the Conduit to Space in keeping the distance from spaceport to starport short, because the dropships were all zero gravity, and thus had no restrooms.

That was fine for short trips, much akin to his riding to distant track meets on his high school's bus, but with an 18 hour trip out to the training station, Paul was thankful for Davis's insistence that all starships have artificial gravity.

After another 20 minute deceleration burn, the Cougar slowly made its way to the D-4 station, which was an altogether different version from the starport. This station was much larger, and instead of having gravity cylinders it was equipped with gravity discs, two smashed flat on top of each other like pancakes and rotating in opposite directions inside a mutual casing, meaning that the rotation wasn't visible from outside.

Six of those discs were visibly attached into a spine-like zero gravity section like CD cases being set into a vertical holder. The front half of the discs were visible, but the back half was sunk into the spine, which extended down further than there were discs. Paul knew that was because this type of station was expandable, with the possibility of adding on more discs and even more sections of 'spine' as necessity required, making it almost like a giant Lego set with no predetermined dimensions.

The docking area was on the far side of the spine, opposite the discs, with no other starships present on the four stubby pylons, widely spaced down the length of the station, capable of accommodating the largest of starships, as well as allowing for future designs of even greater size.

Paul and the others were called back to their seats and strapped in as the gravity cylinders slowly decelerated, returning the starship to full zero gravity to aid in the docking procedure. Once the hard dock was made, any additional internal movement could put additional stress on the small but firm tether resulting in sheering motion, thus all docked ships had to spin down before attaching...at least until the new docking collars were installed. Currently the stronger versions were still in the prototype phase, going through an extensive series of tests before being sanctioned for use in the field.

After unstrapping his duffle, Paul followed the attendant out of the ship and into the training station much as he'd done at the starport, except there were no civilians milling about, nor were there recreational facilities. The inside of the habitat was a long series of hallways connecting workrooms in a very Spartan design, only interrupted by emergency bulkheads that would auto-seal in case of an atmospheric breach so that the whole spine of the station wouldn't vent out.

White illumination strips were everywhere, with colored ones popping up at random locations for direction and identification of particular sections of the station, which stood out in stark contrast to the otherwise snow-white demeanor of the design aesthetic.

The attendant's dark blue uniform clashed with the environment, making her clearly visible against the environment as a white uniformed training officer met up with the group and took possession of the trainees.

"Quarters are this way," he said with the usual formality. None of their trainers could ever be described as chatty.

The ten trainees followed the man down the spine until they came to the third disc transition station, which was essentially an elevator terminal that carried them along the inside of the disc case to the center of rotation. Once there, the elevator began to slowly rotate, matching the spin, then attached to the disc and opened its door.

Paul, Megan, and Brian floated out into the center of what looked like a hamster wheel slowly spinning around them, reaching for the ladder handholds on the walls and pulling their feet onto the rungs while slipping their duffles over their shoulders. A tiny gravity pull resulted, which barely increased as they walked down the ladder to the floor of the hamster wheel, gently resting their feet on the grippy surface.

There was a doorway a quarter of the way around, which Paul gently walked toward, feeling like he was going to launch himself up with each step, but thanks to a wall railing he kept himself in place and exited the elevator terminal just as Jason, Kip, and Emily arrived behind them.

On the other side of the doorway was a claustrophobic staircase that led down to the first of the micro-gravity levels, which had the same basic geometry as the gravity cylinder in the Cougar they'd just arrived on. A few steps away was another elevator station, this with four units facing in on each other like you'd typically find in a skyscraper on Earth.

The trainer stood in the hallway and handed Paul a keycard. "Level 4, room 26," he said, pointing to the elevators.

"Thanks," Paul said, walking slowly with long gentle steps as Megan and Brian received their cards. He got to the first elevator and hit the call button, then waited for the others to catch up.

"This feels so weird," Megan commented as the elevator door closed on the trio.

"But cool," Brian added, grabbing the handrail as they suddenly felt the artificial gravity increasing as they moved farther 'down' and out on the spinning disc.

"It's going to be hard to maneuver like this," Paul commented, starting to feel his legs again. "Every twitch I make wants to send me flying into the ceiling."

"It'll certainly take some getting used to," Brian commented.

"Which is why we're here," Megan reminded them as the elevator door opened and they walked out onto imperceptibly curved floors with normal gravity. "I don't know about you two, but I'm gonna grab a hot show and take a long nap. Either one of you care to join me?"

"For which part?" Paul asked, knowing which she meant.

"The nap," she said, giving him the evil eye. Her body temperature ran a predictable .8 degrees below normal and as a result she always complained of feeling cold, making either an electric blanket or snuggle-buddy her best friend while sleeping, the former of which she carried in her duffle.

"I'm not really feeling tired, so I'm going to explore a bit," Paul said, shrugging in gentle apology.

"Alright vamp," Brian said playfully, "I'll let you suck up my body heat, but no tickling this time."

Megan punched him in the shoulder none too gently in acceptance. She hated that nickname.

"Room 23," she told him as she headed off down the hallway.

"When do you think we're scheduled to begin?" Brian asked Paul as they waited for the others to catch up.

"They'll probably give us a few hours at least to settle in," he said as the elevator opened and three more of them walked out.

"8:00 am," Jason answered, overhearing the last bit of their conversation. "Then we get to take a bite out of the Os' lead."

"Let's get to it," Paul agreed, fist-bumping his teammate.

6

Adjusting to the zero gravity hadn't been as hard as Paul had previously thought, but it was an odd set of motions to learn. Every movement he made had to be scaled down and he constantly had to be reaching for hand or footholds. There was no 'standing' still, because even when he nulled out his motion every twist of his neck or flick of his wrist would start him listing. In truth, he felt overpowered for the environment.

But fortunately the station's designers had been wise enough to take this into consideration when laying out the interior. The more Paul looked around he realized that there were handlebars, rungs, indentations and edges *everywhere*, and once his eyes knew what to look for he began to develop a subconscious rhythm to his movements.

That rhythm was 80% arms, 15% twisting, and 5% legs...which was also odd to Paul because in gravity he did almost all his movement with his legs, but here they were almost a detriment to him unless he had a long span of clear hallway to shoot down, which he and the others had fun trying to get maximum speed and accuracy out of their 'jumps.'

After a day of running through the zero gravity obstacle course set in the spine of the station, which ironically also looked like a kids' playground, Paul and the others were brought into a completely empty room, ten times larger than anything else on the station. There were small handholds on the padded walls of the giant white cube, but nothing in the open airspace to latch onto.

Everywhere else on the station there were polls, grating, or even just wall protrusions extending out to avoid this type of open space, but here there was simply nothing to work with and Paul felt a sense of unease wash over him. Glancing at his teammates he saw similar concern on their faces.

Their lead trainer, named Gent, pushed off from the wall near the entrance and floated up towards the center of the gymnasium-sized room as one of his assistants toggled a wall-mounted control board, causing a thin rod to extend down from the 'ceiling' into the dead center of the chamber. Gent grabbed hold of it then hand-walked himself down to the nub. Once settled, the assistant retracted the pole, leaving Gent floating in the center of the room.

"You need to remember," he began, making tiny hand movements to steady himself, "that every twitch you make has an effect. Even turning your head will cause you to rotate, so you need to be aware of everything you do before you do it. You also need to adjust to your environment…in this case, that means the air. You're not free floating in vacuum, so you have some limited means of movement. Use it," he said, beginning to 'swim' through the air.

He didn't go far, but to Paul's surprise Gent began moving, imperceptibly at first, then gaining speed as he traveled towards the wall. Above them on the 'ceiling' a clock started counting up from zero, timing the trainer. When he eventually made it to the wall he twisted about, grabbed a handhold, then walked his body down to the center and pressed a hidden button, stopping the clock at 48.2 seconds.

"How did you do that?" Jason asked in wonder.

Gent smiled cruelly. "Figure it out. 020, you're up first."

Jack nodded and waited for the stabilizing rod to extend, then, using the skills he'd practiced yesterday, leapt off the wall like a bullet and shot towards the center of the room. He missed slightly, but caught the rod with his arm. He steadied himself facing the wall next to the others.

"Wait for the signal to begin," Gent said as the assistant retracted the rod. A moment later a chime sounded and Jack began swimming through the air much as he would have done in the water.

Problem was, he wasn't going anywhere. Instead he was spinning about uncontrollably, every twist of his body enhancing the problem and making his movements more erratic.

"Null it out!" Emily shouted.

Taking her advice, Jack forgot any attempt at movement and curled up into a ball. He tried to analyze the direction he was spinning and reached his left arm out from his chest, then moved it to the left, slowing but not stopping his leftward spin. He continued for another minute, trying to move his hands sideways through the air, then turn them flat against the motion to try and steady himself, only minorly succeeding. When Gent finally ordered the stabilizer rod extended Jack was out of reach by a few inches, struggling with forced patience to swim his way to it.

Suddenly there was a blur in Paul's peripheral vision as Megan leapt off the wall and flew towards Jack. She thumped him on the back as she passed, knocking him into reach of the rod while skewing her own trajectory. He got a handhold on the rod and she the far wall, then both pushed off to return to the group clinging to handholds near the corner entrance in the padded cube chamber.

"021," Gent called out.

"Oh boy," Randy said under his breath, launching himself off the wall towards the center point. He grabbed the rod and carefully steadied himself, nulling out as much micro-motion as he possibly could before the rod retracted.

When the chime sounded he didn't move at all. He just floated there, arms extended, studying his situation. After a long moment he reached both arms forward, much as the trainer had, then tipped the angle of his hands and brought them back along his sides trying to cup as much air with them as he could.

He moved forward immediately, but not from the air he was moving, but rather from the counterbalance of his swinging arms. However, when they reached the end of their swing, their momentum tugged on his body and nulled out his motion, with a slight lateral twist thrown in that frustrated Randy to no end. He tried again and again, but couldn't manage any controlled movement, though he did succeed in accidentally drifting off the center point towards the far left wall.

After several minutes Gent looked at the other trainees. "Someone go get him," he ordered.

"I'm next anyway," Kip said, jumping off the wall and grabbing onto Randy's arm as he passed, which pulled them both over to the far wall. Kip waited there until the rod was extended again, then floated over to the center point for his try, which ended up equally fruitless.

Emily came next, and started rotating around uncontrollably right from the start. She tried different arm movements, half steadying herself, but with each motion she made it seemed to send her on a slightly different trajectory than she'd expected, nulling out a twist but adding a corkscrew motion that either cart-wheeled her side to side or flipped her head over heels. Neither her arms nor her legs were attached to the center of her body, so creating straight lines of momentum was virtually impossible.

She tried the next best thing, doing the mental math and approximating the direction each twist would send her before she made it, but it was no use. No matter how close to neutral she got, she could never null it all out, let alone provide any thrust. Emily knew the key was in moving the air, but it was too thin to cup with her hands, though if she could smooth out her motion enough it should work at least a little bit, and with successive motions her momentum would build, but she couldn't tell if she was making any progress or not without some point of reference. With the rod gone there was no way of knowing if she'd moved an inch forward or back, leaving her no way to measure the tiny movements that were plaguing her.

She blew out an exasperated breath, frustrated with her failure, when she noticed herself rotate slightly in a new angle. She frowned, but otherwise didn't move, still listing about uncontrollably. There had been no arm movement to trigger that, and she was pretty sure she hadn't twisted her torso or head.

Then the epiphany hit her. She filled her lungs with air then blew out hard...resulting in a small, but significant rotation backwards.

From the 'ground' Paul and the others watched as Emily made no progress, and he wondered what he could do differently. He would be the next one to go, and if he didn't figure something out he'd be spinning about just like Emily was...

Paul frowned. "Is she..." he whispered to Jason.

"I think she's figured it out," he whispered back as Emily, still tumbling uncontrollably, suddenly had a lateral drift manifest...and it was steadily growing faster, moving her over to the side wall.

"That a girl!" Brian yelled as it became clear that her sideways movement wasn't an accident. She was still spinning about, but drifting steadily towards the wall, continually picking up speed until her flailing left arm hit. With the reflexes of a cat, she twisted about and swiped at the wall, brushing her fingers against the clingy pads and pulling herself to the nearest handhold. From there she made her way to the center and energetically punched the finish button. The clock stopped at 2:34.6 and she launched herself back towards the group.

Megan reached out and grabbed her arm as she came close, pulling her up to the wall. "How..."

"Use your breathing," she said to everyone, but looked at Paul. "Like a low power jet engine."

Paul smiled and pushed off towards the center rod, ready to use Emily's breakthrough and get a decent time logged for the 2s. He thought through what the best procedure would be, dismissing Emily's tumbling. She'd been blowing out each time she rotated around, but there had to be a better way than that.

Paul remembered what Gent had done, then a thought suddenly struck him as he grabbed the rod. He pulled himself out flat to the 'floor,' head down in a superman pose then released his grip. The rod retracted and he waited for the chime.

When it sounded he slowly breathed in through his mouth, then exhaled through his nose for several seconds, thinking that would be as close to his centerline as he could get his thrust. He sucked in another breath and repeated the process, sure now that he was moving forward at least a little.

After the fifth breath he spotted the small grid-like grooves in the 'floor' and used the end of his nose for a reference point, finally able to visually confirm that he was moving forward. He continued adding bits of speed with each breath before finally reaching the wall and grabbing a handhold. He raced his way over three meters to the center button and slapped his left palm on it, then glanced up at the clock just over his head, but he was too close to make out the numbers so he twisted and looked at the side wall.

1:22.4

"Better," he said to himself as he flung himself sideways and down, floating slowly towards the others.

"In through your mouth, out through your nose," he told Jason, who was up next. "Tilt your head for vector adjustments."

"Will do," he said, launching off the wall.

"Nice work," Megan commented, bumping into his shoulder as she floated beside him.

"Not as fast as him," Paul pointed out, glancing at Gent.

"We'll work it out," she said confidently.

By the end of the training session all of the 2s had their times under 40 seconds, with Jason scoring the fastest of any trainee to date the following day with a 26.4 second run, further chipping away at the 0s lead with a team average of 34.8 compared to the 0s' 35.9 and the 1s' 38.2, with the other seven teams' attempts waiting for upcoming training missions.

7

With the first of three training segments completed, the 2s moved on from zero gravity training to low gravity drills, which required them to adjust all over again, but more so than before, since there were a range of artificial gravity levels available throughout the station and their training drills didn't always occur on the same level.

Their quarters were based on level four, near the outside of the rotating disc, with every level closer to the center being a progressively lower gravity. This size of 'disc' contained 20 levels, not counting the small transit chamber they had arrived through, which unofficially was level 21.

They started their training drills on level 16, which had approximately 1/3 gravity, which was enough to keep them on the floor, but not enough for them to walk about normally. Every step they took wanted to vault them into the ceiling, but thanks to the days they'd spent in the zero gravity training, they'd learned a soft touch.

The problem was moving fast and begin agile. Their challenge for the day was to navigate an obstacle course for time…while getting pelted with fist-sized dodge balls from auto-tracking turrets spaced at vulnerable points around the course, like the narrow balance beam they had to walk across.

Paul's reactions to incoming objects, whether they be paintballs, dodge balls, darts, or any of the other training devices used to keep them on their toes were geared for normal gravity, making him an easy target for the little red balls if he tried to control his movements. On the other hand, if he reacted normally, he'd careen out of control up to the ceiling or off the apparatus he had to navigate through. A balance had to be reached, and their reaction times reset, before any of them would be able to successfully navigate the course on time.

One trick they'd learned early on was that they could alter the artificial gravity by running with the spin of the disc or against it, giving them more or less grip. And while that wouldn't help them if say they were on Luna or any other planetoid, it would work on any rotating station or starship.

That bit wasn't always helpful, because some of the obstacle courses moved laterally, also some of the sections where they could have used more grip required them to move against the spin of the disc, causing them to actually have less. Regardless of whether they were able to turn that factoid into an advantage, Paul and the others learned quickly that they had to be aware of the changes at all times.

What was fun about the whole thing was the fact that they essentially had superhuman strength and jumping ability on the course, which was designed accordingly. The room they were currently in was double high, meaning that it encompassed two levels, allowing for some climbs and jumps over barricades that the trainees never would have managed otherwise.

Paul had quite a blast with the hangtime at first, then cursed the vulnerability it gave him when the turrets tracked his way, because he couldn't move again until he touched down. Many a time he got pelted in the back or stomach while he was jumping over obstacles. After a few bruises he learned to side jump the barricades or go over head first, keeping his body in as low an arc as possible. Superman jumps were a straight up invitation to getting pelted.

Dan adjusted the best to the course, and got under par time before the rest of them did. Paul didn't get the pillar walk for some time, which was the second to last obstacle on the course consisting of 10cm tall pillars spread out over a 20 meter stretch of hall that he had to pass through without touching the ground, which would result in immediate disqualification. He'd gone through the course 5 times and kept failing on this section before finally getting the knack of making small, quick steps side to side.

The dodge balls were coming from the end of the obstacle, with two small launchers extending down from the ceiling. At first he'd tried to long jump over most of them, but had found that made him an easy target and the impacts would knock him down and off the pillars, resulting in a DQ.

After that he'd tried smaller jumps, but still couldn't dodge the balls coming at him from straight on, and since this part of the course was enclosed, he didn't have the luxury of watching his teammates' attempts, though Dan did give the group some pointers after his first successful completion. They needed everyone getting under par today, else there'd be a points penalty for the team.

It finally sunk in to Paul that the point of the pillars and turrets was to force him to sidestep his way through, making complete redirections of his momentum with 1/3 the normal grip he'd normally have. Once he had that concept firmly implanted in his mind, he took to the course again and approached the pillars slowly, dodging a few balls that came out after him before he even got to the first small octagonal steps.

Paul ducked to the left, then stepped up to the first pillar, barely large enough for his one foot, then he stepped to the right as a ball flew through the spot where he'd just been. When he stepped down on the right, he launched himself diagonally up to the next step less than a meter ahead of where he'd previously been, smiling wide as he dropped down in a crouching pose as another ball flew over his head. Like a lot of the challenges being thrown at the trainees, this one was deceptively simple, and now that he knew how to attack it he wasn't going to have a problem.

That said, he still had to move quick or get pelted, which happened about halfway through, but since he was staying low to the ground and taking short hops it didn't completely knock him out of place and he was able to catch himself with a very long and flexible reach with his left leg over to the next pillar, which he immediately pushed off of and landed in a more normal position on the pillar to his right.

He went through five more diagonal hops before he passed underneath the turrets, which were unable to depress low enough to hit him at point blank range, thankfully. Paul jumped over a small barricade and moved on around a corner, never having made it this far, and saw the finish pedestal ahead of him.

It was, however, on the other side of a large red section of floor that he instantly recognized as a disqualification pad. He was going to have to jump over the entire thing...and there were four turrets, two on the right with another two on the left, waiting to shoot at him.

Paul thought it over for a few seconds, deciding that speed was his best ally and backed up as far as he could to get a running start, which was more like a 'loping start' in the low gravity. Just before he took off, however, he added a slight variation to his plan as a thought struck him. Using his left foot he pushed off on the wall to add some initial momentum and lunged forward, running up to as quick of a sprint as he could manage.

But instead of running straight on, he angled to the left in the last few steps and jumped towards the wall in between the two turrets, taking a nearly point blank hit on his left hand that he deftly placed in between himself and the turret in mid air. He let it knock his arm aside, but kept as much of the momentum off his torso as he could so as not to affect his alignment as he began to fall downward.

Before he could hit the floor, he bounced himself off the wall, redirecting his motion back to the right and getting a half jump extra out of the maneuver. He landed face forward on the far side of the disqualification pad, managing to roll out of it in a somersault and get back to his feet and 'run' the last two steps to the finish pedestal, which looked more like a giant, slow motion leap with a pogo hop enroute.

Paul smashed down the finish button and quickly looked over at his time, posted above where the rest of his teammates were standing...

1:27.8

He blew out a tired breath, relieved. Par was 1:40, which meant he wouldn't have to go back through it again today. The individual time trials would be tomorrow along with the team run, which had everyone on course at the same time, with all having to finish before the clock would stop. Seeing as how he was one of the slowest today, he guessed that he'd be the team's dead weight along with Randy, who had only managed a 1:34 about a half hour earlier, though he'd gotten the hang of it far sooner than Paul had.

Jason inquired as to whether they could get any more practice time in today, now that they'd all gotten under par, and the trainer informed them that they could if they wanted, but that any times they registered wouldn't count towards anything. Jason nodded his understanding and urged the others over to the start line.

"Let's start with pairs," he said, pointing at Dan and Brian, the fastest of the bunch so far, "then we can work up to more. I have a feeling we can use each other to get over some of these obstacles faster than going it alone."

"You mean like throw Paul over the pillars," Megan teased.

"Actually..." Jason hedged, "I was thinking something like that for the balance beam."

Kip smiled widely. "Brilliant," he said, thinking through various possibilities.

"He's right," Dan added, "there's potential for assistance on several spots."

Paul quietly laughed to himself. So much for being done for the day...but Jason and the others were right. They needed to practice more, especially for the team run. According to the 0s' and 1s' results, their team course times were considerably slower than the individual ones, so maybe they hadn't thought to work together. If that was the case, and the 2s could manage to shave off a chunk of time, it'd be another opportunity to close the points gap.

"I'm all yours," Paul joked, teaming up with Megan for their pair run. Dan and Brian had already taken off, not bothering to start the timer, so Paul assumed they'd all get out on the course together to try and sort this out. He let the pair get a twenty second head start and glanced at his teammate.

"Let's go," she said, game as always for another challenge.

8

The next day they started with the individual runs with unlimited tries within a two hour time block. Paul took two, shaving his time down to 1:22.9, placing him 7th out of his teammates and 25th out of the 30 trainees to test so far. When all was said and done, the 2s had an average of 1:19.3, ahead of the 1s' 1:20.2, but trailing the 0s' 1:18.5 and losing a few points to them.

The second part of the day's challenge was the team run, again with unlimited tries confined to a 1 hour block. What points they'd lost in the individual challenge they needed to make up here, and based off their practice runs yesterday, they figured they should be able to beat both the 0s and 1s by at least 10 seconds, which would be a huge swing in points if they could pull it off.

"Ready?" Jason asked everyone as they stood on the start line. He received nine curt nods, then depressed the start button with a tone sounding in sync, informing the others that the challenge had begun.

As practiced, Dan and Brian sprinted out into the lead with the long, loping steps that proved most effective in the 1/3 gravity. They came to the first obstacle, a gauntlet tunnel, staying side by side and locking arms as multiple dodge ball launchers pelted them from both sides. Using each other as leverage, they managed to stay on their feet and make good time while providing a distraction to the turrets.

With them playing decoy, Emily, Megan and Kip slipped through in single file behind them, having to fend off only a few balls flung their way coming from behind, which when they hit only propelled them forward even more, though askew. Without having to worry about getting hit from the front, thanks to their blockers, they were able to anticipate the hits and keep their momentum throughout the 45 meter gauntlet.

When they exited that section the course took an abrupt left turn into a monkey bar horizontal ladder over a disqualification pad. Emily took to it first and quickly made her way across, double swinging the bars thanks to the lesser gravity and her lighter frame, smallest of all the 2s but with just as much length of limbs as the rest of them. She dropped down on the far side several meters ahead of Dan and took off to obstacle three, leaving the others behind.

The balance beam came next, and required her to walk across a 10cm wide beam for 20 meters while being targeted by two slow firing turrets, one on each side that fired randomly, never letting you know from which direction or at what time you would be shot at. With that unpredictability, it was difficult to reposition your weight to deflect a hit, and usually resulted in the trainee being knocked off onto the disqualification pad below...and in the team run, one person's disqualification meant a points deduction at the end, which none of the teams could afford.

Emily got to the beam early, with several seconds lead over her teammates, and had a few options available when crossing. Some previous successful attempts had been to crawl across, keeping handholds on the beam so that the balls wouldn't knock you off. It was slow, but effective for the ones that kept falling off.

Another tactic was to walk slowly and try and bat at the balls coming your way, absorbing the impact on the arms like shock absorbers and keeping them off your torso. The third and most popular method was to just charge ahead, jumping out and trying to leapfrog your way across, hoping to not get hit at all. Most of the time this technique failed, but when it didn't it provided the quickest method of crossing.

They couldn't gamble with the team run however, given that they needed everyone across and statistically speaking it was likely that at least a couple would go down if they attacked the obstacle in that fashion.

When Emily reached the beam she didn't hesitate, they'd planned out each obstacle beforehand and she immediately leapt into what looked like a long jump attempt, flying through the air and landing on the center of the beam as a ball pelted her in the back, tipping her over to the right.

Fortunately she'd already been collapsing down on top of the beam by design, so the impact didn't knock her off. It spun her about as she grasped the beam like a monkey and swung about underneath, then crawled inverted almost all the way to the end, continually getting shot at by the turrets and swaying back and forth with each hit, but her crossed legs and arms held firm and the balls couldn't dislodge her.

Barely two meters from the end she held position and took the hits, providing a distraction for the turrets as Dan quickly walked across the beam, stepping over her legs and arms and jumping for the platform at the end, drawing one shot from a turret that came too late. Now that he was in the safe zone, the turrets rotated back to pick up the next closest target...which was Emily still hanging underneath. They hit her again, swaying her back and forth, as Megan made her way across uncontested.

With the turrets distracted, the rest of the team made good time getting across with no one falling. When Randy passed over her, she knew he was the last and it was time for her to crawl back up on top of the beam. Keeping an iron grip, she continued to get hit by the annoying red balls as she swung back up and walked on her knees over the last two meters. When she'd gotten to her feet in the safe zone the others were already out of sight around the next corner on the wall climb, all going according to plan...

By the time the group reached the pillars they were slightly ahead of pace, Jason guessed, based on the fact that Emily was in the rear but had already caught up and passed Megan and Randy over the wall jumps. Usually she lagged behind and caught up on the pillars, being the best on that particular section, but she arrived 8th in line just as Dan lifted Brian up on his shoulders in the safe zone on the far side.

Brian held his hands up in front of the turret, messing with the motion trackers and blocking any balls being shot out, causing Dan some grief trying to balance the two of them in the low gravity, but thanks to ample practice the other day they'd gotten the 'cheat' tactic worked out, and effectively cut off one of the two turrets from the 'kill zone.'

Ivan and Jack came next, dodging the one active turret carefully until they crossed into the safe zone with Ivan drawing most of the shots. Jack got across almost totally free, but had to dodge a couple on the last few steps. Once he was in the clear he gave Ivan a boost and they blocked the second turret, freeing up the pillars for their less agile teammates.

That meant Paul and the others who'd had the most trouble with this obstacle...but now that there were no longer any balls flinging their way they didn't have to zigzag at all and took a straight line through the tiny pillars, crossing the whole thing in a handful of seconds. Megan was the first to make it across and she immediately hurdled the low wall and moved on to the final jump, wanting to clear it early to avoid a bottleneck of bodies that would cost them precious seconds.

The others made a single file line across the center of the pillars, save for Emily, who literally danced around the outside of the slowpokes and slipped by Dan's legs while

Randy came across, saving the group another 1.5 to 2 seconds.

The blockers disengaged as soon as their teammates were past and caught up to the others just as Kip landed on the far side of the long jump area in the final safe zone. Before he even landed and the turrets could readjust their aim, Paul took off and did his wall hop double jump, grabbing a hold of Megan's outstretched hand as she pulled him into the safe zone and out of the way of Jason who was jumping straight through the middle a split second behind his teammate.

He took a hit to the midsection, but his momentum was enough to carry him through, though he landed in a heap on the edge, with Kip hauling him out of the way of the others.

Ivan and Jack came next, simultaneously jumping to save time with Randy jumping a second behind them. Aside from Paul he was the worst jumper in the group and the team needed to distract the turrets as much as possible so he could make it across, given that he hadn't perfected Paul's wall hop.

He barely made it across, even without getting hit, but an outstretched Megan quickly grabbed him before he even made the safe zone as she was supported out over the disqualification pad by Kip's firm grip on her waist. She yanked Randy into the clear and he ran on down to the finish line where the others were waiting.

Dan and Brian came next, simultaneously jumping with Megan and Kip each waiting to help them across if they got hit askew. Brian did, but Kip grabbed his foot before it could dip down and hit the red pad centimeters before the end and tugged his teammate into the safe zone, where he landed on his face, but without a disqualification. He quickly got to his feet and ran for the finish with the others as Emily easily leaped across last with distance to spare.

She got hit twice, but it didn't matter. She came down on a knee, then loped her way to the finish button and slapped it down quickly, looking up at their time.

1:33.4

Jason let out a cheer, which was quickly echoed by the others. That was a good 3 seconds faster than any of their training runs, and the best by far over the 0s' 1:52.9 and the 1s' 2:12.8…it was even under Randy's individual time from the first day.

"You think that's enough?" Megan asked the group.

"It'll be close," Paul commented, referring to the amount of points they would gain on the 0s.

"Should we go again?" Emily asked. "We've still got plenty of time."

"Not sure we'll do better than that, but yeah," Jason said. "Let's get as much as we can here, or we might regret it later."

"Agreed," Randy said, nodding. "We've got another ten runs easy to experiment with. Let's see if we can tweak the order a bit, Kip was holding us up on the monkey bars."

"Yeah, let me switch with Jason at the start," Kip agreed.

"Alright," Jason said, pointing over to the nearby start area. "Let's get to it."

9

In the end their extra efforts paid off in terms of a 1.2 second reduction and a 4 point increase for the challenge, leaving them 17 points ahead of the 0s in cumulative total and moving them up to 2nd rank out of all ten training groups. They were still over 600 points behind the 7s, but they were putting up some good scores that the lead team would be hard pressed to match later on.

The following day Paul and the others moved outward on the discs and went through similar challenges with 2/3 gravity, with Paul finally finding his feet. Moving about seemed easy to him, now that he didn't have such a long hangtime and his legs functioned more like normal. In fact Paul rose to the top of the individual charts, both for his team and the overall list, telling the others it felt just like the Matrix and wondering why they weren't doing as well as him.

When they progressed through the second day of testing, his skill with the 2/3 gravity held and he cemented his top spot, putting up an obstacle course run a good 7.3 seconds faster than anyone else and earning some much desired gains in the individual cumulative scores, and while his position of 13th didn't change, the gaps did, climbing him up relative to the others.

The odd thing about both the team scores and the individual ones was that no one was dominate at everything. Star Force's training was wide and varied, and the trainees were learning the value of knowing where their strengths and weaknesses lie, and using their teammates' attributes to cover or enhance their own. Even though Paul gained a few points on the others in the latest round of challenges, there was no guarantee that would continue to the next, and as such both he and the others sought out any opportunity to suck up additional points.

The final third of the mission involved high gravity training on the outer levels of the discs with a maximum of 1.2 gravity on level 1. Here the obstacle courses took on new challenges as the superhuman leaps of the low gravity disappeared and became backbreaking just to execute a normal hop over a low wall. Everything felt slow and heavy, like you were wearing a weighted vest.

In addition to the obstacle courses, there was also a second track in the station, in addition to the one at normal gravity, that ran the entire circumference of one of the discs. Paul and the others were given two days to get accustomed to 'running heavy' before they were timed in a mile run going with the direction of rotation, meaning the faster they went, the slightly greater gravity pull they would have to fight.

Like Paul, several of the 2s had been in track and were accustomed to training runs ranging from easy jogs, to long runs, to medium distance/medium paced tempo runs, up to interval workouts that literally left your legs screaming in protest...but running in high gravity was something completely new altogether.

They all had trouble at first, given that their step timing was off. By the second day they'd adjusted somewhat, but it was clear to Paul that what running efficiency they'd gained during their routine fitness workouts in Atlantis had completely vanished with the altered movements needed in the higher gravity, slowing both him and the others down considerably.

His first practice mile came in at a 6:22, with Randy bringing up the back end with a pathetic 7:56. Emily, surprisingly, had the quickest time at 5:54, which Paul suspected had something to do with her lighter frame. All of them were rail thin by now, but her build put her a good 15lbs lighter than their group average all the way down at 117lbs, which considering she stood 6'1'' made her appear toothpick thin. Paul, however, knew not to be deceived by her appearance...the girl had a nasty uppercut and held even with him in sparring matches, demonstrating a muscular strength that her frame didn't show.

She'd originally been a tennis pro from one of the European countries, Paul couldn't remember which, and it made him more than a little embarrassed as a runner to be beat by someone outside his sport. Fortunately for his ego his body eventually rebalanced itself enough to regain some of his coordination, with his time dipping down on the last testing run to a 5:31, but still more than a minute slower than his best normal gravity mile that he'd run in Atlantis.

Emily improved as well, down a few seconds to 5:49, as well as the others with the top time going to Brian at 5:27 within the 2s, but Kevin from the 1s had run a blazing 5:13 a few weeks ago, one that Paul doubted he could match even if he had a few more days to rework his rhythm.

Like most challenges, this one reshuffled the points again. The 2s lost 14 to the 0s, but maintained their overall lead by 6 with the 2/3 gravity and high gravity obstacle course scores added in, however the 1s kept top honors in the high gravity, outscoring both teams by 56 points, though to be fair they did have three of the best runners out of the entire trainee class, which some of the trainers had started to refer to as the 'trailblazers' as they made preparations to usher in a second 100 person training unit at the end of the year.

They'd been told that there wouldn't be any intermixing of the two groups at all...they were even being given separate quarters in Atlantis so that they wouldn't be crossing paths during downtime. They'd also been given orders not to discuss any of the training challenges with the newbies when they arrived, so as not to give them an unfair advantage.

Not that Paul or the others would have...they didn't want them beating any of their established high scores, even though they'd later been informed that due to some of the lessons learned from the trailblazers, the second class's training regimen would be altered slightly, making direct points comparisons invalid.

Paul didn't know if that meant they were going to make it harder or easier on the second group, but he could see some areas where the trainers would want to make alterations after all the problems the 2s, not to mention the other teams, had given them. They'd developed a knack for winning scenarios their own inventive way, using methods the designers hadn't intended for them. To the trainers' credit, they never invalidated those scores, but Paul was sure they weren't going to make the same 'mistakes' twice with future trainees.

Sucks to be them, Paul thought dismissively. He and his team were full steam ahead and weren't looking back. What the next generation of trainees had to go through was their problem, he and the 2s had their own to deal with.

One of those problems was the lack of challenge scores to compare with, given that they were the first class to go through them. Like the current mission, not all the teams went through at the same time and those that came last in the rotation, this time being the 9s, would have the advantage of knowing how everyone else did and could train themselves with an eye towards measuring up...whereas the 0s had no clue what was a good score or not, they just had to wing it and hope for the best.

All the teams were more or less on the same timetable, but none of them were working on the same challenge at the same time, given that they had to share facilities. When one team was on one of the paintball ranges, another would be in the pool swimming laps while another was out on the track or the shooting ranges. The trainers coordinated all sessions so the teams didn't have to worry about anything above and beyond showing up and working their asses off, leaving only downtime for the teams to hook up and compare notes, so to speak.

They of course did NOT give each other a heads up to other challenges. That would be cutting their own throats points wise, but they did discuss in detail challenges that both teams had passed, sharing knowledge, tricks, and stories that all around benefited everyone to some extent.

In some regards they were all on the same side, fighting against the trainers and whatever they would throw at them next, but more than that, over the past six months they'd gelled quickly and efficiently into a team the likes of which Paul had never seen before. They were all friends, with no animosity between them, only competitive fire and a desire to one up the others for brief bragging rights, though down deep they all knew it was really because they wanted to improve, but weren't above having some fun in the process.

And while the other teams were brothers in arms, the 2s had become closer than family for Paul, which seemed strange from an academic standpoint...he hadn't known them nearly as long as his own sister and parents...but they all seemed so alike in mind, body, spirit, and drive that they could well have been clones of one another, allowing them to work together easily, often knowing what the others were thinking without having to ask.

It also made having discussions easy and free flowing. They were all on the same page, but with different perspectives and experiences that, when aired out, usually resulted in better scores for everyone. They learned and adapted as a group, watched each other's backs, and genuinely cared for each other, though they never got sappy about it.

Paul figured this was about as close to being a Jedi as he'd ever get...

He was completely wrong about that, however. The challenges and changes that he would experience in the following years were going to be far greater than anything they'd faced thus far. Though he couldn't see it now, nor could any of the others, they'd just begun what would be a very long, arduous journey, far beyond anything they could imagine.

10

Paul woke up early the final morning and went for a normal gravity run with Jason, trying to rebalance their legs and get in a decent workout before they left on the long trip back to the starport. Neither of them liked going a day without some type of workout, and even though they were sore and stiff from the radical training they'd been going through, they pushed the pace and got in a fairly hard 5k run...though the time wasn't all that impressive given their awkwardness.

Paul felt much better though after the workout and subsequent shower as his body seemed to be shifting back into normal patterns. If there was one thing he'd learned from this little field trip, it was the necessity of maintaining normal artificial gravity when in space as often as possible. His body would adapt to any environment and conditions it experienced, but in the process he realized that he would lose most of his other hard earned strengths.

Davis had been right, more so than he ever imagined. They *had* to have stations and ships with normal gravity, otherwise they'd run into all kinds of health and fitness problems.

That said, he was glad that he'd been able to learn how to deal with the zero and low gravity environments. Even if he didn't have a chance to practice those skills in Atlantis, at least he wouldn't be completely inept the next time he found himself in that situation...which technically would be in a half hour when the 2s transferred over to the waiting *Jaguar*-class starship that had stopped by on a short detour of its routine cargo run a few hours ago to pick up the trainees on its way back to low orbit.

After packing up his duffle Paul left his temporary quarters and grabbed a quick breakfast in the cafeteria two levels up. The slightly lesser gravity didn't bother his eating habits, but he did feel a bit light sitting in his chair. When he finished a stack of pancakes he stashed a couple of individually wrapped snack bars into his duffle for the trip back, unsure as to what food would be available on the cargo ship.

He met up with the others and their escort attendant on level 20 and were guided back through the zero gravity spine of the station to the docking area and boarded the large starship much as they had the Cougar, save for this one didn't have rotating cylinders in a stretched out hull. This starship had a large, thick disc up front, with a zero gravity cargo section stretching out behind, reminding Paul of a giant pizza cutter.

The ship was half as long as the station, and was returning from a circuit of stops in mid orbit during which it exchanged various cargos and personnel like a massive subway train running around the planet. Its previous two stops had been factory stations, dropping off raw materials brought up from Earth and picking up manufactured components to then transport out to other factories or shipyards for assembly.

The ship was also carrying large containers of water which would be used to supplement and rebalance station reserves. In addition to crew requirements, water was also required for several mechanical functions, including hydrolysis that provided both oxygen for breathing and hydrogen/oxygen for fuel cells to power the stations.

Most of the hydrogen and oxygen used was brought up from Earth in pressurized canisters, but each station and ship had been equipped with solar arrays to provide backup power and the ability to refuel their stores using the available water on board in lieu of resupply from Earth. As such, all stations and starships carried water reserves, and not all of them were in full supply yet, given their recent construction.

It was Star Force procedure to bring up water from Earth whenever possible, in whatever large or small quantities they could squeeze onto the dropships in addition to their primary cargo or passengers. That water usually made its way to one of these larger cargo ships, then distributed throughout the Star Force orbital infrastructure.

The Jaguar was the largest starship fielded to date, and massed more than some of the small stations. It had been built in the primary shipyard, situated in geosynchronous orbit, along with its five sister ships, taking approximately one year each to assemble, though construction of their components had begun long before that at various orbital factories.

It carried a crew of more than 50 on a regular basis, and the disc width was equal to that of the training station's discs, though this one was twice as thick and, as usual, was actually a pair rotating in opposite directions encased within an outer shell. Virtually all of the ship's compartments, including the bridge, were located in the disc, with the zero gravity sections...which made up 85% of the ship's interior...reserved for cargo transfer.

On the way back to the starport, Paul and the others got to visit the cargo bays and 'explore' a bit. Inside the cavernous six bays, each situated adjacent to one another in the long 'tail' of the starship, were hundreds of various sized crates, each attached to racks spanning the bay. Fortunately they were only half full, leaving lots of empty spots and making it the perfect place to play hide and seek during the 25 hour trip.

Paul and the others got to practice their zero gravity skills more than they had expected, thanks to an understanding captain, and organized their own obstacle courses in one of the bays, as well as several other challenges to keep themselves busy...including the long range jumps that they hadn't been able to try out on the station.

Even the large training room there was shorter than the length of the bay, and though they had to avoid crates and support structures, Paul and the others found that they could, if they aimed precisely enough, launch off one wall and fly to the other just a little under 100 meters away.

Needless to say, the return trip proved much more entertaining than the 'plane ride' out on the smaller Cougar.

When they got back to the starport they had about an hour's delay waiting for their dropship, so Paul pulled rank, so to speak, and got permission to observe part of the unloading process as the Jaguar transferred over crates to the starport.

Unlike the small docking arm that they'd used to board from the Sparrow, the Jaguar was attached to a much wider port via its own extendable docking pylon that attached directly to the inside of the starport's shell rather than the docking arms emanating out from the zero gravity section in front of the cylinders. Most of the bulk cargo storage was located in the shell anyway, but even if it hadn't been, the Jaguar was too large to squeeze into the primary docking ports without obscuring half of them.

Instead the giant ship situated itself next to the outer rim where the docking bay doors were retracted and extended a grapple arm sideways from its 'tail' segment, just ahead of its engines, which were sticking down below the starport with the disc section poking out above and the long tail connecting the two on the side so as to not block the other traffic coming in and out.

Once the grapple was attached and the small momentum differences between the ship and starport were nulled out mechanically, the Jaguar's docking pylon extended and connected with the inside of the starport's shell with an L-shaped attachment that got up and under the overhang so the actual docking port could still exist within the starport's protective shell rather than being located on the armored exterior.

Paul watched from the starport's side as some, but not all, of the crates were transferred over via mechanical arms attached to the walls of the large docking pylon. They motored their way along small tracks with the cargo in their grip, then very carefully exchanged the packages with the starport's own cargo arms, which then carried the crates down to a processing station.

From there they were moved via sled to the appropriate warehouse compartments within the shell, some having to go all the way around the backside of the cylinders to get to their storage areas on the other side of the starport.

Paul took a ride with one of the workers on a sled back into the well lit but 'dark' areas of the starport where nobody else ever went, just to see what it was like. The sled moved on a track set into the 'floor' while the midsized crate was held down with a series of clamps. The worker stood on a raised platform with his feet in footholds as he drove the sled down the port side of the starport.

Paul stood beside him, hanging onto the rim of the control panel and his feet in a second set of footholds, amazed at how much cargo was being stored and transferred about and impressed with the overall size of Star Force's operations in space. He'd known all along how ambitious they were...after all he'd been living in their largest construction project for the past half year...but given the fuel to weight issues of moving cargo and personnel up into space, he hadn't realized it could be *this* busy.

Midway through his tour of the dark zones, he hopped 'trains' and hitchhiked a ride with a crate being taken into the starport's interior for distribution. The tracks that ran the length of the floor, walls, and ceiling diverged

into a short offshoot that led into the backside of the station where the cylinders were attached to a cargo distribution area.

The crate in question was taken off a sled and moved to a side chamber where it was opened and smaller packages, not quite crates but of a similar design, were removed and sent in groups through the rotational airlock and into the gravity zone of the starport. Paul followed along, seeing some containers being sent to the food prep area while a few others were taken up into the commercial zones. Both contained food, but Paul figured one was meant for the cafeteria while the others probably contained prepackaged snacks that would be made available for sale to the tourists constantly transiting through the commerce hub.

Paul eventually returned to the front end of the cylinders and the zero gravity section they'd first passed through on arrival almost two weeks before. Megan, Jason, and the others were sitting attached to three tables halfway up the amusement park-like reception area, waiting for their dropship to arrive. He joined them and watched the wall-screen view of the Earth and docking area, noting the large slice of the left side that was obscured by the docked Jaguar.

He didn't have to wait too long before an attendant arrived to escort them inside their dropship...another Sparrow that, ironically, was bringing up the 3s for their training mission. They met and conversed with each other briefly, then went their separate ways. Paul and the others boarded the dropship and detached from the starport without delay and nudged away from the space station on thrusters alone.

Once they'd drifted out to a safe distance, the Sparrow flipped over, pointing its engines forward, and began a sharp descent burn, nulling out most of their orbital momentum and dropping them back down to Atlantis's position with very little reentry friction, though it could have stood the heat of a full on reentry had it needed to.

Once down into the atmosphere a pair of hull panels retracted and the small jet engine that the Sparrow contained came online and flew the spaceplane back to Atlantis, where it circled a few times before being given clearance to land on one of the massive runways. More hull panels on the underside of the Sparrow opened and the blocky landing gear extended, breaking up the otherwise smooth, polished chrome visage of the craft.

They touched down without incident, then taxied off the main runway, down a service offshoot, and over to a semi-active terminal, docking with a walkway extension.

Paul unstrapped and stood up, feeling real gravity for the first time in what felt like forever. It was different than centrifugal gravity in a way, cleaner somehow...or maybe that was just his imagination. Either way, grabbing his duffle and walking off of the dropship on sore legs, he was glad to be back home.

Paul frowned to himself as he and the others made their way through the terminal, now free of any handlers, and headed back through the city to their training area and quarters. When had he started thinking of Atlantis as home? Home was supposed to be back in Indiana with his family.

He glanced to his left at Jack, then at Emily on his right, suppressing a smile. He wasn't sure how it had happened, but it seemed that he had picked up a second family and a second home in recent days. That wasn't something he'd expected to have happened, but now that it had, he was glad. It made him even more sure that his decision to join Star Force instead of going to college had been the right one.

Paul glanced at his surroundings and suppressed a laugh. The biggest and most prestigious college campuses on the planet had nothing on Atlantis...not by a long shot.

Nemesis

1

January 13, 2044

Paul stood on the small square platform, looking out over the giant indoor pool surrounding him as he checked his breath mask one last time. The seal on his neck appeared to be in place, and the clingy material had a firm hold on his head, enough to cause a mild headache, but that was good. The tighter the grip, the less water would seep underneath the edges and up to his mask's breathing chamber.

He glanced around one last time, getting his bearings, then pressed the button on the start pedestal to his left. A tone sounded as the bright overhead lights cut out and dropped everything into darkness. Remembering where the edge of the platform was, Paul stepped off into the blackness and fell into the mass of invisible water a half meter below.

Disoriented at first, Paul didn't move until he got his equilibrium reset, which took several long seconds. Tiny bubbles of air exited four pinprick vents on the side of his mask, but he couldn't see the bubbles race their way to the surface...or anything else for that matter. There wasn't a single light on in the entire room, above water or below. Paul was going to have to navigate the first part of this challenge blind.

When he was fairly sure that he had his head upright, he reached a hand up and felt for the line of bubbles. Using them as a plumb line he straightened his angle in the water so he was perpendicular to the floor and allowed himself to sink to the bottom some 18 meters down.

Thanks to his thin and muscular build, sinking wasn't a problem, but since he was on the clock he turned on his forearm thruster tubes and accelerated his descent. Waiting without anything to see or measure his progress by, Paul felt like he was swallowed up in the vastness of deep space, save for the lack of starlight. At the same time the vastness felt claustrophobic, and he was grateful when his feet finally touched bottom with a sudden jolt.

He released the handheld thrust buttons and let them retract on their bungee cords back into the units and out of harm's way. Bending at the knees, Paul reached down and felt for the floor with his bare hands. When he found it, he stretched out horizontally and began swimming about, stroking the smooth surface in a blind search pattern.

After several meters of traveling along the bottom, Paul found one of the shallow ridges that ran out from the center of the pool like a sunburst. Trick was, did he remember which way to go or had he got himself totally turned around.

He was fairly sure the center was off to his right, so he followed the ridge that direction, keeping his hands on it at all times. Even losing contact with it momentarily would cost him several seconds, and since this was an individual challenge, he was competing against the other 99 trainees for points and bragging rights...or in Paul's case, just trying to keep up with the rest. He was one of the poorest swimmers in the group, ranking #98 on all unassisted swim challenges, which included surface laps in an Olympic sized pool.

Fortunately this challenge wasn't unassisted, and he had the use of the forearm thrusters to move him about, which leveled the playing field considerably, but considering how good his fellow trainees were in general, he couldn't afford to lose precious seconds by being sloppy.

Eventually Paul found his way to the center of the sunburst located directly under where the starting platform 'floated,' though technically it was connected by a low arched walkway to the side of the pool, but from within the water it appeared to be a floating island...or at least would have if the lights were still on.

When he reached the center the ridges flattened out and led Paul's hands to a shallow crater, in the center of which was a small navigational add-on for his breath mask. He felt for its dimensions and mentally pictured the angle it was at, rotating it around and lining it up with his right eye. The device snapped into place over the transparent panel, obscuring what would have been his vision in that eye, had there been anything to see.

A small button press activated the echo-location device, and a series of small chirps were audible in the water. Each time the rapid fire sounds emanated from the device, a lingering blip would appear on screen with the computer processed dimensions of the pool and the objects it contained. It appeared to Paul as if he was looking through the rotating blades of a fan, but the greenish blue image gave him more than enough information to begin navigating around the pool in search of his first cube.

He reached over to his left gauntlet and pulled out the hand control, which slipped neatly over his left thumb. Paul repeated the process on his right arm, passing over the small emergency wristband that held a panic button underneath a small plastic case. If for any reason Paul had difficulty with his breathing equipment, he could lift the case, press the button, and within 13.5 seconds the entire pool would drain out through hidden grates covering the floor.

It was a reassuring backup for Paul and the others, and alleviated some of their discomfort at having to train underwater...that, and the equipment upgrades that they'd made three months ago.

The trainers had started them off using standard scuba gear, with pathetic goggles, a breathing mouthpiece, and a pair of awful air tanks strapped to their backs. Paul had had the worst trouble, with water continually going up his nose, as it did every time he went in the water, but the subsurface drills didn't allow for him to clear his airways like he could swimming laps on the surface, and as a result the first few training runs had been a nightmare for him and some of the others.

Even the best swimmers were complaining after the first day. The equipment wasn't designed for speed, agility, or any basic functionality aside from floating in place and looking at the scenery. After three days of complaints, which apparently echoed up through the Star Force ranks, Davis had come down to 'trailblazer' territory...the large sector of Atlantis where the trainees lived and trained...with a team of equipment engineers to assist the trainees in designing their own equipment.

They'd self delegated the responsibilities for the designs to Ben, Mark, Jason, Zak, Ian, and Paul, the three best swimmers and the three worst out of the group, while the others would exhaustively field test the designs and offer feedback. All their underwater swimming training was suspended, with the allotted time redesignated for the equipment work. They spent a total of 24 days on the project, with the engineers planning out and fabricating their designs within a matter of hours using the wide array of industrial resources available to them in Atlantis.

At the end of it all, they'd created the breath mask that Paul now wore, the vest-like air tanks that were smooth, form-fitting, and neutrally buoyant, the tube-like forearm thrusters, and even the echo-location device, among a variety of other equipment that Paul wasn't using at the moment. In fact, the only other piece of equipment that he wore was a pair of black, knee-length jammers courtesy of Speedo. That was one piece of equipment they hadn't needed to redesign.

With the echo 'eye patch' in place and functioning, Paul pointed his right arm in the direction of a slowly swimming box taking laps in the pool at about 2/3rds depth, and partially depressed the soft trigger. Inside the tube attached to the outside of his forearm, six tiny fan blades spun up, creating a small jet engine-like effect to provide him with propulsion.

Paul pointed his other arm at his feet and activated it in reverse, adding to his forward momentum with his arms offset, which would have looked like a superman pose had there been any light to see him with. He made minor corrections with the angles of his arms and goosed the speed of each thruster accordingly to intercept the automated underwater 'rover' that held his first objective.

When he got to the turtle-like device he swam up over it, right arm held out and keeping his pacing, while he deactivated his left thruster and reached out to grab the small cube on the rover's back. It was firmly stuck into a slot, and Paul had to put his foot on the rover's back to pry it loose, but with a little pressure it came free, lighting up with a bright orange glow in the process.

Paul's left eye blinked against the light, while his right was still obscured by the echo-location device. As his eye adjusted, four fruit loop-like hoops lit up in the distance, indicating where he had to go next.

Unable to hold the cube in his hand and thumb the acceleration button at the same time, Paul reached over and manually set the speed knob to setting 4 out of 5, then added adjustable thrust from his left thruster as he jetted away from the rover toward the nearest of the hoops, sliding through it with ease and twisting his arms to the left to make a sweeping turn.

He about missed the second hoop and had to cut all thrust from his left arm, but he managed to swing through the second with the cube in his grasp, registering each passage and deactivating the hoop lights when completed. When Paul finished the quartet, a small pedestal on the floor near the north end of the pool lit up with an orange ring around its square top, and Paul jetted off towards it as fast as he could, kicking up his right thruster to 100%.

That said, he couldn't take an entirely straight line to the target. There were still many underwater obstacles in the way, visible only to his echo-location device, two of which he accidentally brushed up against. They held firm on their floor-mounted tethers, of which Paul also had to be careful to avoid. They didn't show up on the echo-location device save for extreme close range.

When he made it over and down to the pedestal, he saw an empty slot in the top for the cube he held alongside another identical one. He slid the orange cube in, with its light cutting out upon contact and the other simultaneously activating with a neon green glow. Four more hoops lit up the same color.

Paul swam off and through those as well, cradling the green cube as he swam. After completing those four 'hoop loops' a green square illuminated on the underside of the starting platform. Upon reaching it and setting the cube inside the empty slot, a blue one activated and he repeated the process three more times. When he finally finished with the yellow cube hoops, the top of the rover lit up and he swam back over to it and replaced the cube in the single empty slot on top.

When he did so all the hoops in the pool lit up and Paul, now without the cube to cradle, jetted off at maximum speed towards the nearest one, passing through it and another almost in alignment on the opposite side, with each deactivating as he passed through. Going for maximum speed, he began knocking off others, trying to line up 'strafing runs' that would hit two or three at a time, avoiding the painfully slow turnabout that would cost him several seconds for each reversal.

As he swam about in a hurry, the lazy rover redirected from its predictable lap path and swam up a bit towards one of the hoops Paul had deactivated. When it passed through it, the green hoop lit back up…meaning Paul would have to pass through it yet again.

"What the…" Paul muttered inside his breath mask when seeing the stupid rover turning the hoops back on. He had a small pocket of air directly in front of his mouth and nose, plus two expandable pouches just below each ear that would puff out as he exhaled, making his respiration almost normal inside the mask…as opposed to the 'sucking air through a straw' feeling of the original scuba equipment.

"Damn it," he said, speeding off to the next hoop, mentally plotting out the quickest route to get to the remaining ones. The rover seemed to be picking hoops randomly, which meant Paul wouldn't have a straight-line path to go through to deactivate those for a second time. He was quicker than the rover by at least double speed, but he knew that forethought would be required to get all the hoops deactivated as quickly as possible. If he didn't plan out his attempts, he'd chase individual ones at random and end up adding a lot of unnecessary time to his run.

He was also worried about the power charge on his thrusters depleting before he finished, in which case the rover would become almost as fast as him, or maybe even faster if Paul had to hand swim the rest of the course. Either way it would mean additional minutes to his time, which was something he couldn't afford and would have to quit the challenge and restart again…something that had become taboo for the trainees.

Selecting the best course available to him Paul swam off, both arms extended before him, and rose up to the blue hoop almost at surface level, bending at the waist in a V-shape and grabbing the hoop to pull himself through and redirect his line of momentum back down towards a sweeping, descending turn of three almost aligned hoops of various colors.

He deactivated those in quick succession, then turned around in one of the slow 180 degree turns, passing through one of the deactivated ones in the process. As he did so, it turned back on as well.

"Doh," he criticized himself, learning another wrinkle in the new challenge and swimming back through to deactivate it for a second time.

2

Staying ahead of the rover proved harder than he thought. The device was slow enough, but it maneuvered in whatever lines it wanted, thanks to four omni-directional propulsion pods. Paul, on the other hand, was using long, high speed turns to zip about, which ironically took more time to pull through than the rover doing a direct, thrust-reversing turnabout.

It wasn't until halfway through the set that Paul realized going full out wasn't the quickest way and began feathering the throttle experimentally, saving full thrust for any long segment, but otherwise being as nimble jumping from hoop to hoop as he could be.

He also took a cue from the Rover and tried a few direct reversals, either reversing thrust with the hand controls or just moving his arms from in front of him down to his sides and accomplishing the same thing. It killed Paul to do it because he felt so inefficient, but towards the end of his run he realized that staying as close to the hoops as possible was key and his big turns had just been wasteful.

Paul followed the rover through the last hoop and deactivated it before the stupid machine could get to the next one. As soon as he did the floodlights came on and suddenly Paul could see everything in the crystal clear water with his good eye...the other one was still obscured by the echo-location device.

He swam back up to the start platform and found a short, four rung ladder and climbed out of the water and back on top, prying his finger up under the edge of his neck-wrapping breath mask. Once he had a leverage point he stretched the thick, yet pliable material until he had a hole big enough to fit his head through, then wiggled his way out of it. He detached the O2 line and carried the black mask in his hand as he walked across the arch-like gantry back to the control station where a trainer and four of his peers were waiting for their turns.

On a small scoreboard imbedded into the wall his finish time was displayed in red numbers.

7:43.3

Paul sighed. That was more than four minutes over par, hence the red numbers.

"Wow, that sucked," Jack said as Paul walked up.

"Thanks," he offered sarcastically.

"Any suggestions?" Larry asked, about to make his first attempt.

"Trim your lines and stay as close to the hoops as you can," Paul said, sitting down next to Kevin and Steve as he pulled off his tank vest.

"And pick a better line than he did," Jack added, who'd already made par on the course another day and was coming back to try and up his score. "He was all over the place."

"Will do," Larry said, heading out and closing the door behind him. On the wall of the control room was an array of display screens, all of which showed the underwater hoop configuration shifting to new, randomized positions as the trainer reset the course.

"024...are you sticking around for another go?"

"Yeah, sure, why not? I'm not due for my next session for another hour and a half."

The former Navy Seal nodded approvingly. "Give it some time and you'll get the handle of it. Took me a while to figure out those damn gadgets you all made, but nifty little things they are none the less. Wish we'd had those back in the day," he said as the lights in the chamber went out and all the underwater cameras switched to nightvision mode as they watched Larry stumble his way into the pool.

"Did I look that bad?" Paul said as Larry obviously struggled for some type of balance underwater in the pitch dark.

"Pretty much," Jack jibbed him, being the only one of his teammates present. The rest of the 2s were off tackling other individual challenges, with each of them progressing through their personal lists at their own rate. Some of the harder challenges had to wait until prerequisites were finished first, but otherwise each of the trainees could move through hundreds of different scenarios in whatever order they wanted. Given that they all had to share the same facilities, they tried to spread their attempts out as much as possible.

Paul had taken to his strengths first, primarily running and agility drills, but he'd also gained an aptitude for some of the martial arts. After digging as deeply into those as he could, which took time regardless of how skilled he *thought* he was, he spread out his allotted training time to focus on his worst areas, in which all forms of swimming qualified.

When looking at the posted scores of everyone else, he'd realized that he needed to gain more points in his weak areas than he conceivably could in his strengths, both because his strengths were lesser in number, and because he needed to diminish the points' gap put on him by his teammates in his weak areas.

After a year of training his individual rank had leveled out at 15th overall, with considerable point gaps above and below him. When looking over his options for advancement he'd concluded that his efforts would best be spent in tackling his weaknesses first and getting those out of the way early, not to mention trying to scrape up more points in the challenges he'd already made par on, such as Jack was attempting to do on this one.

Paul still hadn't gotten through half of the challenges yet, but he was nearing the end of the level 1 list, with this swimming challenge and three others remaining, along with a pair of marksmanship drills that he didn't think he'd have a problem with. One trick he'd picked up from talking with the others was to pick one or two disciplines at a time to focus on instead of spreading out training sessions over multiple weeks. It seemed that they all learned better when there was less downtime in between bouts, hence Paul had been doing a dreadful lot of swimming in recent days.

But better to bite the bullet now rather than have it hanging over his head for latter.

He watched Larry on his run with interest, trying to learn what he could from it and the others that he observed before it came around to his turn again. Jack succeeded in trimming four seconds off his previous best and left satisfied. The others each took two tries and called it quits for the day, leaving Paul alone on the course and able to make multiple back to back runs, only stopping to swap out equipment for fully charged units.

After five attempts he succeeded in making par, but only barely. Still, it was a pass, and opened up another level 2 underwater challenge, one that he would not be tackling for some time. He needed points, and while passing additional challenges did give him and others a points surge, it didn't last when the rest of them went through the same challenges later.

Those trainees who at first sought out only to pass just above par on as many challenges as they could found themselves with an early points lead that eventually faded when the rest of the group got deeper into the challenges and the fast starters found they couldn't easily pass the level 2 challenges...not without first sharpening their skills on the level 1 scenarios.

All in all, Paul was pleased with his progress and his current ranking, but not satisfied. He knew he'd have to do better just to graduate from the program, let alone maintain his rank. There wasn't a single slacker out of the 100 of them, and if he or any of the others started to take it easy they'd be passed up in good order. All of them were making steady progress up the charts, and if he was to keep pace with the others he had to continue improving on a daily basis.

Today had been a success, and with the par time achieved he vaulted 302 points higher, but that was still 135 behind Kerrie, and based on her progress...which Paul watched intently...she was nearing the completion of another challenge of her own, which would boost her lead over him yet again.

After finishing up his swimming challenge, Paul caught a quick shower then met up with the rest of the 2s as they ran through a cross country obstacle course in one of the 37 training 'parks' located inside Atlantis, each mimicking a different style of Earth terrain.

Paul and the others ran through one of several forest environments that dominated the parks, this one consisting mostly of tightly packed evergreen trees and no open grassy areas...on top of which it was snowing lightly, thanks to the climate controlled indoor environment. The size and scope of the training parks were jaw-dropping, and fit in with the overly ambitious design of the city which, on the surface, was sitting in 102 degree weather...while here inside, Paul and the others were running through two inches of snow!

The point of the drill was two-fold. First was the basic problem of navigating through dense forest. There were markers spaced out designating the route they had to travel, but in between each of the two-pole 'gates' were long stretches of forest without any premade paths to follow, so the trainees had to gage the quickest routes, as well as avoid getting lost.

The second point of the drill, as always, was time. Navigating your way through a forest environment was one thing...doing it quickly was something else entirely, especially given the irregularly spaced snow packs falling down through the trees in almost random locations, meaning they didn't have an even amount of snow on the ground to adapt to. Some areas were bare dirt while others had a half foot of snow to deal with.

The trick of the team run was to get everyone through the course as quickly as possible, but to do so in a way that was advantageous to the slower runners, else it would just be a challenge for the slowest person on each team. Paul was the second best runner in the 2s, after Jason, and both of them had been assigned to pace the slower runners. Jason had Ivan trailing him, while Paul led Megan, picking the route they would run while she only had to focus on keeping up with him.

By the time they'd finished their run...of which they only attempted once today, due to the high energy expenditure involved...they'd gotten their team time a good twelve seconds faster than Megan's best individual time, putting them 7th out of the 10 teams at present.

That wasn't going to be good enough for the 2s or Paul, who knew that the better his team did, the more points he'd score in his individual ranking. Star Force philosophy valued teamwork as an important individual skill to possess, thus 10% of the points available in the individual trials came from a trainee's team score...meaning someone couldn't ignore their teammates and hope to climb up the individual ranks on their own.

Paul didn't think any of them would have done that anyway, but the points spillover, which worked both ways, served as an ever-present reminder that they were a part of a larger endeavor, and the stronger they became as individuals the stronger the team would be and vice versa as they learned from each other and explored how they could surpass themselves by teaming up, such as on this cross country run.

Thoroughly exhausted after trouncing through the snow in skimpy bodysuits, Paul and the others retreated to the communal shower rooms back in their residential quarters, finding that the 4s had beat them there and were already occupying 10 of the 40 stations. The 2s took up ten more of the enclosed mini-bathrooms that had everything from a shower, toilet, mirror, sink, bench, and drying unit to a hamper chute that led down to an automated collection shaft that took their snow- and sweat-soaked clothing over to the laundry, which was also automated, save for folding the clean and dried clothes and returning them to the trainee inventory, which had to be done by hand by the quartermasters.

At the far end of the long 'shower hall' was a wide wall with numerous closets and drawers filled with fresh clothes and racks of sandal-like casual shoes, which they all shared. Paul grabbed a set of clothes and shoes in his size and retreated into one of the open shower stations as the 5s came in and began claiming their own stations.

15 minutes later Paul walked out in a fresh set of clothes and headed over to the cafeteria while Frank from the 6s took his shower as he and most of the other teams were waiting their turn at the end of the training day. He was a bit sore from slipping on the snow, but he was originally from Indiana, so running on the white stuff wasn't exactly new to him.

The rest of the 2s met up and occupied two of the 5 seat tables in the cafeteria and were halfway through their overly stuffed food trays when the 7s came in with obvious looks of frustration on their faces. They weren't talking to anyone else when they came in, which was normal for the teams since downtime was their only chance to mingle...which suggested to Paul that their ill mood was probably a result of their recent team challenge, of which the 7s were the first scheduled to tackle.

As per mutually agreed protocol, teams wouldn't discuss new challenges with other teams that had yet to pass them, so as to not give them an advantage in the points war, but while that was true the trainees always had individual challenges or past team challenges to discuss, or even their unofficial video game tournaments to talk about...so it was immediately obvious to Paul and everyone else in the cafeteria that something was wrong with the 7s.

As they walked by the 2s enroute to the food stations, the 7s said nothing at all, but Greg looked over at Paul and gestured with two fingers pointed up at his eyes as he walked by.

Paul frowned, now sure that something was up. In their hand signal code, created entirely by the trainees to give themselves the ability to communicate during challenges without the trainers being aware, the 'two fingers over eyes' gesture meant 'keep your eyes open,' suggesting there was danger or mischief at hand.

"Wonder what that's all about?" Emily whispered after they were out of earshot.

"What challenge did they just run?" Dan asked the others.

"G-2C," Jason answered. "The same we go through in two days."

"Bunker defense?" Brian asked, based on the identification code. "I wonder what the trainers have up their sleeve this time."

"If it's got the top dogs spooked, it must be something big," Megan pointed out.

"Guess we'll find out in two days," Paul said, biting a chunk out of his extra-large, blue iced sugar cookie...one of three on his plate, along with a stack of other sugar and carb-heavy foods. The amount of calories they burned through in a day was more than 3 times the norm and Paul and the others found themselves eating as often as they could, with sugary snacks being the lifeblood of their daily diet.

"Yeah," Jason said distractedly, still looking at the 7s as they filled their trays. Something was definitely up.

3

Two days later...

Kip knelt down and pressed his back up against the low upper bunker wall and held the single-shot paintball 'shotgun' up at an angle aiming back over his head. The butt of the thick weapon was set on the floor and with an iron grip Kip adjusted the angle as Randy gave him instructions.

"Five meters port," Randy said from his spotter position up in the corner of the squarish cupola that topped the bunker the 2s were tasked to defend for half an hour against continual trainer onslaughts. "Ten shallow."

Kip used his two arms as levers and marginally adjusted the angle of the weapon then nodded at Brian, who was squatted down on the opposite side of the paintball gun. With Kip holding the barrel in place, Brian pulled the trigger and the oversized paintball flew up into the air and out of sight.

Randy watched it land a meter short of one of the trainers on high ground who was sniping the hell out of the trainees. "Trajectory on...one shallow."

Brian recycled the weapon and Kip made the barest of adjustments to their improvised mortar, then gave his teammate the go ahead to fire, launching another green ball up into the air.

"Splash damage!" Randy reported.

"Has he moved?" Kip asked.

"Yep."

Kip released his hold and shook out his arms as Brian picked up the shotgun in a more traditional pose and walked up to the wall and took position in the nook between two castle-like wall protrusions, exposing only a piece of his head and the barrel of his weapon. Down below him Megan fired off a similar oversized round at one of the trainers trying to advance toward the bunker through a cluster of boulders set on the grass just outside the bunker.

It caught the man in the right calf and forced him to crawl back behind cover while three other trainers took the opportunity and opened up on the first level wall, causing Megan to duck down as they plastered the bunker with a volley of the fast firing, normal-sized paintballs.

Kip and Randy ran back down the inside ramp in the cupola and emerged in the northwest corner of the small bunker just in front of the mission end pedestal that the trainers were trying to get at. The 2s had to defend it for 30 minutes against 30 trainers equipped with the standard issue semi-automatic weapons that the trainees usually used...however, the ten trainees were only given two of the slow firing, over-sized shotguns to use in defense, leaving them seriously outgunned.

Their only other means of disabling the attackers was the stun sticks they were all equipped with. Barely an arm's length long, the silver rods looked like short lightsabers without the glow, ending with a rubberized hilt. The 'blade' was metallic and ended in a curved cap, but otherwise was just a long silver cylindrical tube that charged with stun energy then released on physical contact.

It gave the trainees a means of hand to hand combat, but that meant they had to wait for the attackers to get inside the base, which was problematic because all they would have to do to beat the trainees was rush forward and tap the button on the pedestal once.

It was a tough challenge, but not something overly complex. The trainees were meant to be huddled up inside the bunker as the trainers made their way across the boulder-strewn park that greatly resembled 'blood gulch' from Halo, where upon a hand to hand fight would ensue for possession of the bunker...at least that's what it had been intended to be, but the 2s weren't going to play that game.

Using the shotguns as mortars had been a trick the 4s had perfected on an earlier challenge, then shared with the other teams after the final scores had been tallied. It gave the trainees a way to break up any sniper positions as well as being able to fire back without exposing themselves directly to the attackers' mass fire. The larger size of the shotgun balls also meant additional stun potential, meaning a direct hit on a cluster of targets could disable them all with a lucky splash.

That said, the shotguns had to be recycled after each shot, making them poor choices for hand to hand fighting against multiple opponents. You could take down one target with even a glancing shot, but you'd be exposed to the others too long with the slower rate of fire, meaning their best use would come in fire support.

Knowing that the challenge would inevitably end in a fight inside the bunker, the 2s had decided to change the ground rules. While Kip, Brian, and Randy kept the attackers distracted with the mortar fire and Megan made sure they couldn't just run across the open areas with impunity, Paul, Jason, Dan, and Emily quietly snuck out the back entrance of the bunker and split up in pairs, one going north, the other south.

Paul and Emily headed north and kept behind the rocks and trees as much as they could as they flanked the trainers who were approaching from the west end of the park. This was the first time the 2s had run this scenario, but not the first time they'd been on this training site. Paul knew there was a series of small paths through the bits of forest that bordered the north and south edges of a wide open grassy area that encompassed most of the park and made for an intense free for all engagement zone.

The 2s had beaten the 8s three weeks earlier in one such throw down...with the temporary bunker having been removed. Paul had gone down in that engagement, but thanks to Jason's skills the 2s had come out victorious and earned a few bonus points, even though he'd been the only man left standing.

How familiar the trainers were with this park, Paul didn't know, but the three that he and Emily were coming up behind either didn't know of the paths or they just didn't expect the trainees to leave the bunker...at least maybe not on the first go around.

Big mistake. The trainers should have learned by now to expect the unexpected.

Emily exchanged glances with him and gave Paul a 'shove of her fist with thumb and pinky extended' hand signal towards the three trainers who were starting to inch their way forward, looking like they were going to make a break towards the next available cover, which was probably the clump of trees cattycorner right.

Paul nodded his agreement. They would rush the group together.

Emily slid to the side and up behind a tree, waiting for Paul to get in position. When he did, he pulled his stun stick out of his belt holster and thumbed on the power button. A slight crackle/pop sounded as the weapon charged, but the trainers didn't notice. Paul counted down on his fingers so Emily could see, starting at four and dropping his hand on two. They both continued the mental countdown in sync, then jumped out of cover and ran towards the backs of the trainers some 15 meters away.

One of them heard them coming and turned around just in time for Paul to kick his weapon out of his hands, followed by a quick jab of his stun stick into the man's chest, dropping him to the ground unconscious. Meanwhile Emily took her target down with a slap across the back of his shoulders, never having seen who hit him.

The third man turned and took a pair of shots at Paul, but he ducked behind cover as Emily came up on the man from behind. A quick whack on his butt and he was down as well, with the trainees graciously appropriating their paintball rifles.

Paul took the extra weapons and headed back through the trees as Emily crept her way along the flank to harass more of the trainers. When he got back to the bunker he gave the extra rifle to Jack and they took up firing positions in the bunkers, spraying the trainers with suppressive fire while the rest of their teammates slowly picked apart the trainers.

There were nine opponents still active on the battlefield when the thirty minutes expired and the challenge end tone sounded, with only Ivan going down among the 2s. Paul and the others were proud of passing the scenario on the first try, which would bump them ahead of the others in the training rotation and temporarily put them ahead of the 7s in points.

Unlike most other challenges, this one had simply been pass/fail, with 1000 points awarded for completion, so there was really nothing to gain or lose to the other teams here, just the prestige of beating it before anyone else had.

Still, a lead was a lead, and it was the first time the 2s had risen to the #1 ranking, and even though they knew it statistically wouldn't last, Paul and the others took it as a sign of things to come. They had gradually whittled down the 7s' lead to the point where this leapfrogging of the score could start to take place, and they were chomping at the bit to close the gap even further.

Later in the day, after all their training and challenges were finished, Paul was in the main lounge working on a snack and some navigational calculus drills on a datapad when Greg and Scott walked over to him with grim expressions on their faces.

"Well?" Greg asked.

Paul put the pad down and glanced up at him from his comfy, overly plush chair. "Well what?"

"You went through G-2C today, right?" Scott said pointedly.

"Yes," Paul answered, a bit confused by the breach in protocol. Neither the 5s nor 7s had beaten the challenge yet, as far as he knew. "We got it on the first try."

"How'd you take him down?" Greg asked in disbelief.

"Take who down?" Paul asked, getting more and more confused.

Greg and Scott exchanged glances. "You should know who if we're talking about the same thing. G-2C, bunker defense scenario?"

"I know what it is...what are you talking about?"

"You didn't fight the Black Knight, I take it?" Greg finally asked.

"What Black Knight?"

"That's a no," Scott confirmed.

Greg shook his head. "I don't get it...the challenges are supposed to be identical."

"Will someone please tell me what's going on?" Paul demanded.

"Ok," Greg said, lowering his voice to a whisper and slipping into the chair beside Paul. Scott stood and leaned on the back of another. "I know this is a breach in protocol and probably looks like the 7s are trying to get a leg up on the 2s but it's not, I promise."

"Go on," Paul said, remembering the heads up Greg had given him earlier.

"When we went through the G-2C challenge the trainers threw us a skiffer...a 7 foot tall, black armored trainer armed with what we're guessing is a stun sword. He jumped us in the bunker and knocked us all unconscious. When we came to he was gone and the trainers wouldn't say a word about it."

"Same thing here," Scott added. "He didn't even go for the pedestal. He went after all of us, even chased Kerrie down through the woods until he got her."

"He is unnaturally fast and swings his sword like it doesn't weigh a thing," Greg continued. "Our two teams got hit by him, but the 8s didn't...and apparently you guys didn't either."

"No, we didn't see anything like that," Paul said, thinking hard. "Some sort of trigger you tripped?"

"We thought about that, but we haven't come up with anything. A few of us even snuck back inside last night to look for motion trackers or pressure plates but we couldn't find a damn thing," Greg admitted.

"8s didn't pass, did they?" Paul asked.

Greg shook his head.

"You said this guy was wearing armor? Were you able to stun him at all?"

"That's the worst part," Scott said. "Brad wacked him good with his stun stick, but it didn't take him down. I saw him do it and the guy barely twitched."

"We were told that the stun energy soaks through everything," Greg continued. "Now armor should lessen the bleed through, but we hit him with two shotgun balls and three stun sticks in less than 10 seconds and he didn't go down."

"Oh..." Paul said warily, realizing that things had gotten to be a bit too easy lately, "this is not good."

"But why didn't you guys get hit?" Scott asked.

"Good question," Paul agreed. "I think this is something everyone needs in on."

Greg nodded, already thinking along those lines. "Team reps in my quarters in half an hour?"

"I'll help spread the word," Paul said, putting the last bit of snack in his mouth before he left to track down the others.

Whatever this new training element was, he had a sneaking feeling it was some kind of payback on the part of the trainers...and given how much trouble and embarrassment they'd caused them, this could end up being one hell of a karma-induced ass kicking.

4

Three weeks later...

Jack and Paul walked side by side down the narrow desert canyon, feet crunching slightly on the hard packed dirt/sand that made up the dry creek bed as they watched the nearby rocks for movement. The rest of the 2s were also patrolling the park in pairs, cleaning out hidden turrets that the trainers had placed in random locations. Given the narrow confines of the erratic canyons, the pesky turrets could literally have been anywhere...and the team had been tasked to clear them all out in the minimum amount of time possible.

This was the third attempt the 2s were making on the course, set in one of three desert environment parks in Atlantis. Their first attempt had been a learning exercise, with them taking it slow and getting a feel for the challenge while coming in well above par time. The second time through they'd rushed it, making par but losing half their team in the process, which incurred additional point penalties.

Paul jerked back just as the barrel of one of the turrets came into view, with a paintball flying through the space where his head had been and splattering against the side wall of the canyon. Jack went evasive as well, then regrouped with Paul a few meters back and exchanged some quick hand gestures. They'd recently learned that a lot of the turrets had hidden mics so that the trainers could listen in and anticipate their tactics if they spoke them aloud.

Paul guessed that this turret was on auto...no trainer could have responded that quickly to him coming into view, but now that he'd been spotted one of the trainers in the control center could assert control over the quad barreled pain inducer and give the targeting a personal touch.

Paul and Jack weren't going to wait that long and split up with Jack running over to the side of the canyon and Paul darting ahead into view again. He dove and somersaulted on landing behind a boulder near the creek bed, drawing fire as a distraction while Jack leapt over the angled rock the turret had been hiding behind and fired into its deactivation sphere at point blank range.

The turret attempted to swivel back around to face the rock but didn't have time before Jack filled it with enough charge to permanently deactivate it with a confirmation tone sounding.

Paul nodded his congratulations towards Jack when he saw his teammate's face widen in surprise. The sound of rocks/gravel falling prompted Paul to spin around just in time to see a huge black figure come sliding down the side of the canyon and drop to the ground a dozen meters behind him.

Jack peppered the figure with paintballs, half of which missed as the giant stood up out of his landing crouch and ran towards Paul, pulling a long black tube from a clasp on his hip and shoving it into Paul's sternum as he awkwardly fired back into its midsection.

Paul hit him with at least three shots, but the man was so fast he was on top of him before he could move aside. The end of the stun sword knocked Paul back against the rock...after that he remembered nothing.

Jack stood by the deactivated turret and filled the air around the black armored giant with a hail of paintballs, then took off running back down the canyon the way they'd come, knowing that he had to stay out of range of that sword.

The Black Knight saw him run off and took after him, covering the ground in large, fast steps. Jack's face went white with shock when he turned around and saw him closing rapidly. As a last resort, Jack tried to double back at an angle to avoid the intercept and fired off a few close range shots one handed as he tried to slip free...but the narrow canyon didn't leave him many options.

It wouldn't have mattered regardless. The Black Knight deftly spun about, reversing direction and ran Jack down in three steps, slashing diagonally across his butt and up to his right shoulder. Jack fell hard, bouncing off a boulder and breaking his nose.

The next thing he saw was the synthetic sky atop the park with three heads partially blocking his view. One was a med tech, the other two were Jason and Paul. He tried to twist his head to the side, suddenly feeling a painful tightness in his face. As the anti-stun injection cleared his senses he also tasted blood on his lips.

"Remain still, 020," the medic said calmly as he dug through a supply satchel. "You have a broken nose."

"I don't know, Paul," Jason said casually. "Might be an improvement."

"Can't get much worse," Paul added deadpan.

"Your compassion is touching," the medic noted as he pulled out a small, shiny metallic...something.

"What is that?" Jason asked. Paul was equally curious.

"The proper name is Kich'a'kat," he said, placing the device on the bridge of Jack's broken and bloodied nose. "But we usually refer to it as a level 1 regenerator."

"Dino tech?" Paul asked. The medic nodded as the small silver/gold device appeared to melt into rivulets that ran down the sides of Paul's nose, then solidified. With a painful 'crunch' that made Paul jerk in sympathy, the device realigned the pieces of bone in Jack's nose.

"Can he feel that?" Jason asked when Jack didn't so much as blink in response.

"Shouldn't...it numbs the affected area first," the medic explained as the skin on Jack's nose regrew impossibly fast, sealing up the cracks where the blood had been leaking out. When the device finished a little over a minute later, the metal rivulets flowed back into the main housing and the suction-like grip on Jack's nose released, with a small blue light winking on, indicating that the injury had been healed.

The medic picked the device up, which still lightly clung to Jack's face, and placed it back in his equipment bag. Paul wondered what else he had stashed in there.

"It will take a moment for the numbing to wear off," he explained, looking down at Jack. "Your new tissue will be weak, so try to avoid landing on your face again in the near future."

Jack tentatively reached up and touched his bloody nose, then wiggled it back and forth experimentally. The pain was indeed gone.

The medic offered Jack his hand and pulled him to his feet.

"Thanks," he said gratefully.

"You guys have been giving us some extra business lately," the medic noted.

"The Black Knight?" Jason guessed.

"Is that what you're calling him? Hmmn, yes, he does seem to be causing an abnormal level of injuries."

"Who is he?" Paul demanded.

"Can't say...I've never met him. But I hear he's been kicking the crap out of you guys."

"We only met today," Jason clarified.

"Did he get all of us?" Jack asked.

"Oh yeah," Paul answered. "You took the worst of it."

"Just out of curiosity," Jack asked the medic. "Will that thing heal a broken neck if he tosses us off a ledge?"

"Not this one, but this one can," he said smiling, pulling out a much larger device that was equally shiny.

"Really?" Paul asked, a bit concerned. "So we're free to get our bodies broken up as much as we want so long as you can put us back together again afterwards?"

"I wouldn't say that. These ranges were designed to minimize the hazards, but there will always be some amount of danger associated with the type of training you're doing."

Jason looked around at all the sharp edged rocks and cliff walls. "Minimized, huh?"

The medic smiled ironically. "Why do you think there's no water or deep sand in any of the environments?"

Jack caught his meaning first. "So we don't suffocate when we're stunned."

"Bingo," the medic said, sealing up his satchel and walking off down the canyon.

The three trainees let the man go, then turned to face each other in conference. "The others were right," Jason whispered. "Whoever this guy is, he's good."

"And stupidly fast," Jack added. "I don't see how he can move so quick in all that armor, let alone for his size."

"Are our weapons doing anything to him?" Paul complained/asked.

"I don't think so," Jack said, remembering how many times he'd shot the guy before he'd been offhandedly bounced into that rock. "I lit him up after you went down. He didn't so much as twitch."

"I think you're wrong about that," Jason differed. "Me and Ivan met up with Emily and Dan before he took us down, and several times I saw him duck into cover to avoid being hit. If his armor makes him immune to the stingers then he wouldn't need to shy away from weaponsfire."

"He didn't shy away from mine," Jack argued.

"There were four of us firing on him," Jason reminded his recently wounded friend. "I'd bet you 100 laps in the pool that we can take him down with enough hits."

"Like a super turret," Paul added, not liking the concept at all.

"That attacks us at random?" Jack said, kicking the toe of his shoe in the dirt. "Doesn't exactly make for a level playing field between teams."

"Actually it won't affect the team scores," Paul said, suddenly seeing the logic in it. "It may delay us and the others, but as long as he isn't showing up every time in the same challenge we'll all have a chance to pass uninterfered with."

"So what, he's just screwing with us?" Jason asked.

"It might be just that simple," Paul said, wishing he was wrong. "Another way to keep us on our toes."

"Well that's just wonderful," Jack said, placing his hands on his hips in frustration. "What are we going to do about it?"

The three of them were silent for a moment, then Jason finally responded with a fiery confidence in his voice. "We're going to find a way to take that bastard down."

5

Five weeks later...

Paul held position just outside the stairwell with Emily as Jason and Jack slowly walked up, overlapping their narrow shields for cover against the waiting paintball turrets on the next level up in the new training course the trainees had dubbed the 'tower.'

A completely 'urban' course, the tower was 15 levels of staircases with a finish pedestal on the top level. There were no windows inside the 'building,' buried deep within Atlantis's inner structure, but there were heavy floodlights on some of the levels...offset by dimly lit levels and others with intermittent lighting, making it hard to spot turrets and trainers.

Today's challenge was turrets only, with few barricades in the otherwise open levels. Each corner of the square rooms held a stairwell, either going up or coming up, with its opposite direction facilitated by another quartet of stairwells situated back to back in the center of the room looking like a large pillar that blocked the view of the opposite corner. That way, in order to climb higher, the trainees had to cross each roomful of hazards, though they could advance up any of the four stairwells they chose.

There were a few low barricades spread out across each level, but everything else was just open space and an easy kill zone for the turret columns situated along the walls, next to the center stairwells, and a few random ones placed out in the open to create additional fire angles. Normally the trainees would have sniped at the turrets to deactivate them from afar...problem was, they didn't have their rifles in this challenge. They were only equipped with stun sticks and the new, but handy, personal shields.

That meant in order to deactivate the turrets they had to close to point blank range...or else just try and make a run for the next stairwell and ignore the turrets altogether. Neither was a good option, as usual, which made the 2s work hard for each level up the tower they advanced.

Paul heard several shots hit his teammates' shields as they were only partway up the staircase, meaning there was a floater turret placed directly in front of the stairs...

"Paul!" Jason yelled.

"On it!" he answered back as he passed by Emily and put his foot on the bottom stair, looking up at his teammates hunkered down near the top, deflecting a steady stream of stingers that were thumping off their shields in mechanical rhythm. He flicked the power button on the stun stick in his right hand, hearing the soft crackle/pop as the 'blade' charged with stun energy. He repeated the process on Jason's stick, which he held in his left hand. "Ready...give me the angle."

"Half meter left," Jason said, holding his and Paul's shields tight together as he rotated the one on his right hand about in preparation. He glanced at Jack, who was brushing up against his left shoulder, pinched between the sides of the stairwell coming up from below floor level.

Jack nodded and looked forward. A moment later he and Jason leapt up four steps and into view of the wall turrets on their flanks. They pulled their second shields over to cover the additional turrets, trying to scrunch up in between the corner of the too narrow shields. With a well placed shot the turrets could get through the gap, but it was a risk they had to take.

When the pair had run up the steps they'd also split apart, leaving a narrow gap between them that Paul ran towards. When the turret directly in front of the stairs came into view he shovel threw one of the stun sticks forward, trying to keep as much rotation out of it as possible, then let himself fall face down onto the steps and out of the line of fire.

The stun stick passed between his teammates, almost hitting them in the shoulders, and flew true to target. The silvery 'blade' hit the target sphere atop the turret and on physical contact released its stun charge. The stick bounced off the sphere and fell to the floor, bouncing across the carpeted surface until it hit one of the waist-high barricades.

Jason and Jack readjusted their shields to the sides, providing better cover now that they didn't have to defend against the immediate forward arc, though there were a pair of turrets flanking the inner stairwell directly ahead, but at the moment they weren't aimed at them.

On the two adjacent stairwells the rest of the 2s were gathered and distracting as many of the turrets as they could. Jason and Jack had poked up last of all, hoping to avoid most of the attention, and as of now only four turrets were pelting their shields with paintballs while the other two groups were getting most of the turrets' attention.

"Emily?"

"I'm ready," she said, standing directly behind Paul and activating her own pair of stun sticks.

"Jason?" Paul asked.

He glanced at Jack again. "Go!" he yelled, stepping up out of the stairs and onto the floor to the right. His two shields blocked everything above his knees, and he hoped the turrets would track his center of mass.

Jack did the same thing on the left, opening up the stairs and further distracting the turrets as Paul and Emily ran up and out, hurdled a low barricade, and each smacked one of the turrets guarding the inner stairwell with their stun sticks before running halfway up the stairs and out of view of everyone except Jason and Jack, who quickly retreated back into their stairs to cover their exposed shins and feet.

With two of the four center turrets down, the fire on the other groups decreased, allowing them a little breathing room, but not enough to try and break free. It was up to Paul's group to take out the rest of the turrets on this side of the room.

Emily exchanged hand signals with Jason, then took off running back to their position. He and Jack walked up and out again, distracting the few turrets aimed at them and clearing the way for Emily to slide feet first back onto the stairs. She skidded down several on her butt, but she avoided getting hit by any of the stingers.

Paul followed her a heartbeat later, but ducked down behind the barricade, midway between staircases and waited. Meanwhile Emily came back up with Jason and Jack covering her in a wedge of shields. They sidestepped to the right, then backtracked along the edge of the stairwell opening towards the wall, careful not to fall down into it, for there was no railing.

From there they advanced to the nearest wall turret, blocking paintballs at point blank range. Emily jabbed one of her stun sticks out in a narrow gap between Jason's shield and the wall, poking the turret's sphere. The stun charge deactivated it and the three man 'turtle' moved down to the next one.

One of the turrets tracking Megan's group suddenly turned away and aimed for the threesome, now under remote control from one of the trainers. The barrels dipped down and shot at their legs from a distance, hitting Jack in the shin.

"Down!" he yelled, half falling into Jason, but Emily grabbed hold of him by the waist to keep their shield wall intact. The three of them knelt down, covering the incoming fire but unable to move forward.

Emily's torso popped up suddenly and she side-armed one of her stun sticks into the turret they'd been heading for, now only two meters away and took it out, clearing that half of the wall so Jason could readjust his shield angle for better cover.

Meanwhile Paul had leapfrogged to another barricade and ducked down again. There were two turrets left in this quarter of the room, on the wall beside Megan's group. One held an auto turret shooting at Paul's guys, while the other was the trainer-overrided turret, now doing likewise.

Before Paul had a chance to act, Megan chucked one of her stun sticks out from their now clear left angle and hit the trainer's turret, leaving only one left shooting at his group. Once they'd knocked it out, it wouldn't be difficult to clear the others out and secure a path to the next level.

About to rush the last turret, Paul's peripheral vision caught sight of another floater to his left just in time for him to reverse his course and drop back down behind the barricade as it swiveled and shot over his head.

"Damn," he whispered, scolding himself for being so sloppy. The others hadn't had a chance to take that one out yet.

Jason stepped aside from Jack, who was now sitting on his legs behind his two shields, protecting Emily as they crept away from their wounded teammate, walking on their toes with their knees almost pinned to their chests toward the last turret on this wall. Emily caught a glance of Paul moving between barricades just as a sliver of splattered paintball caught her in the forehead.

It immediately numbed her senses, making her a bit lightheaded, but she stayed on her feet. A few seconds later and they were right in front of the turret, where she jabbed out again along the wall when Jason created a gap and took it out of play.

"You hit?" Jason asked as Emily slumped against the wall.

"Yeah," she said, grimacing. She pointed to her forehead. "Just a piece."

"Stay put," Jason said as Paul jumped up, ran forward, and dove at the floater turret, slapping it inactive, then taking cover behind its base. "Here," he said, handing her one of the shields. "You're out of the heavy fire now."

"Get it this time," she said, gripping one of the shield's handholds and snugging it up in front of her knees and chest. Jason left her alone and moved off to help the others, meanwhile Emily rubbed the numb spot in her head, trying to disperse the energy into the surrounding tissue and blood, thus diluting the effect. The tip of her index finger went slightly numb in the process, but that only meant less charge in her head, so she accepted the tradeoff as she waited out the denumbing process. Regardless, she was going to have one hell of a headache afterwards.

With one quarter of the level clear of turrets, the attack angles favored the trainees, who were able to overlap shields to greater effect and carefully pick off the rest of the turrets after a brief confab between Jason and Paul, who had gradually become co-team leaders of the 2s over the past few months. They were currently on level 14, with only one level more to go and the defenses increasing the higher they went.

This was farther than they'd gotten in their previous attempt, and though they were down a man from earlier, plus having Emily and Jack partially incapacitated, they mutually decided to clear out this entire level so they could approach the final room from all the stairwells, as well as be able to move about below to reposition people for multiple confusion if the trainers chose to take direct control of the final set of turrets...which they knew they would.

With 8 team members fit to continue fighting, for now Jack was back on his feet though limping heavily, they split up into pairs and probed the final level's defenses, walking slowly up the final flight with shields held above their heads.

They received incoming fire almost immediately, signaling that there were turrets on the ceiling this time. That wasn't something they'd had to deal with on the lower levels and would provide a different challenge. Paul was trying to gage the distance that he'd have to throw from behind his shield when the impacts suddenly stopped. Jason frowned at him, and he returned the gesture, wondering what was going on.

Suddenly something heavy hit his shield from the side and knocked him into Jason, with both of them falling backwards down the stairs, tumbling on top of their shields and stun sticks...which fortunately had been turned off and reattached to their belts.

When Paul twisted around and got to his feet he looked up the stairs but saw nothing, then heard a similar clamor on the far side as Megan and Dan took a tumble down their set of stairs.

"What the hell?" Jason asked, quickly grabbing his shield and hitting the stairs. Paul followed a step behind him but neither of them was shot at as they ascended, which he wondered might be a trick on the part of the trainers until his head cleared the last step and he saw the finish pedestal in the center of the room...with the Black Knight stalking about beside it.

"You think those turrets are really off?" Paul whispered as the others emerged from their stairwells and stared down their opponent, who was keeping close to the pedestal and making no move towards them.

On the other side of the room Brian walked sideways, keeping the Black Knight locked in his vision, and tapped one of the turrets with his stun stick. Likewise, the other trainees spread out the room, still hiding behind their meter-long shields, and deactivated all of the wall turrets.

Paul threw one of his stun sticks at the ceiling, hitting one of the low riding turrets there and let it fall to the ground beside him, resisting the urge to catch it out of the air and potentially stun himself. With Emily's stick held in front of him warily, he reached down and picked up the other...all the while the Black Knight walked about impatiently, never getting more than two meters from the finish pedestal that would end the challenge in a victory for the 2s.

Ivan and Kip deactivated the other ceiling turrets, with Paul getting the last one. Now that they had made sure they were out of the equation, they looked at the Black Knight, unnerved by the sight of the 7 foot tall monster...but equally freaked out by the fact that he wasn't attacking them. In every other encounter they'd had, he was constantly in motion, taking them down with lethal precision and never giving the trainees a chance to breathe, let alone plan out a counterattack.

Paul slapped both stun sticks together, making a loud clap that got everyone's attention, then he went through a series of hand signals before dropping his shield and thumbing both sticks on. He spread his arms wide in preparation and walked toward the pedestal.

The Black Knight stepped in between it and him, holding up his long black stun sword in a guard position. When Paul got within three steps of the Knight he leapt forward and slashed sideways in a faint with his silver rod, less than half the length of the Knight's sword.

The Knight ignored the faint and spun his sword around his body, stepping forward once as it completed the circle and lashed out at Paul's side. The trainee brought both stun sticks up in guard and wisely deflected the Knight's 'blade' up and over his head, with him having to duck to avoid the arc. The power behind the Knight's swing was mind boggling, and there was no way he could have stopped it with brute force.

The blade swung up over the man's helmeted head and came crashing down on where Paul had been a moment before, missing his retreating shoulder by inches. Twin stun sticks slapped at the blade, trying to delay its movement as Dan jumped out from the wall and tried to make a run for the pedestal...but the Knight was ready for him and reversed his direction of attack in a blur and jabbed his sword out across the pedestal and caught Dan in the ribs, knocking the wind out of him and dropping him to the floor unconscious.

Paul threw one of his sticks at the Knight's back, but his impossibly fast blade whipped around and knocked it aside and into Brian's shield, where it discharged, sending a tiny pinprick tingle through the barrier and into his hand. He thumbed off his own stick and tossed it to Paul, then picked up the live one the floor, hearing the crackle/pop as it recharged once the blade broke physical contact...a safety mechanism to keep the stick from emptying its power source uselessly.

A moment of calm resumed, with the Black Knight stepping across Dan's unconscious body and continuing to pace around the short perimeter.

Jason signaled the remaining 6 trainees, realizing that their odds of success went down with each team member lost, so they had to maximize their chances now.

Paul moved first and swung wildly with alternating arms at the Black Knight, who deftly parried each, almost toying with him as all the others rushed forward a split second later.

The Knight battled Paul's blades aside easily, then swung about and knocked Megan's shield side, inverted his sword, and brought it behind his back catching Brian in the knee, knocking him down less than a meter away from the Pedestal.

A whirlwind twirl of the intimidating black blade knocked Kip and Randy back, but they managed to hold onto their shields and avoid being stunned. A quick flip of his wrist brought the blade around again and down on top of Jack's head as he clumsily rushed the giant. He fell to the floor, accidentally hitting Jason in the knee with his stun stick, taking him out of the fight.

A silver stun stick flew through the air and hit the Black Knight in the back, bouncing off his armor and refusing to so much as make him twitch, but it did prompt him to turn around and slash at Paul, who barely managed to be able to duck underneath.

Kip and Randy charged forward shield first and dove into their opponent, attempting to knock him off his feet. They felt like they hit a stone wall on impact, with Kip ricocheting off and Randy succeeding in buckling the Knight's knee, but he didn't go down. Instead he ignored them and jabbed out at Megan as she tried to hit the challenge end button on the pedestal.

His blade caught her in the neck, and she fell face forward, her arm brushing against the button but not forcefully enough to press it down.

Randy wrapped himself around the Knight's legs, trying to take him to the floor or at least pin him in place, but he was too close to the pedestal and slashed at Paul as he tried to make for it, hitting his stun stick parry and forcing the trainee back a step. The Knight's blade then twirled around and slashed down on Kip as he was getting to his feet, then came down on Randy, rendering them both unconscious.

Paul made one last leap for the pedestal, but the Knight freed himself from Randy's grasp and stepped forward, catching him by the throat and stopping his arm from reaching the button. Paul jabbed his stun stick into the Knight's arm, but his grip didn't slacken, so Paul hit him again and again, with the third time resulting in a buckle at the elbow, but then the pommel of his sword came down in front of Paul's face and the base of the blade tapped him on the head, knocking him out.

On the floor below Emily heard the sounds of combat, but no turret fire, wondering what the hell was going on. She got to her feet and meekly walked across the room to the bottom of the stairs, her head so awash in disorientation that she had trouble walking in a straight line, just as the Black Knight stepped out in front of her.

She froze...less from her numbness and more from the fact that she had no weapon, only her shield.

The Black Knight didn't hesitate and batted away her shield with his armored fist, then slashed down diagonally from overhead with his blade. The force of the blow knocked her aside, where she dropped to the floor unconscious.

The armored warrior deactivated his sword and reattached it to his belt, walking off and leaving the bodies where they lay in testament to yet another promising challenge run thwarted by the mysterious nemesis that had become the trainees' bane.

6

Seven days later...

"Run!" Paul yelled at Megan, who stood holding the Black Knight's heavy sword awkwardly, unsure of how to use it against him. From past experience they knew a single strike from their stun sticks wouldn't take him down, but who knew about his own sword.

Megan twitched with sudden understanding and wheeled about, running away to the nearest stairwell in the tower and headed back up, getting the Black Knight's weapon as far away from him as she could.

Paul leapt forward and slashed at the black armor with his stun stick, getting in two quick hits before he was kicked out of the way, flying back a good two meters as the Black Knight struggled to regain his footing as Dan and Brian had him half pinned to the floor. Jack and Jason were already down, but the four of them had managed to knock the Knight off his feet and luckily his grip on his sword hadn't held, with it flying away on impact.

Megan had promptly snatched it up and, if she had any smarts about her, would take it all the way back up to the top level, where this inverted version of the tower run had started, with the team having to fight their way *down* through the levels and turrets...which in some ways was harder than going up.

The Black Knight had jumped them on level 6 and taken out Emily, but missing Dan in his first strike. He'd called out an alarm and everyone had retreated up a level.

When the Black Knight followed the four of them had tackled him coming up the staircase, but his superior strength was showing through as he tossed the trainees off him one by one.

Paul lay on the floor with the wind knocked out of him...and maybe a cracked rib...watching as Ivan, Kip, and Randy stunned him repeatedly on the arms, legs...whatever they could reach with their stun sticks. As soon as he got to his feet the repeated blows finally got to him, dropping him back down to a knee, but he wasn't out of the fight.

With his left arm, which hadn't taken many hits, he caught Kip's stun stick when the trainee swung at his head and pulled him off balance. Kip fell with the Black Knight holding the 'blade' and shirking off the stun charge, claiming the weapon for himself until Randy landed two quick hits on the arm holding it.

The Black Knight's grip slipped as his arm numbed and the stun stick dropped to the ground as Ivan slashed at his back yet again.

Suddenly the bulk of black armor leapt up and forward, knocking Randy down and getting the Knight momentarily away from Ivan's reach as Paul climbed back onto his feet to help his teammates. This was the best opportunity they'd ever had of taking the bastard down and he wasn't going to let a little injury rob them of the chance.

Stumbling, but still quick as ever, the Black Knight retreated a few steps to get clear of the downed trainees and set himself, wobbling slightly, but after a moment it faded and he was rock solid as ever. Ivan and Paul ran towards him as Kip picked up his stun stick and rejoined the fight, jumping over Randy who was just clearing the stars from his spinning head.

The Black Knight waited for them to come to him, crossing his arms and touching the inside of his wrists together. Paul thought he heard a crackle/pop and realized a split second before he lost consciousness that they hadn't completely disarmed their enemy.

Paul's blade landed on the Knight's shoulder, which he let hit in order to punch at Paul's chest before being batted at by the other two. Paul fell to the floor unconscious as the giant turned on the others and delivered quick blows to body and arms, surviving Kip and Ivan's stun hits long enough to tap them out. Belatedly Randy came at the Knight, not seeing what had just happened, and swung hard towards his midsection which, with the height difference, was just in front of his face.

The Black Knight caught the blade with a distinctive electrical crackling sound typical of stun blade charge trying to discharge on stun blade, holding it steady in between the two as he brought his left fist around and lightly punched Randy in the head, dropping him to the floor alongside the others.

A flying stun stick hit the Knight in the chest, causing him to stagger a bit. Another followed it before Dan and Brian came at him after picking themselves up off the floor. It hit as well, missing his too numb hand as he reached to knock it aside. Dropping to a knee again, awash with stun energy, the Black Knight fought to stay on his feet as the remaining two trainees swatted at him with more of the stun sticks that were now littering the floor.

In a move that was half inspiration, half desperation, the Black Knight leaned forward off balance and jumped towards the pair with outstretched arms, one each toward the two trainees. They collided and all three fell in a tangled pile.

Several long seconds later the Black Knight slowly pulled himself out of the mess of bodies and stood, shaking off the stun charges he'd been absorbing. He took a moment to clear his head then walked off towards the staircase, gaining strength with each step, as he went to hunt down Megan and retrieve his sword.

"Heard you came close," Greg asked Paul and Jason as they came into the lounge area late. Jason had stayed with Paul after the challenge while the medics had repaired his six cracked and one broken rib, and as a result had been last in line for the showers.

"Not really," Paul said, appropriating a nearby chair and spinning it about to face Greg's. Jason likewise grabbed one.

"I heard you took him to his knees," Greg went on, "after stealing his sword?"

"Don't ask me, I was unconscious at the time," Jason said after a questioning glance.

"We succeeded in stunning him enough to make it show, but we didn't hit him enough," Paul said, thinking back through the brief, but intense fight for the 6th time since being revived from his stun-induced coma. "But I think we have another problem."

Greg stiffened. "What?"

Paul and Jason exchanged glances. "I think he might have stun gloves."

"Gloves?" Greg asked.

"I don't remember being stunned, unless I accidentally hit myself after he punched me," Paul explained. "I also think I heard him activate them."

"Which, if true," Jason added, "means we can't disarm him."

Greg thought hard. "How would gloves work? Did you see him turn them on?"

"I think there's something on his wrists...it all happened so fast I'm not really sure."

Greg shook his head in dismay. "He's never lost his sword before, which is probably why we've never seen him use them."

"Still," Jason said, "we've got some idea of what it takes to disable him. What's the ratio of stinger to stun stick?"

"I don't think they've ever said," Greg noted, glancing at Paul for confirmation. "But I'd guess 4 to 1...maybe 2 to 1 for the shotgun."

"Something like that," Paul agreed.

"Well, what's that put us for a shot count?" Jason asked Paul.

Paul mentally recounted the approximate number of hits the Black Knight had taken. "Best guess...50+ to visibly weaken him. I'm scared to think how many it will take to knock him unconscious."

"Still, it's some valuable intel," Greg said, nodding appreciatively.

"Given the right situation, I think we can amass that much firepower," Jason said, already thinking through their options. "It'd have to be on one of the park courses, where we can keep our distance. So far we haven't seen him with any ranged weapons."

"But he is quick," Paul pointed out. "We can't hit him fast enough to keep him from getting at some of us."

"Depends on the terrain," Greg countered.

"Blood gulch?" Jason suggested.

Greg nodded. "That's what I was thinking."

"Problem is," Paul said, "he picks when and where to hit us."

"That doesn't mean we can't plan ahead," Jason reminded him. "Anyone feel like a little extra practice time?"

"I'll grab a few guys," Greg said, getting up, then looked down at Paul. "We'll get this figured out."

"You...stay and rest," Jason told Paul as he started to get up out of his seat. "I'll fill you in later."

"Will do," Paul relented, sitting back down in the lounge chair. He leaned back and closed his eyes, trying to bleed off the mild stun headache. He licked his lips reflexively, then caught himself and stopped. The damn regenerator always left him tasting metallic coconut.

7

The Black Knight continued to harass the trainees at random for the following three weeks on varying team challenges before he finally got around to hitting them again on the 'blood gulch' park course. The 8s were running a 'gauntlet' scenario, in which they had to make it from one end of the park to the other past an undisclosed amount of hidden snipers, when the Black Knight showed up again, appearing from behind one of the large boulders in the center of the park and taking down Nik without warning.

"Knight!" Rafa yelled out, aiming and firing off three quick rounds from his stubby rifle as he backtracked. "Scatter!"

The others trainees, save for Vic, took off for cover, hoping that the snipers would leave them alone until this was finished. That hadn't always been the case, but more often than not when the Black Knight arrived the trainers were content to sit and watch.

Vic was the Knight's next target, and the mass of black armor was on top of him in three quick lunging steps. Trainee 086 was fast enough though to drop his rifle and unclasp the stun stick attached to his belt that the team leaders had encouraged them all to wear when the challenge allowed, just in case the bastard showed up again.

Vic didn't have time to turn it on, as he immediately had to deflect a long reaching slash from upper left. He twisted with the direction of the hit and backstepped in a graceful spin that bought him another meter of distance. Had he wanted to strike at the Knight he never would have been able to reach him, the stun sword he carried had too much length, as did the man's arms, but fortunately that wasn't his mission...buying time for the others to set up was.

Vic danced around as much as he could, deflecting and dodging the furious blows from the black sword, which the Knight swung far too easily for its weight and size. He knew he didn't have long before his luck would run out, but he did hold on long enough to see the first few stingers begin to coat the black armor with spots of green.

He ducked underneath one wicked lateral slash, but lost his balance in the process and landed on his back, quickly trying to roll out of the way but knowing it would do no good. The Black Knight was faster than any of them and Vic knew in a moment he'd feel the tip of the stun sword dig into his chest or back just before he blacked out.

But that didn't happen this time, as a wave of incoming stingers prompted the Black Knight to disappear behind the nearest rock. Vic just caught sight of the back of his armor as it disappeared around the boulder and wanted to count himself lucky, but he knew better and quickly looked around for his rifle.

Rafa pelted the Black Knight with six shots, missing twice more as the Bastard ran for cover. On one level he was glad they'd scared him off and kept Vic in the fight, but Rafa would have traded that minor victory for a chance to shoot him up in the open. Right now he had to reposition to higher ground.

The others were doing likewise, climbing up on top of boulders and atop of ledges...using the terrain to put some obstacles between themselves and the Knight to give themselves a chance to retreat if and when he came after them. Mark took a position atop a pancake-looking angled ledge then immediately jumped off it, completing a full forward twist to awkwardly land on his feet and fall to the ground as the Black Knight raced up the backside of the ledge and jabbed forward with his sword.

Rafa didn't wait till his black armor came into view and started firing at the sword as soon as he saw it extend from behind the boulder blocking the rest of his view. By the time his first stinger arrived the Knight had moved into range and it hit him square in the head, splattering a bit of green over his faceplate. Four more shots from other 8s hit him in the torso as he distractedly swiped at the paint partially blocking his vision and jumped down off the ledge in pursuit of Mark.

Rafa's next two shots missed the moving target, but a few of the increasing number of paintballs zinging his way hit the Knight, but they didn't slow him down. Mark had gotten to his feet and ran towards a group of boulders on which three of his teammates stood firing, but the Knight quickly tracked him down and knocked his legs out from under him with one quick flick of his wrist, accepting the dozen or so hits on his chest to make the kill before darting off again in search of cover.

He didn't completely find it, trading the firing lines of five trainees for two others, who quickly retreated back behind cover when he rushed them, which then brought him into the firing lines of four more of the ever-repositioning trainees. The 8s had practiced this sort of cat and mouse harassment many times with the other teams and knew which spots in the rocks made for good firing positions, as well as where to run when they needed to get out of the way.

The Black Knight wasn't confused, however, and picked one target to track down, knowing that the trainees were trying to distract him long enough to rack up a lot of hits. Rafa recognized this immediately as the Knight jumped up on top of a boulder with stunning ease and height, exposing himself to a hail of shots to chase down Andy who'd dropped off the other side.

That took the Knight out of sight for the moment, but Rafa held his spot, perched atop another boulder, knowing that the Knight would either reappear on his own or one of his teammates would draw him out. Even so, as he waited, Rafa could see and hear several of the others shooting down into the rocks at the target. A muffled groan preceded Oni jumping back off her perch and the Black Knight appearing on top of the rocks in pursuit, suggesting that now Andy was down too.

The Knight took four more hits while passing up into view, one of which came from Rafa. Oni disappeared from view and ran through the rocks, rounding a curve and heading straight for Rafa. Her pursuer appeared two seconds later, charging hard and a bit awkwardly towards the trainee.

Rafa unloaded as many shots as he could into the Knight's chest, firing directly over Oni's head, the last of which was joined by four other shots that hit his black armor just as he caught up to and swung at Oni, missing by inches as she instinctively dove into a somersault and rolled through the grass just in front of the boulder that Rafa stood on.

The Black Knight stumbled as more stingers hit him, but succeeded in bringing his sword down on top of Oni and taking her out of the fight as two more trainees climbed up on nearby rocks and added their fire to the small kill zone in which the Knight now stood. He slashed up at Rafa, but didn't quite have the reach, then fell to a knee as the repetitive stinger hits took their toll.

Rafa pumped his rifle's trigger as fast as he could, adding more and more paint to the already green-plastered black armor, combining his shots to those of the five other trainees as they brought the Knight down to both knees. When his sword fell out of his hand Rafa's heart seemed to do a double pump out of sheer joy, but he knew better than to celebrate and kept firing.

Thirty seconds later Zack lowered his weapon and held up his open palm in a signal to stop. He climbed down off the rocks and cautiously approached the Black Knight, who was lying prone on the ground, apparently unconscious. Rafa and the others also climbed down, belatedly realizing that there were still snipers about, but so far they hadn't opened fire on them. Perhaps the trainers were as shocked as they were that they'd actually taken down the Black Knight.

Vic carefully walked up to the armored giant and picked up his long stun sword and pulled it out of his reach...but the Knight didn't so much as twitch in response. "This thing is heavy," he commented, swinging it about experimentally as a blue paint splatter hit the rock wall beside him. On reflex all the trainees dove for cover.

"We've still got a challenge to complete," Rafa yelled to the others. "Let's make good on it."

The surviving six trainees began working their way through cover, Vic now carrying the Black Knight's sword in place of his stun stick, and tracked down the closest of the snipers. One good thing about the stingers was the paint smears they left behind on the rocks, which made it easy to identify the angles of fire and backtrack them to their sources.

Rafa took down the first sniper from the flank as the others drew his fire. The trainer slumped over in his harness, attached to an elevated branch in one of the trees, and Rafa moved under his position, sighting the next sniper as Vic motioned in the approximate direction. The moving leaves in another tree made for a dead giveaway each time the sniper fired, now that he knew where to look.

He exchanged hand signals with Lens, who was closer to the target than he was, directing him to the spot. On cue, Vic popped out of cover as a distraction, drawing the fire of not one, but two snipers as Lens took down the first.

Now where's the other one? Rafa thought.

Back in the small grassy clearing between the rocks the Black Knight lay still on the ground as his armor slowly absorbed the stun charge saturating its hardened plates. When the stun-hungry material had finished eating up the latent charge, it began pulling the energy out of the Black Knight's body, returning him to consciousness within twenty seconds. He stayed on the ground for another minute as feeling returned to his body and the trainees moved on, tracking down the snipers.

Once adequately destunned, the Black Knight climbed to a shaky knee and held the position, needing a few more seconds before he could walk again. He pulled his arms together and touched his wrists, activating his stun gloves as he listened for the sounds of weaponsfire and deduced the approximate location of his targets.

Rafa and the rest of the 8s were halfway through the park when Hans made a quick dash between rocks and the snipers didn't fire at him. Rafa thought maybe he'd caught them off guard, but when Vic advanced a few seconds later and there was still no shots fired he wondered if the snipers were repositioning to flank them or had pulled back towards the finish area to double up their firepower just when the Black Knight caught up to them, punching Zack in the back before he could even turn around.

Rafa glanced to his right in disbelief as he turned around out of reflex and fired on the Knight. He hit him with two shots before Vic came into view from behind and hit the black armored giant with his own stun sword.

The Black Knight stumbled forward a bit, then casually turned around and caught Vic's next swing on the blade and held it firm. He yanked the sword towards him, bringing Vic with it when he refused to let go. The Knight kicked out his legs and dumped him to the ground while shrugging off the stingers coming from Rafa and now Hans as well. He reached down and punched Vic in the chest, stunning him unconscious.

The Black Knight touched his wrists together, deactivating the gloves and picking up his sword by the hilt before running after Hans, who quickly retreated out of view, but he didn't last long. Without the ability to sustain massed fire they knew they had no chance against their nemesis.

Rafa was the last of the trainees to be taken down, running across the park in a vain attempt to reach the finish area, hoping either the snipers wouldn't fire and give him a chance of winning the scenario, or that they would take him down before the Knight did. Attacking him one on one was futile...at least against the snipers he stood a small chance of evasion.

Neither possibility came to pass. The snipers held their fire as the Black Knight used his superior speed and ran Rafa down some 200 meters before he got to the finish area. The last thing he heard was the quick stomp of boots behind him before a blunt tip lodged itself in his back and everything went black.

8

Paul and Jason exchanged lunges and parries with deactivated stun sticks in one of several small sparring rooms in Atlantis, trying to expand and sharpen their skills. There were three individual challenges that directly involved the short weapons, but it wasn't for the sake of increasing their scores that they were practicing...both they and the other 98 trainees were desperate to find a way to defend themselves against the Black Knight.

It had been four months since he'd first appeared, and to date none of the teams had been able to take him down. The 8s' brief moment of glory had been their last, and no one had been able to render him unconscious since then. It seemed he was learning as fast as they were, and every technique they used to try and counter his attacks he eventually adapted to...if not outright shrugged off.

They key problems when facing him were his speed and skill with the sword. While the Black Knight's lack of a ranged weapon was the trainees' biggest advantage, his speed countered it in most cases, allowing him to close ranks alarmingly fast and dispatch with any snipers they attempted to deploy, and ever since his near defeat on blood gulch he'd taken care to keep out of the open save for when making a kill. As a result, it was nearly impossible to amass enough firepower for a prolonged period of time, sufficient to disable him.

The stun sticks, however, held much more charge than the stingers did, so the trainees could conceivably disable the Black Knight quicker if they utilized hand to hand combat...preferably in concert with ranged snipers. The problem was, the Knight's blade was more than twice as long, and he had the strength to break through any 'stops' the trainees could make with their stun sticks, meaning every attack he made had to be diverted away at an angle since the massive amount of force he delivered couldn't be abruptly canceled out with a conventional block.

Even when some of the trainees had stood toe to toe with him, they hadn't lasted more than a few moves, for the Black Knight wasn't only stronger and faster than they were, he was also more skilled. That, Paul and Jason had come to believe, was where they needed to focus their attention. If they could improve to the point where they could last 10 seconds against him, or 20, or 30...then he would either have to retreat or stay in approximately the same position while their snipers picked him apart. Combat duration, it seemed, was the only way to counter his omnipotence.

The pair of 2s had been sparring for over an hour, utilizing one of two individual training blocks allotted to them during the day. Their schedules varied wildly, but they always had at least one 2-hour training block during which they could increase their base fitness or hone their skills. There was no testing involved during these hours, and the trainees could proceed as they chose. Paul, as well as most of the others, got in a daily run of at least 10k under 40 minutes. Some of them went longer, some shorter, but 6.2 miles seemed to be the agreed upon standard.

Paul had already completed his run first thing in the morning, then had 3 hours' worth of individual challenge work, followed by an hour of 'Dino class' in which the trainees were continually updated on discoveries made within the Antarctic pyramid, which mostly consisted of additional parts of the database being translated. There was so much information already available to them that they had a backlog of material to work through, but neither they nor their instructors were rushing through any of it.

Each day they would have a new lesson covering a tiny piece of the greater mystery that was the V'kit'no'sat and their empire. Today's lesson had been an introduction to the species known as Hjar'at...otherwise known as the Stegosaurus, including images from the distant past that were considerably different from the conceptualizations made by paleontologists and movie directors. The bone-like spines on their backs and tails were in fact clear as glass and, like a Human's fingernails, would regrow when broken off.

They also were not fat and cumbersome as pop culture portrayed them. Their bulk was muscular and lean, lending them far more agility than their size inspired. Paul was shocked when he saw an image of a small one roll up in a ball and do a somersault forward, resting only on its back spines, which he realized must have been made of incredibly strong material.

But most remarkable of all was the images of the Hjar'at at night. Somehow they could induce their spines to glow a neon blue, from which they appeared to also emanate some form of energy arcs, leaping from one spine to another. So far the researchers in the pyramid hadn't been able to recover any information about that particular attribute, and the instructors had encouraged the trainees to form their own speculations.

After their class had finished the trainees had a brief lunch, then more academic work. The 2s had a navigation class, which delved heavily into the mathematics of inertial force, gravity, and thrust. The class was a prerequisite for entering the naval warfare challenges, of which the 2s were scheduled to begin approximately 5 months later, if their current score progression held.

A short team workout on the 'ring out' course followed, with one serious attempt at upping their best score on the playground of elevated platforms connected by suspension bridges, zip lines, and flat topped pillars...all of which had no guard rails of any kind and were constructed several meters above thick red mats that spread out beneath the course like the water beneath an erratically constructed dock.

They managed to chip off three seconds, which increased their team score a negligible amount, then they split up for more individual training, with Paul and Jason opting for some creative sparring practice.

They'd found that if one wasn't careful, their movements would become repetitive and predictable...something that they truly could not afford, and while there were specially assigned martial arts instructors that they could practice with, Paul and Jason had developed a knack for figuring out the capabilities of each new piece of equipment given to them...some of which the designers hadn't foreseen.

The stun sword that the Black Knight used was *not* part of their current equipment inventory, and it was debated whether it ever would be, so the trainees had to do their best to create sparring challenges with the short stun sticks to simulate the longer sword...which never truly worked.

At the moment Jason was using two stun sticks against Paul's one, trying to force each other into unfamiliar defensive and offensive patterns, figuring that the more comfortable they were with the weapons the better chance they had of improvising against the Black Knight's blade, thus the point of the current sparring exercise was to make the opponent as *uncomfortable* as possible.

The trick of the matchup was in overcoming the leverage force applied by the single blade vs the double strike capacity of the pair, and vice versa. When engaging the Black Knight the trainees were automatically at a leverage disadvantage, given his superior strength, so Jason was being forced to deflect Paul's attacks, whereas Paul had the option of brute force stopping Jason's strikes at any moment, though if he did so he opened himself up to the opposite blade.

It was an awkward arrangement at first, but with successive days of practice they'd both gotten fairly good at their combat 'dance' and continued to press each other as often as they could, marking each other with light bruises from their successful blows. Paul always kept to the single stick, and Jason the double when sparring with each other, but they each practiced with different combinations, including the use of handheld shields, when sparring with other trainees, most of whom were 2s given the differences in team scheduling.

After the first week Paul had to admit that there was a lot of room for improvement in what had originally looked to be very simple, straightforward movements...but he also realized with a measure of disgust just how much time it would take to become proficient with the weapons. Skill had to be earned, he knew, with time and training...and despite the huge gains he and the others had made since the beginning of their training, it was painfully obvious how far they still had to go.

He hated to admit it, but in some ways he was still just a newb.

That thought more than anything drove him to work harder and longer at sparring practice, a mindset that Jason shared. The Black Knight had taken their egos and smashed them flat dozens of times, showing them in painful clarity just how skilled they *weren't* and never relenting in his vicious determination to see them fail. That personal aspect to the ambushes ate at the trainees even more, given their inability to settle the score.

That said, they had no choice in the matter. Their training and challenges continued on, with most of them not interfered with by the Black Knight. His appearances were truly random, as far as the trainees could deduce, or rather failed to deduce any pattern to his attacks. They had to go into each team challenge with the knowledge that he might show up, and then have the guilt of their anxiety to deal with when he didn't. It seemed he was in their heads even when he wasn't on the course.

The trainers, however, absolutely loved the situation, though they denied it and the Black Knight's very existence when questioned about it. Their most common response was 'What Black Knight?' followed by an uncongenial smile.

Paul and the others had to admit, in private, that when training to face the overbearing dominance of the V'kit'no'sat at some point in the hopefully distant future, the Black Knight was giving them excellent practice in the art of getting one's ass kicked. Someday Paul hoped he could meet the mystery man outside his armor, at which point he'd shake hands, mount a step stool, and punch him in the face.

One other lesson the trainees were learning was that of hate...both the advantages and disadvantages of the emotion. Up until now Paul had never truly understood the word, but given the four serious injuries inflicted upon him, and the dozens of others received by his teammates, Paul had an intricate understanding of the concept and the powerful motivation it provided...which was also why, he figured, that a lot of the Dino class lessons centered on the bloody history and oppression of the V'kit'no'sat. Not only to inform them of the dangers they faced, but to allow them to feel a connection to what otherwise would appear to be nothing more than a farfetched storyline.

Several recordings of atrocities against both Humans and other races contained within the pyramid's databanks had made that connection all the more real, distant in the past though it was.

Altogether, the magnitude of the task placed before them was overwhelming, but the Black Knight had given them a tangible, superior opponent to face and adapt to, unlike the V'kit'no'sat who were distant and unknown. That fueled the trainees' competitive fires and laced their reactive instincts and would, in time, come to be seen as the most beneficial part of their training...though only in retrospect. At the moment, each of the 100 trailblazers hated the bastard with a passion that drove them to find a way to defeat, or at least survive, one of his attacks.

When Jason and Paul finished sparring, they split up and finished their last hour of training with swimming and Jujitsu, respectively, then hit the showers with the others at the end of the day, swapping stories, playing games, and sleeping for those needing a few extra hours of shuteye. For the 2s, the following day would see them advance into a new series of challenges, of which the 7s, 3s, and 9s had already progressed.

Tomorrow their mission would be to escort a non team member through a new course to a finish location, protecting him/her in the process, as well as using the individual's technical skills to make their way to target. Paul was leery about that aspect of the challenge, but knew it was something they would have to get used to. Star Force employed a wide range of experts, none of which he would expect to have any training remotely similar to his own, but potentially with skills they would need to exploit in the field.

That said, it was still a step closer to graduation and Paul allowed himself to savor the moment of transition, wondering what Davis had in store for them after they'd completed their training.

Then the thought of the Black Knight showing up tomorrow and beating the sentimentality out of him popped into mind, spoiling the moment.

Paul laid down on his bed, about to go to sleep for the night, as his mind began running through various permutations of known tactics and scenarios. After half an hour of fruitless thought, he forced himself to abandon the exercise and get some sleep, focusing his mind on the resolute fact that while he might not figure out the solution tonight, eventually one of them would, then they'd take that bastard down...hard.

9

Paul met up with the other 2s in the equipment/shower room the next day, dressing in the dull white body suits that had become standard training gear for most of the challenges. The material was both flexible and durable, allowing for a bit of protection against bumps, scrapes, and rolls while maintaining full agility. The coloration made for a disadvantage on most of the courses, but so far camouflage hadn't been a topic of discussion, but Paul figured that would probably change in coming days.

With equally white, and equally flexible boots that attached to the pant legs rather than overlapping, the 2s finished their basic prep and walked through Atlantis to the nearest lift terminal, where they boarded three 'elevators' that carried them laterally through the city over to the park-like training zones. They met up in a mission specific equipment room, one of many in the training areas of the city, and appropriated their safety glasses and weapons...along with their ward.

She was a 5' 5'' extremely cute, extremely blonde computer technician...but the first thing that went through Paul's head was how thin and out of shape she was. Jason was helping her get used to carrying a shield and instructing her how to cover up behind it, but Paul was already running variable doomsday scenarios through his head. He didn't like them having to babysit a non combatant, especially when her obvious lack of skill could cause them to fail the challenge.

"So," Megan whispered to him as she picked out one of the stun sticks from the selection on the wall, along with its holster/belt, "what do you think of your new girlfriend?"

Paul tossed her an annoyed glare. "I'm wondering why they sent someone so frail."

"She's not supposed to fight."

"But can she run? We need to stay mobile, otherwise we'll be sitting ducks when we cross open ground."

"All part of the fun," Megan kidded, picking up a bulky pre-loaded paintball rifle and hitting the power button, which then began charging up the ammo with stun energy.

Paul walked over beside Jason and their 'package' and grabbed a shield of his own. Normally they didn't carry them in the parks, but given that they had to protect Neira they needed something other than their own bodies to block incoming fire with, even if firing the rifles one handed was a bit of a chore.

Dan and Brian chose slightly different loadouts, appropriating small paintball pistols in place of the stun sticks, which also came with a hip holster, along with the newly issued sniper rifles that the trainers had long tormented them with, added to the trainee inventory only two weeks ago. Given the size of the weapons they required a two-handed grip, meaning they couldn't use shields, but they could keep the enemy distracted and confused, which would prove even more valuable than simply blocking paint.

The 2s had learned months ago that a good defense was multifaceted, and since their mobility was going to be limited, they had to make up for that deficit in other ways.

Jason had been assigned as Handler, meaning he was going to be on Neira's hip the entire way, so he appropriated a pistol for his left side, a stun stick for the right, and picked up two of the flat, vertical shields. He was going to let the combat fall to his teammates unless it came to hand to hand, and needed the extra blocking capability to create a 'turtle shell' barrier that he was now practicing with the tech, having her drop to her knees with her shield in front and ducking her head down behind it as he came up from behind and essentially wrapped her inside his arms, with both shields closing her off from harm while using his body to cover her back.

"Looks cozy," Megan teased as she walked up beside Paul, hoisting her shield up onto her back via retractable straps. She and Paul were going to be the skirmishers today and couldn't bother carrying the shield in a conventional manner, needing to keep their arms free and mobile. "I'm surprised you didn't volunteer."

"Was I really that bad?" he asked, half serious.

"Only with the blondes," she said, taking a half step closer and sarcastically kissing him on the cheek. "That was just plain insulting."

Paul looked over at her eyes, darkened behind the safety glasses but still full of mischief. Her dark brown hair was pulled back tight against her head and wound up in a small braided knot at the back. "I'll remember to mention that to Sara sometime."

Jason finished his practice lessons with their partner for the challenge and turned around to find the others geared up and waiting for them. "Let's do this," he said confidently.

"Are *you* ready for this?" Paul asked Neira.

She nodded perkily. "Just get me to the consoles and I'll do the rest."

Paul nodded once, then he and Megan walked to the head of the group and led them out one of six entrances to the equipment room...five of which led to nearby courses. The 2s walked down a long octagonal corridor that ringed the 'terrace' park until they came to their designated entry point, with a trainer waiting at the door.

"Stand by," he said into a small wristbound comlink, communicating with both the control room and the trainers in the field. He waited until they all gathered around the entrance doors, which were sealed, then addressed the group of trainees.

"Challenge D-3A...your orders are to escort the tech to the finish area on the far end of the course, whereupon she will hack into the finish podium to end the mission. The podium will not function as normal until she activates it, thus her survival is required for completion. As usual there are time, kill, and survival bonuses. Any questions?"

There were none, so the trainer stepped aside revealing the start podium. Paul walked up to it and pressed down the large button, starting the clock above the thick doors that split and parted laterally, revealing an urban/garden landscape beyond. Megan ran with him up to the end of the small entrance tunnel, then disappeared around the corners, finding the closest available cover to begin probing out from.

Ivan and Jack came next, hanging back in the tunnel until the skirmishers had moved up a safe distance, then moved out and took up guard positions. Randy, Kip, and Emily came out next and began fanning out, creating a perimeter on the low terrace that led to several higher levels, which formed a small 'hill' over which the rest of the course lay.

When Megan tried to climb the short staircase up to the second terrace she drew the first fire from a hidden sniper, with the blue stinger missing cleanly. As a skirmisher she knew to always keep moving, and had been zigzagging up the steps, off which she rebounded back down to the lower level and found cover against the terrace's concrete retaining wall.

Emily spotted the sniper as he fired at Megan and quickly communicated the approximate location via hand signals to the others. The trainer was hiding behind a line of soil-filled pots each the size of a hot tub up on the third terrace, giving him a view of the stairs while shielding him from most everything else.

Paul, on the other side of the elliptical course, moved further to the left on the first terrace, following the curve of the wall that gradually expanded the width of the park out from the narrow end where they had entered. He approached a symmetrical set of stairs and darted forward, then jutted left just before he got up the second step and slipped back in behind the retaining wall.

No shots were fired. Either no one was covering this side or he hadn't provided them a good enough target. Paul set himself then darted across the stairway opening and slipped over to the other side, hunkering down next to a potted coconut tree that rose up far above his head.

Still no fire.

Paul glanced back and caught Randy's attention, signaling for him to provide cover. He nodded and took aim with his rifle up on the second terrace as Paul jumped out of cover and sprinted up the stairs.

A blue ball splattered at his feet when he hit the top step, followed by three quick shots from Randy that caused the trainer to duck back into cover behind a hedgerow trimmed to geometric perfection. Paul ducked behind a small, dry fountain directly in the path of the stairs and lay flat on the ground, hoping there wasn't anyone on the second terrace nearby, else he'd be a painfully easy target to hit.

He looked around the best he could manage, the fountain rim was only 2 foot tall, but at least he had his shield slung over his back to offer some protection. Off to the right, the direction he was facing, there was a small courtyard with solid benches situated in a square. As quick as he could manage, he jumped to his feet and ran to the downside bench and took up position behind it in a low crouch.

A few seconds later Megan dropped to a knee beside him, having come up the stairway on the opposite side. "Two down, right side. I think we can go up that way if you give me a boost."

Paul looked over her shoulder, trying to pick the best spot. "Alright. Other side of that hedge," he said, signaling back to his teammates within vision range. Some of them were out of sight below the edge of the terrace.

Dan signaled back for them to proceed, aiming that direction with his sniper rifle. Brian wasn't in sight, and must have redeployed to another position.

Paul tapped Megan on the shoulder, signaling his readiness. She set herself for a moment then sprinted off towards the low, green hedgerow, keeping as close to two meter high terrace wall as she could. A mass of potted trees blocked her best route, meaning she was still visible to some of the third terrace positions.

Dan's long-barreled rifle puffed twice, taking down a trainer on the third level as Randy moved up the stairs and onto the second. Whenever one of the 2s moved, the others used the distraction to redeploy, leapfrogging their way forward, which prompted Paul to run after Megan a couple seconds later. If they were going to shoot at her, then he'd have a small window of opportunity.

There was a short rectangular potting box with red and white flowers in his path, but he hurdled it without too much trouble and joined Megan in between two more coconut trees, tucked up against the retaining wall where they were momentarily out of sight. Down below Emily caught their attention, bringing her flat palm up in front of her face and popping her thumb up straight...the signal for an automated turret.

She relayed the approximate location from Brian with more hand signals, who was currently high up in one of the trees with a better vision angle than the rest of them. The turret was hidden behind a tree on the third level and had a clear lateral field of fire across the center placed, double-wide staircase leading up to the fourth and top terrace.

"Give me a peek," Paul suggested. Megan knelt down on her knees next to the base of the wall and placed her hands flat on the ground, tensing her arms and back, making an impromptu bench that Paul stepped up on. Megan wobbled a bit, but otherwise held firm as Paul's head popped up above the edge and looked around.

There wasn't much to see. Two large pots blocked most of his vision, but no trainers were visible...nor the turret, and there was just enough ledge to shimmy up on this side of the pots for cover.

Paul stepped down and huddled next to Megan to whisper in her ear. "Narrow gap between the pots and the edge."

Megan left her rifle on the ground and stood up as Paul cupped his hands together. She put her foot in his fingers and readied herself. Both of them went through three bobbing swings of arms and leg to get their timing right, then Megan jumped up and slithered over the edge with the help of the boost. Paul reached down and picked up her weapon, then fed it into the tiny hand that appeared above him. It reappeared a moment later and he deposited his weapon in it, which also disappeared from view.

Up top, Megan turned over onto her back, laying on her shield, and dipped her right leg over the edge, tucking it up against the concrete and bracing herself with her arm. She also grabbed the rim of the pot, hoping a few fingers wouldn't be enough to attract attention as she flexed her toes upward. A moment later she felt Paul's weight try to drag her over the edge as he used her foot and knee as leverage points to climb up on, but he was quick enough about it and slid up behind the other pot down past her feet.

She slid his weapon over to him and rolled over onto her belly, then carefully inched up into a hunch, looking around as best she could when she heard a grunt from nearby, then the distinctive clatter of weapon falling on rock tile. The others must have downed another trainer.

Paul risked a one second peek up and over the edge, just enough to get his bearings while hopefully not long enough to allow anyone to sight in on him...though if they were looking, they now knew exactly where he was.

"Turret is far left. Not much cover in between. Head up that way and I'll draw fire," he said, pointing down the length of the wall.

Megan crawled off to the left while Paul scurried right, crossing behind the edge of the courtyard that was ringed with shrubbery, the small gaps between which posed some problems, drawing the fire of a sniper up on the fourth terrace, but the 2s' own snipers downed him as soon as he popped up out of cover, leaving Paul to deal with the distant turret.

He pulled the shield off his back and parked it up behind one of the cube-like shrubs, knowing that the stingers could potentially penetrate the greenery, whole or in splatter, either of which would cause trouble for him. With the shield in position to catch most of the paint, he popped up into partial view and fired three shots at the sphere atop the turret.

Only one of his shots hit, but as predictable the barrels swiveled left and fired on him, though its aim was no better than his. Then again, with four barrels firing rapidly, it didn't have to be.

Paul hunkered down behind his shield, hoping not to catch any flack on his extremities that the narrow shield didn't cover and waited out the firestorm. After several long seconds and more than 40 stingers pelting the now blue shrubbery, the leaflets stopped moving as the turret retargeted on Megan for a few shots, then fell silent.

"Clear!" Megan yelled out for him, knowing that he was out of hand signal line of sight. She did motion to the others, however, and got them moving forward. Dan repositioned first and took out the trainers on the 4th level, the top of the artificial hill, clearing the threat from this end of the course.

Jason watched from the entry tunnel as his teammates moved up the stairwell and onto the top terrace, then moved laterally to secure firing positions. He turned and looked back at the now closed doors at the far end of the tunnel where the technician was waiting behind her shield.

"It's clear. Let's go."

10

Neira knelt down next to the door control panel and pried it off with a tiny chisel-like devise from her belt-mounted toolkit as Jason stood behind her with his twin shields, nearly obscuring her from view. They were nearly 2/3rds of the way through the park course with the widely spaced park sidewalls beginning to narrow down again, confining and reconnecting the multiple paths available through the center region.

The door they stood before now was at the base of a 5 meter high wall and composed of thick metallic segments...too thick to kick down or break through in any other manner. Neira was their only way through, as she had been for two other impasses. After she got the panel and numerical pad off the concrete wall, she pulled out a clump of wires and attached a small interface line that led to a palm-sized data device, whereupon she began to hack into the computer controlled door lock.

The high wall ran the entire width of the park, with 7 different access points, two of which actually went up and over the wall via catwalks that would have left them vulnerable to attack, essentially suspended up in the air for all to see. Paul and the others had concluded that as long as they had a hacker in the squad, they might as well make use of her and take the road less traveled, so to speak.

This door entrance was on the far right side, tucked inside a small sunken courtyard surrounded by potted trees and shrubs. Jason stood protecting Neira while Megan and Paul stood ready at the door to deal with anyone on the other side while the rest of the 2s were fanned out creating a protective perimeter, covering both the danger zone to their left and the 'pacified' areas behind.

Up on the highest perch he could find, Brian scanned the path behind with his sniper scope, leaving the closer surveillance to his teammates. On occasion the trainers would try to flank them, especially in a park this large, by circling around from behind, so they could never assume any area was totally safe. Brian had adopted a 'check everywhere' rhythm to his scans and was startled when he spotted someone far behind them, coming up and over the first 'hillside' they'd crossed over half an hour ago.

He looked away from his scope and signaled back towards Emily, holding up his hand and extending his middle finger...their signal for the Black Knight. He followed up with his hand touching his chest then jutting out to full arms reach pointing two fingers away, meaning 'far off.'

Emily relayed the signal through the others, reaching Jason just as Neira was finishing up her hack.

"Figures," he muttered. Everything had been going well up until now. He turned his head to the side so his low voice would carry better, but he kept his eyes focused on the area behind them, knowing how fast their nemesis was. "Can you lock this door after we come through?"

"If there's a panel on the other side, yes, but it will take a while."

"What about from this side?"

"But we have to go through? Someone would have to..."

"Can you do it?" he reiterated, knowing time was short.

"Yes, I can. But someone will have to input a second code from this side...hold on. I've got it."

Megan and Paul repositioned immediately, training their weapons on the closed door.

"Open it," Jason said, moving to block her from the doorway. "And get that other code."

The metallic door groaned open, sliding into the thick concrete and out of view. Megan pushed through immediately, followed a second later by Paul. Jason couldn't hear any weaponsfire, so he assumed the area immediately on the other side was safe. He signaled to Ivan to pull back, who relayed the order out to the others who were still some distance away.

"What do you want the code to be? I have to write a new one."

"How long?"

"Any sequence will do."

"The number 2."

Neira tapped rapidly into the data device, then suddenly stopped and disconnected. "Done," she announced, crudely sliding the panel back into place. It hung slightly ajar, but she didn't bother with it further.

"Emily, hold up," Jason said as she and Kip came back to the door. "Give me your stun stick."

Without hesitation she unclipped it from her belt, trusting her teammate completely.

He dropped one of his shields to accept the second weapon. "When everyone is through, hit the number 2 to close and lock the door, then run."

"I understand," she said, walking over to the panel and setting her shield down so she had a free hand.

"Come on," Jason prompted Neira, leading her through just as Jack and Randy arrived.

Dan came through last, hefting his long sniper rifle across his chest. "Twenty seconds," he said as he ran past, indicating how far behind them the Black Knight was.

When he was a good two steps through the doorway, set inside the three meter thick concrete wall, Emily tapped the '2' key and the door promptly slid back into place. Grabbing her shield and rapidly turning about, Emily ran across the courtyard and up onto a large elevated patch of mulched dirt and trees, eschewing the path that the Black Knight was coming up. She dropped behind one of the larger trunks and hid, hoping he'd pass her by, but knowing that if he didn't she'd still be buying time for the others.

She first caught sight of him running into the courtyard, sword still attached to his belt, as he went up to the door and tried to input the open code. Emily found it mildly curious that he would know what it was, but when it didn't work he didn't waste any time with a second attempt and took off to the left, backtracking slightly and crossing over to another of the available passages through the wall.

Emily blew out a steady breath of relief at him having missed her, then began tracking after him from a distance, alert for other enemies laying in wait.

After fighting through a nest of well imbedded trainers on a diagonal terrace full of outcroppings to provide them cover, Jason dispatched half his remaining team to intercept the Black Knight behind them and buy time. He, Paul, Megan, and Dan escorted Neira up towards the final climb that led to a small square surrounded by columns and imbedded inside the park sidewall at the end of the course.

Dan found himself some decent cover and held position, covering the advance of the skirmishers while Jason stayed with his ward, keeping her down and out of sight behind another of the giant pots holding tropical trees. His teammate's sniper rifle puffed once and a trainer abruptly stood up from behind cover, his left hand covered in green paint.

Paul downed the careless man with two quick shots to the chest and ran up one tier, drawing out another trainer which Dan then downed. Megan came up along a different path and took out one of her own, with Paul flushing two more, which Dan promptly took down. A few moments later Paul signaled back that the finish area was clear.

"Move," Jason said quietly, but firmly, picking up Neira by the arm and almost dragging her forward. Her feet caught up to the motion within a few steps and she slowly ran forward, carrying her shield with her. Dan went with them, running ahead and taking up a sniping position to defend the hacker against the other trainers still out on the course, who could be redeploying to this end at any moment.

"Megan," Jason said, gesturing for her to come to him as Neira got to work on the pedestal.

With a careful glance towards the other end of the course, Megan broke cover and ran over to Jason.

"Stay with her," he said, handing her his shield.

"Good luck," she offered, accepting the shield in addition to the one she still wore on her back and ducking down behind the tech to cover her otherwise exposed position directly in the center of the square.

Jason unclipped his second stun stick and activated them both as he started to run back towards the fight in the distance. "Paul!" he yelled, jumping down from one terrace to the other.

"Right behind you," his teammate said, dumping his shield as well and brandishing his single stun stick.

The Black Knight, already finished with their teammates, save for Brian who was at a distance sniping in an attempt to distract the bastard, met them halfway, intent on getting to the hacker before she could win the challenge for them. Jason took at him with both stun sticks slashing, keeping his body moving about as the Black Knight blocked his attacks and swung back.

Paul got there a few seconds later and circled around to try and attack from the back, but the Knight's long sword swung around in a circle, causing him to step back to avoid getting hit.

Jason pounced on the opening, brief as it was, and jabbed into the Knight's midsection, then ducked and rolled left to avoid his return swing. He batted at the incoming overhead blow, barely deflecting it in time.

Paul jumped in from behind and jabbed into the Knight's back, then retreated as he was swung at again...staying in the fight and buying valuable seconds.

Seemingly perturbed with the trainees lasting more than a few moves and the fact that the hacker had reached the finish area, the Black Knight ignored Paul completely and ran bodily into Jason, taking the quick hit by his stun stick and kneeing him in the chest, knocking him to the ground. He also took four quick strikes on his back by Paul as he inverted his sword and drove it down into Jason's chest.

A fifth and sixth hit by Paul caused the Knight to stumble, but he swung around awkwardly, prompting Paul to retreat a step, during which the black armored giant righted himself and brought his sword up. He ran towards Paul and slashed him across the leg after four quick moves, stunning him unconscious and out of the fight.

Another stinger hit the side of the Knight's helmet, causing him to stagger again. Two more followed to the chest as Dan added to the massive amount of stun charge already delivered to the saturated black armor. Ignoring the snipers, the Black Knight slowly ran up the stairs to the next terrace, two below the finish area.

Megan saw most of what was happening and dropped her shields, leaning one up against Neira's back as she picked up her rifle and ran out, seeing the Knight wobbling and knowing that every stinger delivered would bring him closer to falling.

"Got it!" Neira shouted, prompting Megan to skid to a halt just as she reached the entrance columns. She did an abrupt about face and ran back to the pedestal and smacked down the finish button.

A 'challenge-end' klaxon blared out across the park as all the sunlight equivalent ceiling lights turned blue, indicating that the challenge had been successfully completed. Megan, not completely believing it, walked back out onto the terrace and looked for the Black Knight, wondering if even the end of the challenge would stop him from beating them unconscious.

She found him standing one terrace down on the steps, just staring back at her through his opaque faceplate.

Behind him Emily ran up and around, making sure to stay out of arms reach, tossing him a one-fingered salute as she passed by, but he didn't see her. He just continued to stare down Megan for a long ten seconds before finally swinging his sword around in a vertical circle and smoothly reattaching it to the clasp on his belt, breaking eye contact and walking off back into the center of the park.

Brian caught up to the others a few seconds later, never taking his eyes off the giant. The trainees had never finished a scenario with the Black Knight, and it was unnerving to see him up close and not attacking. They were used to waking up to the face of a medic with the Knight long gone.

"Well that's a first," Dan said, walking up beside Megan.

"About time," she echoed, finally turning around and looking for Neira, who was waiting by the pedestal, unsure of what to do next. "Nice work."

The petite blonde smiled widely. "Happy to be of help."

Just then a hidden doorway in the back of the square opened and a squad of medics ran out and passed by the trainees, though one lagged behind with the group.

"Any of you hit?" she asked.

Megan glanced around then answered for the others. "Nope."

The medic moved on, taking her anti-numbing injections to those who needed it.

Behind them an unfamiliar man walked out of the doorway and approached Neira.

"Well done," he congratulated her.

"Thank you, sir," she said with a muted smile.

"You adapted well, especially with the trainees' unexpected request. Your mission score will reflect that."

Neira nodded then turned and waved gently to Megan and the others as she left with the man, passing by a grumpy trainer waiting in the shadows on the other side of the door to log out the trainees after they were all tended to and flag the course for cleanup.

Paul and the others were revived to the view of a blue landscape, which at first seemed to be a side effect of getting stunned. When their heads cleared enough to look around they realized it wasn't their eyes at fault.

"Did we win?" Paul asked when the others walked down to join them.

"That we did," Megan said, offering her hand to pull him up, "by a whisker."

"How close did he get?"

"About thirty meters," Dan said, walking over and helping Jason up. "Nice job with the diversion. You kept him busy longer than I thought."

"That was the idea," Jason said, rubbing his chest and wincing in pain.

"Cracked rib?" Paul guessed.

"Oh yeah," Jason confirmed. "But worth it."

"We'll get you fixed up inside of an hour," one of the medics hovering nearby assured him.

"I'll tag along," Paul added, walking out with his teammate. When he passed Megan she leaned over and whispered in his ear. "Your girlfriend did well."

Paul paused and leaned back. "So much for the dumbness of blondes," he said, returning her sarcastic kiss from earlier and walking off with Jason and the medic.

"We finally beat him," Emily said, stepping up beside Megan.

"Escaped him," Megan corrected. "But yeah, it's definitely a long overdue victory."

"You think he'll be extra pissed next time?" Emily asked, cringingly slightly.

Megan blew out a raspy breath, feeling her elation mildly deflate. "Probably."

The 2s went back to the shower/equipment room, got cleaned up and headed off to lunch, after which they had another Dino class and, aside from Jason, got in another two hours of training time, followed by two more hours of individual challenge work.

Victories, as they'd learned long ago, were never an excuse for laziness or its twin, celebration. Victories were to be stepping stones to even greater skills and abilities, and were best followed up by new challenges.

As the old sports slogan went:

Losers quit before they win...
Winners quit after they win...
Legends never quit...

Trailblazer

1

November 12, 2044

Sean Davis sat in his Atlantis office, leaning back in his chair for a few brief minutes in between administrative paperwork and looked out at the heavy tropical downpour that was soaking his nearly complete city along with the workers finishing up the last bits of major construction. Unique to all of Atlantis's buildings, the spire in which Davis's office was located was the tallest of the lot, standing a good five stories higher than any of the others, though to be honest the entire artificial island was one single, humongous building, but the individual units on the surface were, in their own right, miniature buildings, of which his afforded him an unobstructed view of the cityscape beneath the heavy rain.

His office was a perfect circle, with his simple desk little more than a clear sheet of smoothly curved glass, held aloft by equally clear, spindly support struts, giving the office an anti-cluttered effect which, combined with the 360 degree windows that ringed the mushroom-like top of the spire, imbued a vastness to the workspace that Davis felt both necessary and symbolic of Star Force's grandiose mandate. The view reminded him of the sheer magnitude of his self-assigned undertaking and of all that was at stake.

The center of the office had three heavy support struts that shot up into the ceiling to support the top of the spire where the endless window wouldn't, in the center of which was a simple twisting staircase leading up from below. A man dressed in the rare white uniform of the elite trainers that Davis had hired from all corners of the globe quietly walked up into the office as Davis's back was to him, his mind and eyes on the city beyond the windows.

His hearing, however, was not distracted and even the soft footsteps of his lead trainer were enough to prompt him to spin around in his ergonomically small, yet flexible chair.

"Wilson," he said in greeting, sizing up the man and guessing as to his mood. "More trouble I take it?"

"Frustration is more the word," the tall and muscular former Olympic Decathlon triple gold medalist said, emphasizing the point by placing his balled hands on his hips. "The flight training is progressing well, but the naval challenges are a joke. We've got the trainees chewing us out about them not being hard enough...or accurate enough. They're picking out flaws left and right, and the stupid programmers you sent me aren't keeping up. Honestly I don't think they know what they're doing, and I don't know how to explain it to them because even I don't know how the hell you're supposed to fight in space."

"And therein lies the problem," Davis said, standing up and crossing his arms over his chest while still half looking out the windows at the storm. "We don't know how to fight in space, and what little information we've retrieved from the pyramid's databanks has been mysteriously devoid of any references. We know what their ships look like, and their approximate capabilities, but nothing about how they're used."

Wilson's eyes narrowed. "You have ship schematics? Why wasn't I given that information?"

"Because I don't want to give the trainees anything in simulations that we can't produce," Davis said, showing mild frustration of his own with the never-ending torment of their technological inferiority.

"They need a challenge," Wilson reminded him. "What simulations that we have that are fully functional are downright boring…like playing chess where all that matters is the strength and position of the pieces in the game. We've trained them to be fighters, and now we're giving them crap that some 8th grade geek could handle. Something has to change, and soon."

"Do you have any suggestions?"

"A few. Higgins thinks he can rework the gunnery simulations if you can send us some game designers."

"You already have some game designers on the team," Davis pointed out.

"Aside from Robbins and Mendez, that entire team is a failure. We think it's time to clear house and start over with a new group."

"Are you wanting to keep those two?" Davis said, finally turning his attention away from the rain pelting the window.

"Yes."

Davis nodded. "Alright. What else?"

"The navigational interface has got to go. It feels like math class, not combat."

"It's the same we currently use in the field."

"Well it and a lot of other things the trainees are complaining about, and I can't say I blame them. The whole program feels wrong. We've got to do a major overhaul, and even the trainees are so bored they're starting to design their own challenges and send us the recommendations…and I really hate having to admit to them that they're right."

Davis raised an eyebrow. "They're telling you how to train them?"

"Unbelievably annoying…but I can't fault them on this. We've dropped the ball, big time."

Davis began slowly pacing around his desk. "Then let's turn this to our advantage," he said, ideas beginning to flow. "I've always planned on having them design our military, especially the warships, which is why we're holding off production until they can provide us with the basic designs. So let's give them some challenges along the lines of mission parameters and let them design their equipment and tactics sufficient to complete them."

Wilson considered that. "Possible. The basic physics engine was never the source of their complaints, it was the application of it by the designers. The trainees said they were creating 'cheat units' that didn't match up with the physics when they ran their own calculations, so maybe they are smart enough to use it on their own."

"Would you agree that they prefer to work with modern entertainment tie-ins?"

"Definitely," Wilson confirmed. "They reference them all the time. Hell, I'm pretty sure they got the idea for their hand code from one of their games."

"Good...we can use that as a basis then. I'll get you a new team of programmers, then go through as much pop culture space fiction as you can get your hands on and see if you can copy it into some real life applications."

"That's not the best description you've ever given," Wilson noted, "but I think I see where you're going. Challenge them to make the fiction reality."

Davis smiled. "Well put."

"Thank you...oh, and as far as the new programmers...they went and made a list for that too."

"They did? How?"

"Seems they did a little internet research and compiled a list of names based off the video games they like."

Davis chewed on his lower lip for a moment. "I don't like using non Star Force personnel, but if our people aren't up to the task maybe I can lure a few of the commercial ones

over to our ranks. Actually," he said, glancing over his shoulder as if a good idea just manifested itself off to his right, "if we can pull this off we're going to have to create dozens of games worth of scenarios for subsequent classes to run through, which is more than enough work to keep them employed for the next 10 years creating the ultimate video game. I think under that heading I can attract a professional crew...and I have no doubt with the trailblazers running the show they're going to give us a lot of ideas to flush out."

"You want them designing the challenges for the second class?" Wilson asked.

"Why not? We chose them for their improvisational skills."

"I want to reserve final judgement on what gets added to the training lexicon," Wilson insisted.

"Of course," Davis said, nodding.

"Sounds like a plan, then."

"How are they dealing with Vermaire?" Davis asked, changing subjects.

Wilson smiled slightly. "They've come close a few times, but he's learning as much from them as they are from him, and I think that's really getting under their skin. They're used to adapting to the scenario, not having the scenario adapt to them. Personally, I'd bet they don't take him down prior to graduation...and the second class hasn't got a prayer."

"Still underperforming?"

"They're doing well enough, but they're not nearly as good as the others."

"That's to be expected," Davis reminded him, "we had to water down the prerequisites just to get a second class. We were barely able to field 100 of them the first time."

Wilson shook his head. "It's more than that. The second class has had a year to get it together, but they're not gelling the same way. They're meeting all the necessary standards, but the first class came together within a few weeks and have been damn near telepathic ever since. We're not seeing the same thing with the next generation, sadly, which makes them less fun to pick on."

Davis laughed slightly. He knew competition was a key component in training, but he'd never expected the trainees or the trainers to carry it so far. "Do you think we should reconsider keeping them separate? Maybe social intermixing would do them some good."

"Absolutely not," Wilson said, nixing the idea immediately. "They may all be trainees, but they're separate groups. They're not going to mix any better than oil and water, and to be frank, it would probably just slow down the first class, which we don't want to do, even if it would help the second."

"They're going to have to work together later," Davis argued.

"Yes, but that's later. Right now I want each group focusing on their own training. Bringing in others would be a distraction."

"If you say so, I'll trust your judgement there, as long as the second class is meeting with your expectations?"

"My expectations have been attuned to the first class, so no, they're not. But they are passing the benchmarks we established, though at a slower rate. I estimate it will take them 4 years to graduate, whereas we're looking at two and a half for the first class."

"How goes the prep for the third?"

"I think we could handle three groups simultaneously with the current personnel, but I want to get my trainers experienced before we dilute the squads with more newbs. Besides, doesn't look like we'll even have a full set by the time the first class graduates...unless the numbers have changed recently?"

"Unfortunately no," Davis said, referring to their A7 recruitment efforts, which technically were A7b now, though that was never posted. "We've only got 22 candidates on standby at present."

Wilson nodded. "I don't suggest lowering the standards any more than we have, otherwise we'll run the risk of washouts, and that'll pull down an entire class on the morale front. Better to have a cohesive group fighting their way through and succeeding than to have a Darwinian approach with individuals."

"I didn't want to diminish the requirements the first time," Davis reminded him, "but we sucked the talent pool dry. It was either that or wait another 10 to 20 years for it to replenish."

"I'm confident the second class will make it through, and a few of them are as individually skilled as the others, but it's the team aspect that's really lacking. I suggest we hold off on the third class in favor of quality over quantity."

"You think that's why the trailblazers are so cohesive?"

"Honestly, I think they're sort of a fluke, but yes, I do think that's part of the equation. The rest I doubt we'll ever really know."

Davis considered that. "Do you want to increase the standards again?"

"Ideally yes, but not if we don't have the people to choose from."

"We'll table that discussion for later down the road then. Do you have that programmer list?"

Wilson fished inside a hidden pocket and pulled out a datachip. "It's rather long," he said, handing it to Davis.

"I'm sure it is," he said, knowing how thorough the trailblazers had become. "How's the rest of their training proceeding?"

"Some of them are reaching tier 4 in their individual challenges," Wilson reported with a note of respect, "and their academic schedule is nearly complete. They've still got a lot of team challenges left, but they're passing them on the first or second try now, so I think it's just a matter of scheduling now to get them to the final phase."

"I haven't checked in a while. Who's currently on top?"

"The 7s have a narrow lead over the 2s, but the 6s have had a very good month and are closing in on both. Morgan is still the top trainee and I don't see her relinquishing that spot. Her point lead has been steadily growing over the past 5 months."

Davis chuckled in amazement. "I still can't understand how a girl is beating out all the guys."

"I'll admit I'm a bit surprised too, but I'm actually glad. Physically speaking, males and females are nearly identical, it's cultural differences that attribute for most of the discrepancy."

Davis's brow furrowed thoughtfully. "I believe we had a similar discussion a few years ago about the odds of any women making the cut? You referenced something about Track?"

"The Decathlon used to be a male-only event. The women had a shorter Heptathlon in its place…7 events to our 10 because they didn't think the women could handle the full load. When the change was eventually made their scores were low, which is to be expected with new events, it takes time to adjust, but they eventually came up to respectable levels when some of the men and women began training together."

"But there was still a male bias, correct?"

"Still is," Wilson confirmed. "Women's competition is inferior to the men's."

"Then how do you explain Morgan?"

Wilson laughed loudly. "That is the question of the century, and I've been turning it over in my head many a day. I don't have a straight answer for you, but I think I can narrow it down a bit."

"Please, I'm all ears."

The three time gold medalist began to speak, then stopped himself as he noticed an odd expression on Davis's face. "You know something, don't you? Something from the pyramid?"

Davis smiled. "Perhaps. Go on."

"Well, I was going to say that I think if the women actually competed against the men their scores would improve. Historically, the tougher your competition, the better you become, so women having their own sports division separate from the men actually does the elites a disservice."

"Which we don't have to worry about here," Davis pointed out.

"No, but that was your policy from the beginning with all Star Force personnel," Wilson remembered, beginning to connect the dots.

"So it was."

"Also, I might add," Wilson said, continuing on, "when young, say age 10 or 12, boys and girls sometimes compete against each other in individual sports and there's not much of a difference in ability until they 'mature' later, or so the theory goes."

"You don't agree?"

"No, I think it's mostly cultural. The guys work out, the girls socialize, so it's no surprise who improves physically. The girls that do work out and dedicate themselves to improving end up beating over 90% of the guys anyway, but then they're written off as flukes not symbolic of the whole."

"That could explain why women aren't grossly inferior to men," Davis countered, "but how can they pull even, or even exceed the men?"

"You're having fun with this, aren't you?" Wilson asked suspiciously.

"A bit. Please continue," he prompted with a touch of sarcasm.

"Alright...common knowledge says that testosterone is the key to muscle development. Men have it and women don't...but in truth both do, the women just have less. But I know from experience that the best throwers have smaller muscles than the rest, but those muscles are superior when comparing fiber to fiber. The world record holder in the Shot Put beat out three druggies, discovered after the fact, in the 2028 Olympics even though his testosterone levels were less than half that of the cheaters. Scientists have never been able to explain why, but I think it has to do with the type of training he was doing."

"Anything else?"

"Women tend to be smaller than men, on average, which is why they have shorter hurdles in Track, though that's always seemed unfair when you have the 6'8'' Marshal twins towering over most of the men and they get to run the short hurdles."

"Still a bit of sexism in the sport then?"

"Yes, and that only adds to the misconception," Wilson said, eyeing Davis. "Now, what do you know?"

"Among the V'kit'no'sat's Human slaves, there was no gender division...not a single reference in all the data that we've been able to decipher. Even the visual records show no height discrepancies. That's not to say all the Humans were the same height, but there was no gender trend evident. Some of my people even went so far as to check every image on file and compile the statistics, which were dead even."

"Really?" Wilson said, not sure what else to say.

"It's still a mystery as to why," Davis continued. "One that I'm interested in figuring out, and Morgan is the first clear sign that it may be true of present day Humans as well."

"Some sort of gender degeneration?" Wilson asked.

"Possibly," Davis admitted, "but if it is, it clearly isn't irreversible."

"So are you saying that if we have to fight Dino-slave Humans, we'll be going up against women that are as strong and fast as the men?"

"So the records seem to indicate."

"Then why are you surprised by Morgan being at the top?"

"I guess you could call it a combination of cultural bias and experience. Reading about ancient history is one thing…seeing it happen before your eyes is another. Then again, I'm not so much the athlete as you are, so maybe I'm a bit more ignorant as to the physical potential of the Human body."

Wilson raised an eyebrow. "I thought Vermaire would have opened your eyes by now."

Davis sighed. "I'm still half expecting him to crash and burn."

"It's been seven years," Wilson countered.

"Call me a pessimist, then."

"Ha," Wilson laughed. "You, a pessimist?" he said, spreading his arms wide, gesturing to the city they stood in. "All of this says otherwise."

"Well, it is raining," Davis pointed out.

2

The next day...

"Down on your left..." Randy said over the comlink, "...in the rocks."

"On it," Jason said, tilting his skeet to port while kicking up the vertical jets to gain more altitude. As his T-shaped aircraft rose up over the ridgeline a small outpost came into view, with a pair of turrets guarding a small helipad. One was pointed away, the other to the right. Both began to swivel around to target Jason's skeet as soon as he came into view.

He fired a charged up laser shot into the nearest one, hitting it just below the twin barrels swinging into alignment, but not destroying it. Jason managed one more shot then rolled to starboard and ducked back down into the valley, skimming over the angled rock wall and dropping out of the turrets' line of sight.

"Stay low," Randy said, spotting from his skeet circling high above the simulated battlefield. "The terrain dips after the next bend right in front of the turrets."

"Trench skimming as ordered," Jason acknowledged, dropping his skeet down over the bottom of the valley and the perfectly flat stream running through it. He slowed his forward speed and added thrust to the three vertical jets, located within on each prong of the 'T' in the narrow fuselage. The wingtip engines continued to pull the skeet forward through the valley in a slow hover, staying low and safely out of sight as he rounded the bend.

"Get ready," Randy advised as two more skeets were approaching the outpost from opposite directions perpendicular to Jason's position.

Laying belly down within the skeet's simulator cockpit, Jason glanced up at the charge indicators for his primary and only weapon on the aircraft. Both capacitors were reading full charge, meaning he'd get two shots before having to wait out a brief period for the skeet's fuel cells to supply enough power to refill the power reservoirs that fed the nose-mounted laser.

"Now!" Randy half yelled into the comlink.

Jason pressed down the pedal behind his right foot at the back of the straddle-couch he was 'riding' like a motorcycle. His chest was pressed flat against the slight forward incline of the pads while his legs were hanging over the sides slightly with his feet pressed back against the throttle controls.

Both wingtip jets kicked up their fan blades and pulled the skeet forward while Jason used the right joystick to alter the engine balance and spin the aircraft to the left with the help of a small fan blade in the tail, pointing the clear nosecone toward the rocky wall of the canyon. When he neared a collision, Jason jammed his left foot back hard and kicked in the vertical engines at maximum thrust, launching his skeet up along the angled wall towards the outpost.

Thanks to Randy's timing, Jason was halfway up the canyon when Paul and Kip's skeets crisscrossed overtop the outpost, firing off both capacitor charges into the turret and missing each other by a few meters before pulling up and rolling evasively. The turrets tracked them and fired multiple chain gun spurts in their wake as the fighters danced across the sky then ducked back down into the vast canyon network.

The outpost suddenly flashed into view at almost point blank range as Jason came up over the edge and found himself face to face with one of the turrets...which was still tracking his teammates and pointed away to the right. Jason emptied both capacitors after quickly cutting his forward thrust and managing a sloppy hover barely 50 meters away. His precision firing, thanks to a small swivel angle on the laser mount, hit the turret in the cupola where the gun barrels extended and not the concrete shell below that was already showing a large hole thanks to the strafing run.

The invisible laser shots cored through the thin armor plates, as well as melting the base of the left barrel, continuing inside and penetrating the magazine. Several rounds exploded from the laser-induced heat and popped the top of the turret off in a muffled explosion.

Before the second turret could swing around and bathe him in tungsten rounds, Jason reversed the direction of the idling wingtip engines with a flick of a hand switch and pressed down hard on the right foot pedal, launching him backwards into the canyon. He eased up the pressure on his left foot pedal and sank back down out of sight as the remaining pot marked turret swung around to fire on him.

As it did so Ivan, Kip, and Megan's skeets came in from behind, fired, then peeled off in a variety of arcs, all staying away from a straight passover which would have placed them directly in the turret's firing arc.

Simulated concrete blew apart and a sizeable hole appeared in the armored cap of the turret, but its barrels still swung about, trying to track Megan as Paul circled back around and made a second, more precise strafing run. His single shot hit one of the barrels and when the turret tried to fire on him as he passed nearly straight over the target and rose up spinning into the sky, its slagged barrel reacted poorly to the rounds trying to pour through and detonated the top of the turret in a shower of debris.

"Second turret destroyed," Randy reported. "Convoy clear to proceed."

"Convoy acknowledges," one of the trainers in the control room replied. "Proceeding to next waypoint."

Randy glanced down at the small digital display situated between joysticks and saw a small line of dots start to move again up the road that led past the outpost they'd just neutralized.

"Heads up 2s," Emily's voice said over the comlink. "We've got incoming. Six VTOLs from the northwest."

"We've got them," Dan said as he, Brian, and Jack accelerated towards the targets. "Stick with the convoy. They may be trying to distract us again."

"Six on three isn't good odds," Jason said, lifting up out of the canyon. "Paul, let's go."

"Already ahead of you."

"Good luck," Megan said, splitting off from Paul and heading back to Emily and the convoy with Ivan and Kip.

"Split them up," Randy said, still in his high altitude observation position.

Dan and Brian drifted to the left in response, Jack to the right, but the incoming helicopter gunships didn't alter their straight-line trajectory towards the convoy.

"Ok…" Randy commented. "That's new."

Paul glanced down at his navigational display, seeing his fellow skeets as small blue dots and the approaching VTOLS as red squares just as a yellow blip appeared between them…then two more.

"Missile turret!" Paul yelled as he accelerated to full speed and dipped low to the ground and dropped into one of the canyons.

The missile tracking him lost contact and continued on a straight trajectory trying to reacquire the signal, passing 100 meters over his head as he hovered up against a steep rock wall. Twelve seconds later it ran out of fuel and fell from the sky.

"Report!" he asked as he rose up out of his hover and started getting some lateral speed down the canyon before he popped back up into view.

"Turret down," Jason reported. "Randy got it, but the VTOLs are on top of us."

"Copy that," Paul said, seeing the red squares reappear as he cleared the top of the canyon wall. They were broken up and moving about like a swarm of bees along with the now five blue dots...one of which winked out.

"Dan's down," Brian reported. "They've got seekers."

"Damn it," Paul swore in a whisper as he approached the aerial brawl. The skeets were maneuverable enough to avoid the straight firing missiles, but the ones that could home in on the target were hard to evade.

"You want help?" Megan asked.

"No, stay put," Jason immediately responded. "We've got this," he said, firing on one of the VTOLs from the flank as it fired a pair of missiles at Jack. The rear rotor disintegrated and the gunship fell in a chaotic spiral from the sky.

Jack pulled up immediately, then just as the missiles redirected he slapped his skeet back down hard, causing the missiles to overshoot by a handful of meters...but after they passed by they arced around in a long curve and continued to pursue him, catching up rapidly.

Now behind him, he knew he didn't have a chance of causing them to overshoot again, so he accelerated hard towards the nearest VTOL, fired one shot at it, then flew underneath it as close as he could, causing one of the pursuing missiles to hit the friendly target.

The other missile missed and hit Jack's skeet in the tail, blowing it into simulated bits and causing him to careen out of the sky, but before he hit the ground he managed to kick up his vertical thrust and partially null out the list.

Limping heavily, his skeet wobbled its way down into a canyon and disappeared from the rest of the 2s' scanners.

Sitting in a slow moving hover near the convoy, Emily's sensor board suddenly lit up with two additional contacts far from the combat and directly ahead of the convoy.

"There," she said, feeling vindicated at having resisted the urge to fly out and help her teammates. "Two VTOLs."

"And tanks," Kip noted as four small triangles appeared on the road ahead, about 3 kilometers up the road from the convoy, coming out of a hidden base just prior to the LZ they were heading to.

"Kip, take the tanks," Megan said, already accelerating ahead of the convoy. "Emily, Ivan...you're with me. Get those choppers before they get within firing range."

"Lefty first," Emily said, quickly closing on the not so far off targets, which immediately sprouted missile plumes.

Ivan went to the deck, ducking down into the safety of the terrain while Emily peeled off to the left and ran along the ridgeline, pulling the missiles her way momentarily before ducking down as well, leaving Megan with a free run at the VTOLs. She fired both shots into the left chopper, downing its lightly armored bulk with a pyre of smoke pouring from its slagged engine compartment.

Ivan popped back up into view, much closer than where he'd disappeared, and shot the second VTOL, hitting it twice in the bow, knocking out one of its missile launches, but not taking it out of the fight. Emily took care of that a moment later, then got her hull clipped by a shower of tungsten shrapnel from the hidden base.

"Turret!" she announced, still flight worthy but with a reduction in electrical power. The shrapnel must have hit one of her 3 power cells.

"I'm on it," Ivan said, heading that direction along with Megan.

"Tanks first," Kip reminded them. "They've got heavy armor."

"Right," Megan said to herself as she reversed course. Only one of the four triangles had disappeared from the display screen.

3

The road through the canyons was partially obscured by rocks and trees, but was open from directly above and Megan could see Kip making another strafing run against the tanks. They returned fire with short range automatic weapons, but otherwise didn't stand much of a chance against the skeets…if they were careful enough about not getting too close. The tanks were, however, a major threat to the convoy, which was now less than a kilometer away and closing fast.

Megan flew up from behind the tanks, flying over the carcass of the destroyed one and passing by Kip as he finished his strafing run. She held off fire on the rear tank and the middle one, then emptied both laser blasts into the first, hoping to add to the damage Kip had already done.

Smoke filled the air above the first tank, but it did not stop moving as Megan flew past and began a long circle to come around again after her capacitors recharged. It did, however, mark the position of the tanks with a black plume coming up out of the trees, making it easy for Ivan and Emily to see where they were without having to rely on the intermittent sensor screen.

Ivan raced forward and finished off the first tank, delaying the others as they had to move around and/or dislodge it to get past. Emily, on reduced power, flew up slowly from behind and shot the rear tank, daring it to turn around. Its machine gun turret swiveled about slowly, forcing Emily to fly off over the trees before she could fire a second salvo.

Her first shots had melted through the armor on impact, but only a hole the size of a fingernail, exploding out some of the surrounding armor but not hitting anything vital inside. Trouble was, with an impact point so small, it was virtually impossible to retarget the same hole, and thankfully the skeets' lasers were powerful enough to penetrate on one shot, else the tanks would have been next to impregnable.

"Anyone know where the best place is to shoot these things?" Megan asked, not all that familiar with the interior design.

"Go for the treads," Kip responded. "Easiest way to slow them down."

Megan took his suggestion and aimed for the port side of the frontmost tank on her next pass. Her first shot hit the armor plating, melted through, and did a small amount of damage to the rotating metallic treads beneath. Her second shot did better a few meters aft, suddenly causing the tank to seize up and twist to the side.

"Good advice," she said, thanking Kip, "but we're out of time. The convoy is almost in range."

"Tell them to hold up," Ivan suggested, shooting the first tank in the 'head' as the second one passed it by.

"They won't do that," Megan complained. "Once in motion the convoy doesn't stop until the next waypoint."

"They would if this were real," Ivan argued. "They're just being stubborn."

"And we're about to lose," Emily reminded them, shooting the back tread of the now lead tank, then pulling up out of sight before she literally ran over the second, sitting in place on the road with both its weapons still intact. Machine gun fire followed in her wake.

"Not today," Jason's voice interrupted as he and three other skeets flew in from the north and angled around as a group for a strafing run, passing over the lead convoy vehicle just before they fired into the enemy tank. Eight shots went into its armored head, some of which hit the internal magazine. The top of the tank popped off like a child's toy in the resulting explosion and fell into the trees beside the road.

"One left," Emily reminded them, hovering back into view and firing off a single shot into the aft of the tank with no effect.

Megan and Kip came around and skewered it again, but it wasn't until Ivan's pass that the last of the small triangles winked out. Thirty seconds later the convoy snaked its way into view and skirted around the edge of the smoking hulk.

"Did someone say something about a turret?" Paul asked.

"Up ahead, tucked into the terrain," Emily reported. "Hard to see."

"Randy?" Jason prompted.

"Climbing," he said, getting back up to his previous aerial perch. "Alright, I've got it. Just looks like one this time. Best approach is from the west."

"ETA?" Paul asked.

"Looks like about 2 minutes," Megan guessed.

Paul smiled. "Any other targets, Randy?" he asked as the others were already pulling hard towards the west.

"Nothing on the board...the LZ looks clear."

"Copy that," Paul said, heading off with the others but gaining some altitude as well so he could keep an eye out for surprises as his team quickly took care of the last threat to the convoy.

A few minutes later the simulation ended and Paul's cockpit screens went blank blue, indicating a successfully completed challenge. Their scoring stats flashed up in a grid, which he studied for a moment before lifting the top hatch and climbing off the pommel that he'd been riding for the past 45 minutes.

"Ouch," he muttered, stretching a bit when his feet hit the floor. Dan was waiting for them in the center of the simulation room as the rest of the team climbed out of their individual capsules.

"And?" he asked.

"We won...but our score wasn't the greatest," Paul answered.

"I agree," Jason echoed. "I think we need to try again tomorrow."

"Should be able to scrape up an extra 100 points if we don't get sloppy," Emily added, cracking her neck loudly. "Jack, how did you not go down?"

"Guess you don't actually need a tail to fly," he said, walking up to the semi-circle they were forming in the center of the room...typical 2s' post-challenge debrief. "I kept it off the ground, but couldn't do much more than float and sputter."

"That avoided a penalty," Randy pointed out.

"The 7s were what, 30 points better?" Megan asked.

"34," Jason answered, "but the 6s haven't gone yet, and I don't want to spot them an easy score to match."

"Tomorrow it is then," Brian confirmed for everyone, checking his wristwatch. "We've still got 35 minutes before training session 2. I'm going to go grab a snack, unless you want to hit the gauntlet run again?"

"I think we've had enough seat time today," Jason admitted, feeling a bit saddle sore. It'd only been two weeks since they'd been introduced to the skeets and their unusual seats, and none of them had quite gotten comfortable with them yet.

"Well, see ya," Brian said, heading out of the simulation room and to the nearest of the 24 hour cafeterias that served the population of Atlantis, which had been growing steadily with each passing month. At present, the city was about 75% staffed, but the population would more than double when Atlantis went fully online and accessible to the public as Star Force's primary spaceport, as well as a tourist resort and mid-Pacific transport hub.

Paul and the others broke up, each heading off on their own errands. His morning training session had been spent on hand to hand sparring with Morros, one of the busiest of the martial arts instructors, so Paul headed over to the track to get in his daily run. When he arrived there were eight other trainees already running laps, most of which he never usually crossed paths with. He looked at who was available and sized them up by what he knew of their speed scores, then jumped into the flow running alongside Morgan, who was about dead even with him in the running challenges.

"Hey," she greeted him as he fell into step outside her as they moved into the first turn. "Congrats on breaking into the top 10."

"Thanks...what are you set at?"

"7:15...I've only got three laps left. Don't usually see you down here at this hour?"

"Darth Mo has a busy schedule. I had to skip my morning run," Paul said, keeping on Morgan's shoulder and subconsciously trying to avoid stepping on the green running lights moving along the lane 1 boundary lines, visually marking where she should be on the track to maintain the desired pace. The moving square lights were buried in the track with nothing above the surface to trip on, but for some reason Paul didn't like stepping on the continuously moving dot.

"Your challenge scores in that area are solid," she said with a note of approval. "Are you going specialist or trying to scrape up a few more points?"

"I'm just tired of getting my ass kicked by the Black Knight. Don't worry, your points lead is safe from me," he said with a joking smile.

"At least until you learn to swim," she argued, not entirely kidding. Had his free swimming scores even been average, his overall rank would have easily been in the top 3.

"Don't hold your breath," Paul said with the intentional pun as they swung out into lanes 2 and 3 to pass by Sam who was following his own pair of blue light markers, set probably at 8:00 pace if Paul had to guess.

"Where did you just come from?" Morgan asked, her short ponytail whipping back and forth with each step.

"Simulator room. We finished up a few minutes early."

"Have you heard the news?"

"What news?" Paul asked, frowning.

"I'll take that as a no...they just announced an hour ago that all the naval challenge scores are going to be nullified and we're going to have to start over again."

"No, I hadn't heard that. I don't like them reneging on the points but it's about time they did something. Did they give any specifics?"

"Yeah, there's a brief posted. Looks like they're going to give us access to the sims so we can design our own ships to meet mission requirements."

"Really...did they give any examples?"

"They gave the rundown on the first team challenge, V-4A. It's a recreation of the Naboo blockade. We have to figure out how to lay siege to a single surface city from orbit."

Paul's curiosity immediately perked up. "Now that sounds better. Anything about the individual challenges?"

"Not yet. They said they'd have more info within the week, but we're scheduled to start the team challenge on Thursday."

Paul sensed a hint of concern in her voice. "You worried?"

"If it's fair, no...but my confidence in their workmanship is lacking at the moment."

"If they're resetting the points, how does that affect your total?"

"Negligible," she said, allaying his own rising concerns. "We all got nearly perfect scores so no real points gain or loss should occur."

"So what's eating you?"

Morgan glanced over at him, surprised that she was letting it show as much as his ability to pick up on her mood. Her 6s teammates knew her well, but the others not so much. "I don't like them changing things up as we go along. Makes me feel like they don't know what they're doing."

"They don't," Paul declared as if it was common knowledge, which in the case of the naval challenges it was.

"They did until recently...either that or they hid it really well."

"With our help they'll get it sorted out sooner or later," Paul assured her.

"That's just it, they shouldn't need our help. They're supposed to be training us, not the other way around."

"Why is that a problem for you? I mean, besides the obvious."

"It makes me wonder if what we're doing is important or just playing games. Until recently I've believed that each challenge we've faced had a purpose behind it, but when the naval challenges started it all started to feel wrong."

"Just the naval, or are there others too?"

"No, just the naval, but it makes me wonder about the wisdom in the design of the others."

"Gamer/designer issue?"

"Exactly."

Paul considered that for a moment and didn't respond until they completed the homestretch. "I suppose the problem might lie in the fact that we've...by we I mean Earth...have never fought in space. They have no reference material or experts to call on, so we probably know as much as they do."

"You'd think the V'kit'no'sat knew a thing or two about it," Morgan differed.

"True dat," Paul said colorfully, figuring the Aussie wouldn't catch the reference. "But until they give us records access or cover it in class we have no way of knowing what's really buried under the ice."

"I wish they'd let us inside," Morgan complained. "Even if it was just for a day or two."

"Same here," Paul said as they approached the finish line for the second time.

"Last lap for me…you want to keep the pacer?"

"Yeah, thanks."

"All yours," she said, accelerating into a hard run when her foot hit the line and easily pulling away from Paul. He watched her accelerate again on the backstretch 100 meters later, then again at 200 meters before finally reaching a full sprint over the last quarter of the lap. She coasted past the line, arcing around to the right and slowing down to a walk, leaving the track before Paul even caught up to her.

The pair of green lights flanking Paul eased ahead of him a few centimeters as he came into the first turn, prompting him to accelerate slightly to catch back up. 7:15 mile pace was a challenge for Paul, given that his normal cruising speed was 7:30, but at the moment he was feeling good and decided to stick it out for the remaining 22 laps of his 10k with him being the fastest trainee on the track now that Morgan was gone.

Ego aside, he always seemed to have a little more energy available whenever he was the top dog, and he certainly didn't mind showing off a bit when it resulted in a better workout.

4

The 'Naboo' challenge started out completely different than anything Paul had gone through to date, with little more than a mission objective to begin with and as much time as the team needed to ready themselves. The thing of it was, they couldn't run through it the first time until they'd designed their force deployment, all the way from tactics to individual ship designs, meaning that this new naval challenge was going to involve a lot of theoretical design work before they would even begin to get to the action.

The basic mission was to blockade a single city on the surface sufficient to stop one ship from escaping the planet. Within the simulation that they were given access to there was simply a point on the surface and a termination 'line' in high orbit...everything else they had to design, making the whole exercise feel less like a challenge and more like homework, furthering Morgan's sentiment that the trainers didn't know what they were doing.

The other 2s didn't take to the simulation with much enthusiasm either, but as always they were game for more point scoring opportunities and used their first 2 hour block of 'challenge' time to brainstorm ways of implementing a blockade and getting used to the physics engine. When they eventually broke for lunch they left more confused than they'd entered, and equally disillusioned.

They'd gone along with the movie guidelines and created basic ships, little more than block-like markers with weapons on them, and began to run a few simulations against the single ship preprogrammed to rise up from the city and try and break through the blockade...

Problem was, the Star Wars version of a blockade was laughable, which was made evident when they tried to repeat the 'tactic' in the simulator, finding it impossible to form a 'line' of ships in the sky. First off, closure speeds were so fast that a ship lifting off from the surface, by the time it made orbit, would fly right by any blockade in the blink of an eye, and unless there was an accidental collision, the blockading warships were of no use at all.

Second, there was no reason for the fleeing ship to fly up to that particular point in the sky when it had thousands of miles of orbit to choose from, meaning that even if sitting ships could stop the 'blockade runner,' they'd have to have a fleet numbering in the tens of thousands, if not millions, to lay a coverage net large enough to cover the orbital tracks over that section of the planet. And the idea of covering the *entire* planet was downright insane. Paul found himself reluctantly lowering his appreciation for George Lucas's work as he began to see the outright ridiculous concept for what it was.

So where did that leave them? Was this an impossible challenge that the trainers were throwing at them ignorantly...or was it something difficult, but doable in the long run? Paul took it on a leap of faith to be the later and downloaded a simple copy of the physics engine into a datapad for him to work on during his downtime, as did a few of the others, but it was Paul who was soon consumed with working out the mechanics of it all.

Two weeks passed, with none of the teams even attempting a run, having made little or no progress in coming up with a viable strategy, until Paul finally came through with a breakthrough, staying up late that night and pounding on Jason's door at 4:07am.

Being a light sleeper Jason woke on the first knock and quickly pulled himself out of bed, wondering what was up. When he opened the door Paul tossed a datapad at his chest and walked in.

"I think I've got something," he said as Jason fumbled the toss but recovered quickly enough to keep the device from hitting the floor. Then he noticed that Paul was still wearing the same clothes he'd had on in the evening.

"Have you slept yet? We've got that bunker assault in," he checked the clock on the datapad, "less than four hours."

"I'll manage," Paul promised as Jason looked through the information. A few seconds later his head came up, now fully awake with adrenaline creeping into his veins.

"Have you..."

"38%," Paul answered before he could finish the question, "but with us doing the piloting instead of the computer, I think it'll give us a 50/50 chance."

"I'd settle for 10% right now...this is genius!"

"I have my moments."

"No, I'm serious...I'm already seeing additional modifications that we can make."

"It does open up a lot more possibilities, especially when they get around to having us stop more than one ship."

Jason finally looked up from the diagrams. "Well done, Admiral," he said, shoving the pad back into his chest. "Now go get some sleep, if you can."

"I doubt it," Paul said, smiling as he left. Jason was so pumped that he doubted he could get back to sleep either.

After the door closed, Jason sat down on his slightly heated bed and let the significance of what Paul had just designed sink in. Multiple wheels of thought began to spin as he planned out different ways they could use what Paul had just given them, knowing that this could very well be the key to taking the lead away from the 7s.

After more than an hour of planning, Jason forced himself back into bed and tried to get what sleep he could, but his mind never fully adjusted to the task. He got back up an hour later to begin his normal morning routine, starting with a quick shave then a 10k run over on the track, then a shower and a bit of breakfast before meeting up with the rest of the 2s in one of the desert parks for their bunker assault run.

The Black Knight showed up again and spoiled the challenge, as usual, but even that couldn't quell the anticipation the entire team had for the afternoon session. They followed up the failed challenge with more showers, then another Dino class before spending most of their lunch break quietly refining Paul's plans and readying themselves to make the first real attempt at the Naboo challenge.

The first hour of their 2 hour block was spent programming as they uploaded Paul's ship designs and tactical formations into the simulator's mainframe, along with making a few modifications they'd mutually discussed. After that they all entered their individual simulator booths and closed the hatches behind them, cutting off any non-comlink communications, despite the fact they were barely two meters away from each other.

Inside the booths was a simple command chair and control board, with a large display screen taking up the majority of the inner space, making it appear almost as a tiny personal theater. On the board were a variety of controls, allowing multi-tasking options for a wide variety of craft. Paul reconfigured the board, rotating a joystick down on the moveable panel until it was directly in front of him. He could have used the keys, nub controls, rollers, or any of the other interface devices, but he preferred the joystick, given that he was going to be one of the 'hounds' today.

Once he had his controls set up to his liking he thumbed the 'ready' button and waited for the others to do likewise. A few seconds later his screen lit up with a 10 second countdown timer overlayed onto a picture of a simulated Earth. When it expired the planet seemed to shrink until it no longer filled his screen, leaving him looking down on the globe from a distance.

Paul experimented with the controls and rotated the view of his ship, thrusting slightly to port. The screen spun slowly, with the Earth passing across in front of him until it disappeared against the star field. Paul nulled out the turn and set his 'interceptor' tail down to the planet.

In the lower right corner of the display screen was a sensor display, which showed the position of three other interceptors nearby, though several thousands of kilometers apart. Paul toggled the sensor controls and expanded the view, zooming out until several other dots appeared in a familiar grid.

He and the other three interceptors were arranged in a square, sitting in geosynchronous orbit over the target city on the surface of the planet. In the center of that square was a larger ship, full of sensors and communication equipment, which was piping out the navigational data to all of the others, allowing them to track and coordinate their efforts against the tiny ship now beginning to rise up from the surface.

Four other 'control ships' were situated in geosynchronous orbit around the Earth, staggered so that they could track all objects in orbit and have clear lines of sight between them for transmission. They were one of Paul's brainstorms...taking the long range 'radar' equipment out of the other ships and using a data uplink to give the 'hounds' the necessary information without having to tote the extra weight in equipment, making them a bit faster.

And the speed of the interceptors was critical, given that the blockade runner was little more than a ballistic missile, capable of achieving significant acceleration and with a massive fuel supply. Also, it wasn't constructed as a normal ship would be, with an out and back design philosophy. It was simply a one-way device, and if it expended all fuel putting it on an outbound trajectory from Earth and could never get back, so be it. The point of the mission was to break the blockade...not what would happen thereafter.

The 'break away' point was high orbit, meaning that even if an interceptor was right on the heels of the blockade runner, the mission would end if the ship hit that particular altitude, which was too far away to worry about, well past the moon. However, if the blockade runner got a significant lead, and the computer calculated that an intercept was mathematically impossible, the challenge would immediately terminate, saving hours of needless waiting or requiring the trainees to quit the scenario, which was something that they never wanted to do on principle.

Paul had thought a long time about what Morgan had said about the trainers not really knowing what they were doing, and it'd bothered him why they had set the termination line so far away from the planet when a blockade was something up close near the surface...until he discovered the truth of the matter, something that the trainers designing the program obviously had been aware of.

An up-close blockade was a fools' errand, given the speeds involved, though that had been the 2s' aim from the get go. They'd been referencing science fiction guidance in how to go about setting up a blockade and had suffered a psychological blind spot because of it. Star Wars and others, he assumed, had taken their blockade philosophy from history and used a water navy as an example. Reasonable, from a certain point of view, but totally inadequate. A space navy, as Paul was quickly realizing, was another type of beast entirely.

For starters, ships couldn't just float above the planet...at least not anything that Star Force had available. That meant all ships had to be in orbit, which meant lateral speeds far exceeding the rotation of the planet unless you put them in geosynchronous orbit, which was about 35,000 kilometers away, or just a little shy of a tenth of the distance to the moon. So the idea of sitting ships in space above a target city to blockade it was totally absurd.

The 2s had attempted to bypass this fact by placing orbiting ships in sequence around the planet, so that one would be passing over or near the target city at all times, but one ship was hardly a blockade, and even if they had 10 or more, the 100+ kilometer high cone of atmosphere that sat between them and the target would allow a huge area in the lowest possible orbit for the blockade runner to evade them in.

Missiles were the next logic step, using the low orbiting ships as launch platforms to fire at the escaping ship, but again the math didn't work out and there was just too much area to cover, not to mention that the direction of orbit made a huge difference in missile launch. If the blockade runner took off in the opposite direction, then the latent speed of the 2s' ships would essentially make missile closure impossible, even if the blockade runner passed within a few kilometers.

That meant they'd have to have double the ships orbiting in opposite directions, if not multiple directions, considering that the blockade runner didn't have to take off in a lateral trajectory. It could rise up in a polar orbit or at any other angle. It could even eschew orbit altogether and blast off straight up and through the blockade, given the engine power it possessed.

Which was why Paul had placed four interceptors along the vertical trajectory in geosynch orbit, encouraging the blockade runner to make an orbital ascent, else they'd be waiting in the wings to chase down the ship as it passed through the middle of their widely spaced formation.

'Chasing down' was the crux of the matter, and Paul's biggest breakthrough. While a water naval blockade might be able to sit still and physically block off escape routes, a space naval blockade had to be designed to chase down a fleeing vessel before it could get too far away from the planet, and given that insight Paul had repositioned most of their assets away from extreme low orbit and into better ambush positions.

In fact, all but four of their ships had been placed above where the 2s had been placing their previous blockades, and those four ships were meant to corral the blockade runner into preferred zones of intercept rather than to keep the target on the planet. The four interceptors, none of which were being flown by any of the 2s, were skimming just above the atmosphere on orbital tracks that, if chosen by the blockade runner as an exit vector, would make use of the interceptors' latent orbital speed in addition to their significant engines to make an attempt at a quick convergence as the fleeing ship hadn't yet reached significant escape speed.

That decent chance of early success almost guaranteed that those orbital tracks would NOT be chosen, thus Paul's tactical formation could eliminate vast tracks of orbital space and concentrate their efforts on the more likely avenues of escape.

Those likely avenues were being covered by missiles ships in an orbital grid 2000 kilometers in altitude on a wide range of orbital angles. The net, by necessity, covered the entire planet, else the gradual rotation of the Earth would eventually bring any focused zone out of alignment. Paul supposed he could have cheated for this particular scenario, given that there wouldn't be time for that to occur, but he hadn't wanted a single use tactic for this challenge alone, but a comprehensive blockade plan that they could use in others, as well as gradually modify as they gained more experience with this new aspect to their training.

The missile ship net wasn't 'tight' by any stretch of the imagination, but it did create zones that that the blockade runner needed to avoid, thus further limiting its escape angles and bringing the odds of a catch for the orbiting interceptors up another notch…or potentially making a kill if the ship chose not to avoid them.

The interceptor grid was another 1000 kilometers higher, with each of the 25 ships on individual orbits, hoping that at least one of them would be in line with the escape route the blockade runner was choosing as it slowly rose up through the atmosphere. The further it got, the better the control ships could estimate its course, sending out continually updated projections to the 2s, all of whom were manning their own interceptors, along with the computer controlled ones.

Paul watched from high above, knowing that it would take some time for the blockade runner to reach him even if it came straight up, which it wasn't. It was angling into a spiraling orbital escape trajectory…one that was nearly aligned with three of the low orbiting interceptors.

Paul keyed his comlink to one interceptor in particular. "Ivan, looks like it's heading your way. Get your ass moving now or you won't get close enough."

5

"Will do, Admiral," Ivan joked, using Paul's newly bestowed nickname, as he selected a point on the projected flight path as an intercept and the computer calculated the heading and thrust necessary. He didn't have time to finesse the math and went with his best guess, realigning his heads up display trajectory marker with the flashing icons indicating the computer's continually updated navigational intercept tracker.

"Here we go," Ivan said to himself as he kicked in the four massive engines sitting aft of the pilot, fuel, and weapon pods. The solid rocket fuel engines quickly accelerated the 'hound' towards the blockade runner...or rather where it was supposed to be several minutes later, given that it was still in atmosphere at the moment.

The interceptor's fifth engine, a small plasma unit similar to those used in the starships, was silent and would be used later if needed for navigation, but it was up to the primary 'candles' to provide the thrust necessary to run down the blockade runner, which was also burning several candles of its own, one of which dropped off as it began to leave the atmosphere, reducing its weight and increasing acceleration as the discarded stage lazily drifted into a low and unstable orbit.

The flashing icons on his screen slid off to the right and Ivan quickly readjusted his heading to match, but found it difficult to keep them in his center marker. "Guys, what's up? I can't keep my heading."

"It's altering course," Jason immediately responded. "If we can't predict exactly where it's going, it's going to be a lot harder to catch."

"Anyone with even a remote chance of intercept start getting some altitude," Paul added, studying the situation from afar. "It can't drastically change its course this far out, so we have some idea of where it's heading. Put yourselves in the vicinity and hope we get lucky."

"Will do," Megan said as five other orbiting dots began to reposition. The rest of the interceptors remained motionless, not responding to the blockade runner unless it came within a pre-specified distance. Two of the computer controlled ships were pursuing, along with Ivan, but the rest were already out of the game.

"Paul, I'm going to play a hunch and reposition now," Emily said from one of the three interceptors in formation around the geosynch point.

"Go ahead, I'm going to hold off a while."

"What are you thinking?" she asked, hearing something odd in his tone.

"I think they've got a trainer flying that thing, and he's flying erratically just to screw with our computer projections."

"So much for a predictable first challenge," Emily said, not really disappointed. She, like all the trainees, enjoyed a challenge, though their expectations for this one had been lowered due to recent design flubs.

"We still have a chance," Paul reminded her. "Take your best shot."

"Alright, here goes nothing," she said, mentally plotting an intercept course, thanks to those painfully tedious navigational math classes. Once she had her first leg approximated, she activated her interceptor's four main engines at partial thrust and began moving in closer to the planet.

"Where do you want us, Paul?" Randy asked on behalf of himself and Kip, the other two geosynch pilots.

"I don't know yet. Let's wait and see when he enters his coast phase."

"What if he keeps the engines burning the whole way?" Kip asked.

"Then he'll run out of fuel before he gets to us...and he'll really get predictable."

"Alright, we'll sit tight," Randy confirmed. "Let us know when you want us to go."

That was the question, wasn't it? Paul hoped it wouldn't come to that and watched the display screen as Ivan chased after the blockade runner with both craft continuing to accelerate as they neared. The interceptor was on a slightly higher orbit, with the runner coming up from below almost as if it intended to rendezvous with the attacker, but another slight directional realignment pulled the computer generated intercept line off of Ivan's trajectory again, leaving him with little maneuvering room.

The interceptors were, by design, faster than the blockade runner, but not by much and now that the two ships were pointed in approximately the same direction, there wasn't much closure rate between the two, given that they were both accelerating at full power. With each course alteration the blockade runner made, and subsequent deviation for the interceptor, Ivan's ship had to dedicate more thrust to lateral movement, which then took away from his forward acceleration, which was currently pegged at a consistent 56m/s or 5.8 Gs.

The blockade runner, now free of its second stage, was accelerating at 4.8 Gs, given that it was a larger ship about four times the size of the interceptor, and still several hundreds of kilometers distant, gaining altitude on a spiral trajectory around the planet.

Paul watched the speed numbers for both craft, guestimating their remaining fuel loads while assuming they were at maximum thrust, for every kilogram of fuel expended the craft would lighten and the acceleration rate would tick up slightly, meaning both would be at their fastest the moment before they ran out of fuel.

He knew their specifications by heart now, especially those of the blockade runner, and he guessed it still had half its third stage fuel remaining. That meant that it would have to cut engines and coast before too long if it wanted to save some thrust for later maneuvers…then again it couldn't start conserving with Ivan so close behind. Even if he couldn't take it down, he could force the blockade runner to expend its fuel earlier than planned.

"New plan, guys," Paul said, keying for an open comlink instead of the ship to ship links he had available. "Run that bastard out of fuel making course corrections. Don't let him coast."

On Randy's tracking display the ever changing projected course of the blockade runner showed it looping twice around the planet before it got to their altitude, and thanks to their geosynch position over the launch point, that orbital spire passed just beneath their position with minimal variation.

Seeing that the second of those projected pass-bys would take place several thousand kilometers below them, Randy pointed his nose down to the planet and kicked in his engines, intent on getting there first so he could line up for a parallel intercept, given that a head on approach would be useless at the speeds the blockade runner was now attaining, in excess of 20 kilometers per second.

"You staying here for our final shot?" Kip asked as he too depressed and headed down closer to the planet.

"Yes, but if he increases his orbital angle enough he'll spiral out well above this position, so do what you can now to spook him."

"Guys, I think he's going to get past me," Ivan said as he was nearing the end of his fuel burn. "I'll try for missile lock, but I don't think I'm going to get close enough."

"Wait until the last second to keep him burning fuel," Paul recommended.

"I've got 32 seconds left," Ivan said, now able to see the blockade runner beneath him as a tiny, sunlight reflecting dot moving slowly in the distance. His rangefinder was decreasing steadily, but he was still 114 kilometers away as he primed his single, long-range missile, knowing that the shorter variety that he had slung under the stubby wing-like struts on either side of the ship would be useless at this range.

The belly-mounted, self-guided missile launched two seconds before the interceptor's engines ran dry and Ivan's forward acceleration ceased. The rangefinder immediately reversed itself and began scaling upwards in a hurry as the other ship continued its heavy acceleration.

The long, fat missile, however, had an acceleration rate far higher and began to eat up the distance between the two. The blockade runner's pilot saw it incoming and made another course correction, adding a bit more distance between the two objects and succeeded in adding a few seconds to the missile's travel time...but the precaution was unnecessary. The missile's own fuel was expended before it even reached the halfway point, though it continued to coast forward a while at superior speed until the continual thrust of the blockade runner ate that up and began pulling away from the now truly ballistic missile that sat a safe 46 kilometers behind the fleeing ship.

"Damn it," Jason swore, sitting in low orbit and helpless to do anything about the situation. The two computer controlled interceptors had already broken off, being further away from the target than Ivan had gotten. That left the four geosynch interceptors and three others rising at potential intercept angles to stop the ship, and two of those were now out of position due to recent course changes.

Brian's interceptor still had a shot, minimal as it was, because he had thrusted directly away from the planet, gaining altitude in the quickest means possible, but wasting fuel as he fought against the planet's gravity as he essentially jumped up to the blockade runner's next spiral around the planet and got there before it did.

Problem was, he didn't have the lateral speed, nor the fuel remaining to acquire it once at the target area, meaning he would be trying to hit a bullet with a water balloon as the runner would shoot past him faster than his eyes could see.

Apparently the trainer flying the ship didn't realize that, because he broke from his fuel-saving coast stage and readjusted course to miss Brian's ship by more than 10,000 kilometers.

Meanwhile, Paul continued to watch and calculate...suddenly wishing for a bunch of rocks he could throw out in the ship's path. Those wouldn't have to match speeds, essentially functioning as ballistic mines which would become more lethal the faster the target was approaching.

Hmmn...he'd have to save that idea for later. It was a messy tactic, and one that probably would require far too much debris to be useful, but the concept was interesting none the less.

Over the next hour the blockade runner's course didn't alter much, though Randy and Kip did manage to spook it somewhat, and Paul guessed it had to be running on fumes by now, but probably retaining just a bit of maneuvering capability. With that in mind, he made his best guess at an intercept and began accelerating at an angle towards the nearest intercept line.

They'd already been in the simulators for nearly two hours now, bored out of their minds with inactivity, but all hoping that they'd be able to pass this challenge and move on to the next one if Paul could in fact make the intercept, so they stayed in their simulator pods and watched it play out.

For Paul the situation was a mixture of tense and boring, reminding him of a chess game, only without the action. The closure of the two ships was a simple matter of math and basic navigation, with small corrections having to be made as the runner made some last gambit attempts to shake off Paul's convergence point, but as the final moment approached it made no further adjustments and Paul hoped that was because it was now out of fuel.

If it was, they were going to win...barely. His remaining fuel was low and the actual convergence occurred 5.6 kilometers ahead of the blockade runner. Paul applied corrective thrust, nulling out his lateral drift and dropping in on an identical outward spiral from the planet, with the momentum of the two ships essentially even until Paul began to reverse course and ever so slowly crawl his way back towards the target.

He would have preferred to travel faster, but doing so would require a deceleration burn once he reached the target...meaning more fuel expended that he didn't have. As he coasted back to the ship, his instruments showed that he had a mere 12 seconds of thrust left and he desperately hoped he wouldn't have to use it.

He was already well within missile range, but given how long it had taken them to get to this point he wanted to pad their chances by decreasing the distance even further, so much so that the outline of the ship finally became visible on his screen. It was a fat conical cylinder on the end of a stubby fuel tube, now completely devoid of the solid rocket fuel that powered both it and the interceptors' primary engines.

Now that he was within visual range, Paul activated his 5th engine, with a thin stream of plasma fanning out like a tail of muted flame behind his ship. It didn't have nearly the kick of the candles attached around the hull, but it did provide decent maneuvering power now that the blockade runner's extreme acceleration was taken out of the equation.

Paul closed half the distance to the ship, then targeted it with short range missile lock...saving the big bertha underneath in case the runner was just playing possum. A blue targeting reticule appeared around the ship, indicating a positive lock, and Paul depressed a trigger on the joystick three quick times.

Three short, fast missiles leapt off the racks and flew towards the target some 2 kilometers away, but still there was no response from the runner. Paul watched with sweaty anticipation as another monitor showed both ships and the missiles traveling in between. A few seconds later they merged with the blockade runner's silhouette and disappeared.

On the viewscreen Paul saw a brief shroud of debris form around the ship and expand outward like the petals of a flower. A moment later a mission end message and challenge stats superimposed over the screen and Paul let out a sigh of relief, leaning back in his seat and wiping a few beads of sweat off his forehead, feeling the gentle flow of the pod's air conditioning tickling his skin as he spun around and opened the hatch.

Up in the control room that oversaw the five adjacent simulator chambers, Gent climbed out of his own simulator pod and stretched as Wilson, who'd just arrived half an hour earlier after hearing of the trainees' unusual progress, stared down through the one-way window as the 2s climbed out of their pods and congratulated each other amidst their own improvised stretching routines.

"That took way too long," Gent said, cracking his back. "I thought this was supposed to be a 30 minute mission, max?"

"More like 20," Wilson said, his brow furrowing as he thought hard. "We didn't plan on them deploying so far out."

"Well it needs changed," Gent reinforced as he finished stretching and joined Wilson at the window. Several other trainers were at the control boards, preoccupied with two other challenges currently going on down past the other windows that ringed the room.

"I agree, but not for this one. We have to keep things even for all the teams."

"Wonderful," Gent said, anticipating several more hours sitting in that chair with nothing to do. "This may be important for them, but it's downright dull. I'm pretty sure they'll say the same if you ask."

"I know," Wilson agreed. "We've got our work cut out for us...but at least we've learned something today."

"What?" Gent asked.

"They just taught us how to blockade a planet," the lead trainer said with an obvious note of respect. "Now we can take that and make it more intense."

"How?"

"I've got a few ideas already, but once we bounce it around with the design team I'm confident we'll come up with something...interesting."

"After the other nine teams get through with this one, you mean?"

Wilson looked away from the window and across his shoulder at Gent. "My condolences," he offered sarcastically.

6

One month later...

Morgan sat in a simulator pod, one hand on a control board roller and the other on a joystick as she fired off medium-sized rail gun rounds at semi-distant moving targets. A hit counter glowed in red numbers in the upper right hand corner of the display screen, counting down from 500. The individual challenge would end when it hit zero and would be scored according to time, with a par of 22:35 needed for passing.

Morgan's counter currently read 167, but there was no clock to keep track of the time, so she had to shoot as fast and as often as she could, slipping into a time-distorting zone where nothing existed aside from her trigger finger and the targets. She was peripherally aware of the count, but tried not to get distracted by it or anything else, knowing that a mental lull would cost her precious seconds. She kept the sluggish targeting reticule moving constantly, predicting where the distant dots were going and firing ahead of them as they crisscrossed the screen on random headings.

Fortunately for this challenge all the target spheres, each the size of a bus, were moving along linear tracks...meaning they weren't maneuvering and their courses were predictable. The main problem with tracking the spheres was that the rail gun, a magnetically accelerated metal bullet the size of her arm, had a delay from trigger pull to impact. This meant she had to lead her targets, which were spaced at varying distances.

The larger the sphere, the closer it was, and vice versa, meaning a short delay for the big ones and a multiple second delay for the tiny ones, which were the hardest to hit. The roller underneath her left hand controlled the zoom function, with her using it constantly to pull in and out as she alternated between close and distant targets. All together, her hands were constantly busy, moving about in the jerky twitches typical of most action-oriented video games.

This 'game' though was based on a real weapons system that Star Force had quietly been field testing at one of its orbital facilities. The medium sized slugs were designed as a basic ship to ship weapon, with the smaller, more conventional 'bullets' used in a rapid fire device primarily used for short range defense. The large slugs, each the size of an Olympic bobsleigh but without the hollow core, were a heavy weapon prototype that had only undergone minimal field testing at low speeds, but enough data had been gathered to extrapolate the dynamics of the firing system and create the gunnery program for the trainees to familiarize themselves with.

Morgan hadn't gotten to the large slug challenge yet, but had already passed the light rounds, using them to shoot down incoming missiles in the simulation. The spheres that she was currently shooting at were designed to represent small ships and a single hit from one of the medium slugs at 890 m/s would be more than sufficient to core all the way through the hull and out the other side of an unarmored ship, while significantly damaging or even destroying a hardened one.

The weapon system had a fire rate of 5.4 seconds, though for this challenge she was shooting from a quad battery on sequenced firing, giving her a shot every 1.35 seconds. Still, to beat par time she had to average 2.7 seconds per kill, which kept her firing constantly with an unlimited supply of simulated ammo.

Her screen was full of moving dots but they were spaced out, some on the far left and right, but also some way up and down, meaning Morgan had to continually tilt the turret using the joystick to even be able to see all the targets. Random as their movements were, they appeared in clusters, and after the first two tries she had established a dance-like pattern to her targeting movements where she would zoom in on an area, fire off several shots ahead of where the dots were moving, then roll her view back to a wide screen view, select another dot filled area, joystick her way over to it, then zoom in again.

This left her not even able to see if her shots hit the targets or not, because by the time the simulated slugs got to the spheres she was already firing at others.

Which was why she occasionally glanced up at the hit count to make sure she wasn't missing. She had to trust in her accuracy…which was usually spot on…but given the varying distances, angles, and speeds of the spheres she had to make a mental recalculation almost every shot she took, though that wasn't altogether unlike the other marksmanship challenges she'd gone through, but these new naval gunnery simulations were the most target rich environments she'd seen to date.

Her high score on the light rounds currently had her in 8th place, though that could change as others went back and tried the challenge again, as she might if time allowed, but for the moment the best gunners weren't in the overall top 10 rankings, save for Jason who currently sat in 9th, but he wasn't a real points threat to her lead at the moment, given that Morgan's other gunnery scores traded off with his, keeping her overall lead intact.

Prior to the rail gun challenges Morgan had worked her way through the other two space weapon systems currently available to Star Force…lasers and missiles, though they too were primarily in the developmental stages. After going through all three varieties, Morgan found that she highly favored the lasers for their accuracy and range, even if they offered the least kill power. There was no visible lag from trigger pull to impact with the beams traveling at the speed of light, unlike the slow moving slugs that she was currently firing or the even slower missiles.

In fact, it was Morgan who had insisted on the 6s using laser weapons to pass their first naval team challenge less than a week ago. The 2s had passed the blockade challenge early on, but the other teams had spent two weeks trying to figure it out before the 8s finally found a way. Morgan and her 6s had been almost the last to pass, beating out the 1s by a day, and having to use an extraordinary amount of resources to do it...which incurred a heavy points penalty.

Her team had eventually come up with the tactic of saturating low orbit with thousands of small armed satellites over the target zone...which thanks to the mechanics of this challenge could be accomplished by placing them in the appropriate orbital positions at the beginning of the simulation instead of having to deploy them around the entire planet. It was a bit of a cheat, but Morgan and the others knew that passing and moving on to the next challenge was the bottom line, so they'd pulled out all the stops and threw everything they had at the endeavor.

Using missiles to track and down the blockade runner had been their first tactic, but the gaps between satellites had been too large and the speed of the fleeing ship nullified most of the missiles' usefulness unless they were pre-fired towards an estimated intercept point...which had been their second idea.

After days of repeated failure Morgan had insisted that they try long range lasers and 'sting it to death' with the low powered weapons. After working on the firing program and filling the area with as many satellites as the simulation would allow, which pegged out at 5,643, they ran through the first simulation, watching as the satellites auto-fired on the target with no manual input or flying required.

The blockade runner flew through the satellite field and escaped in short order, taking a few hits in the process. Morgan and the others ran it again and again, making alterations in the distribution pattern of the satellites and tweaking their designs until, on the 36th attempt, their defense grid succeeded in getting a lucky hit on the aft end of the cockpit that triggered a small internal explosion which destabilized the thrust and sent the blockade runner spinning about erratically...granting them a 'win' on the scenario.

Their points score was extremely low, as were those of all the teams save for the 2s, who had succeeded in snatching the overall team lead by tripling the 7s' score and besting the 6s' by a factor of 5. They had, not unexpectedly, been mum as to how they had achieved such a high score and moved on to the second team challenge, and then the third while the others struggled just to pass the first.

As of now, there were four available team naval challenges, all of which the 2s had passed, and while they waited for the trainers to release the 5th they were wisely using the spare time to go back and try to scrape up additional points on the completed challenges that allowed for multiple retries, some of which were more than a year old.

Morgan envied their success, which she had heard was due in no small part to Paul, who had been besting everyone in the individual naval challenges, save for the gunnery drills, which Morgan was using to negate some of the points bleeding. He had risen from 10th to 4th in the individual ranks in less than a month, and even as everyone else began to get accustomed to the space warfare simulations, Paul still maintained a considerable skill gap on everyone else, which was more than compensating for his lack of swimming skills.

That meant trouble for Morgan, though she still maintained a sizeable points lead, because the naval challenges would take up a significant portion of the run-up to their final stage of training, which was due to start in a couple months if their current progression held, though with the setbacks everyone but the 2s had been experiencing, that timetable might get delayed.

They were still going through a myriad of other challenges simultaneously, but if Paul's and the 2s' dominance in the naval disciplines held up, they'd run away with the team title and he might even knock her off the individual lead...which meant she had to buckle down and grab as many points as she could in his weak areas, or in this case his slightly weaker gunnery skills.

Paul's laser scores were currently lower than Morgan's by about 11% and he was currently working on the small missile challenge, which they'd dubbed as 'intercepts' for the little spitballs' ability to track and take down larger, slower moving missiles. Her score there had been average, and she didn't think he'd be able to easily beat it, but she was planning on going back to it and the others later if need be to scrape up some more points.

Right now she was ahead of him in the individual challenge cycle, progressing through simulations that he hadn't worked up to yet or had chosen not to tackle at this stage. Each of the trainees were on their own personal schedule, but Morgan had made a point out of getting ahead of the others so she could take the time if need be and double back to try and raise her old scores, much as the 2s were doing now as a team.

Then again, if she scored extremely high the first time through she wouldn't have to go back again, which was why she was hammering this particular challenge. Though there was no clock to go by, she could feel her targeting mojo flowing and tried to dive into it as much as possible. She was so focused and, to be honest, slightly numb from the constant targeting, that she didn't even realize when she'd finished and visibly shook when the targets suddenly disappeared and her stats popped into view.

It took her a good three seconds to realize what was going on, then smiled slightly when she noticed her time was 19:47...the best to date by any of the trainees, and a score that she doubted Paul would even come close to.

Morgan rubbed her eyes as she assessed her current condition. She wasn't brain fried yet, but her hands were a little numb from gripping the controls with such intensity. She pulled up her watch in front of her face so she could see in the dim light, confirming that she had time for another two runs.

Taking a slow, calming breath, Morgan reset the terminal and readied herself to jump back into the targeting frenzy. If she was going to earn top honors then she needed to stick it to Paul as much as she could, and that meant getting back into the zone before she lost the mojo so, bleary eyed or not, it was time to keep cracking.

She restarted the program and picked up from where she had left off, nailing the first dozen targets quicker than she had the previous time, she thought. There was something to be said for not taking breaks during training, because the body and mind adapted to the task at hand, whatever that may be, and right now it seemed she was adjusting into a rail gun zombie...which was exactly what she needed if she was going to improve over her last score.

Power-napping worked wonders for recovery, but it also would take one out of the zone, which was why Morgan rarely rested during the day and forced herself to stay active until the evening, while most of the others would catch a quick nap during lunch or in between sessions if they finished early. It had been painful for her at first, but she believed that it now gave her a wiry edge to her focus, emotions, and senses as well as an increased ability to delay fatigue when it arose that the other trainees lacked.

That was one insight that she had kept to herself, and no one else had appeared to take notice of her mildly atypical behavior, which was fortunate. If she wanted to be the best of the best...which she very much did...then she was going to need to use every trick in the book to stay ahead of her fellow trainees, for they were truly beasts, in every aspect of the word. Morgan didn't have a single top score in any of the subcategories, with her best being a 7th in agility drills.

No matter how proficient she got in one area, there was always a dozen or so trainees that would best her, even though she tried diligently to outwork them, though not always succeeding, but even when she did it was never enough. They were too good in their specialties for her to match, but she never completely gave up trying.

The single most important reason she was leading in the overall points race wasn't that she came into the training with a load of skills, but that she learned and adapted faster than the others. Second most important was the fact that she didn't appear to have any weak areas, unlike Paul who had swimming as his Achilles heel. Most of the others had at least a couple areas where their scores dipped significantly, but Morgan didn't, due in part to the fact that she worked hard on every new discipline until she mastered it. Passing a challenge wasn't enough for her...she felt that she had to conquer each one to the point where she became confident and comfortable in her skills.

Morgan was nearing that point now with the rail gun challenge, though to attain true confidence she needed to be able to pass the par time repeatedly and not just get by it once or twice out of sheer luck. Though she didn't know it, she did rank first in another stat...that being number of individual challenge attempts. She was running a good 30% higher than the others because no matter what was thrown out before her, she obsessively had to beat it, learn from it, and then own it.

When she eventually ran out of time for this individual challenge session, she left the simulator room bleary eyed enroute to the training parks and another team challenge in the jungle zone. By the time she got to the equipment room she'd shaken off the screen-staring haze and was ready to have at the turret-laden gauntlet run, completely focused on the challenge at hand and not the 36 seconds she'd shaved off her rail gun challenge.

Dwelling on the past was something Morgan didn't indulge in, and celebration had always seemed to fall into that category for her. She preferred to live in the moment, with an eye towards the future and the challenges that lay beyond...always in motion and never stagnant.

With paintball rifle in hand and personal shield slung over her back, Morgan and the rest of the 6s headed off down the connecting tunnel towards the jungle park and the dense foliage that easily hid the annoying turrets, setting her mind to the task of getting past them to the end of the course, scoring more points for both herself and her team.

7

Paul took a seat in one of the desk-like simulator pods, sealed the hatch behind him, and brought up individual challenge F-5C. The lighting turned dim and the wide screen in front of him displayed a large space station similar to those currently used by Star Force, but one much more compact with the rotating disc plate nearly obscured beneath blocky add-ons, most of which were covered with thick armor plates.

It was a defense station…and Paul's mission was to destroy it as efficiently as possible given unlimited resources. On a popup menu at the bottom of his screen was a choice of different ships, weapons, and fighters he could select for his attacking fleet, but he ignored them all and studied the station closely. The key, he knew, was in identifying the defensive capabilities and tailoring his forces to exploit its weaknesses.

He smiled approvingly as he noticed several upgrades to the trainers' designs. Placed on multiple corners of the blocky double-pyramid shaped structure were weapons pods…two heavy lasers coupled with a light chain gun for point defense.

A week ago Paul had passed another individual challenge in which he had to design a small station to defend against incoming missile attack, and that triple weapon pod had been part of his solution. Now it seemed the trainers were going to use his own adaptations against him. He felt a bit of sarcastic pride at having taught them so well.

He rotated the camera view around the station, identifying more weapons emplacements. The designers had gone to excessive lengths to make this a difficult target to take down, equipping it with not one, but two heavy rail guns which would knock a hole in any capital ships that Paul chose to deploy. Furthermore, the defense station had enough medium rail gun batteries and quad laser turrets peppering the hull to rack up heavy damage against any large scale attacking force.

They'd even covered against a drone attack by placing point defense light lasers and missile intercept clusters at strategic positions around the station to avoid any blind spots that the tiny, remote-controlled weapons platforms could hide in. He'd heard that some of the 3s had wreaked havoc with the little devices in the second team challenge when the trainees had been tasked to hijack an armed convoy. They'd successfully chewed away at the escort vessels with their small lasers from blind spots in the ships' firing zones, and based off this station's defensive schematic, the design team had guarded themselves against that tactic being employed again.

Paul pulled up an interior schematic of the station from available blueprints and noted the 5m thick armor plating covering vital areas. The thinnest armor he could find was just under .6m thick, covering the connective 'tissue' between the thicker plates which extended up past some of the intersections like fort ramparts. All in all, the trainers had designed a tough nut to crack this time, and Paul knew that any assault force he assembled would take heavy losses when he assaulted the station.

Fortunately he had another option, and he bypassed the preprogrammed ship designs and went to the customization screen. The program was familiar to him by now, and it didn't take him long to design a new variant of ship. He ordered up only a single unit, placed it at a considerable distance from the station, then began the challenge.

The 'Admiralty' controls, as he liked to think of them, popped on screen around the edges in addition to a selection arrow similar to those used in popular RTS video games. Using the rolling ball on his control board, he highlighted his single large warship and input a flight path directly for the station and kicked in the engines at maximum power.

The heavy ship didn't accelerate very fast, but Paul had included ample fuel reserves in the design, so he sat back and waited while it gradually picked up speed relative to the station. As it did he played with the targeting program and tried to get a lock on the station, but it was too far away for his zoom function to target, plus it was bouncing around a bit from the engine thrust.

Gradually the image enlarged and Paul guessed he could have tried for a lucky long shot with the medium rail guns he had attached to the centerline of the warship, encapsulated in an armored cone three meters thick, which was part of the reason why the ship wasn't accelerating very fast. It was heavier than any of the standard designs, but only protected on the prow, with no armor on the sides, making it a very badly designed warship...or so the trainers probably thought.

Time to teach them another lesson in the art of space warfare.

When the ship's fuel load finally burnt out the jiggling of the targeting reticule stopped as well. Paul used the ship's thrusters to make a minor course adjustment, then targeted the station with the medium rail guns and fired off the full 20-round magazine one at a time towards the station with precisely aimed shots while he was still out of weapons range.

Mathematically speaking, he knew that the ship's momentum would add to the muzzle velocity of the metallic slugs being fired, giving them more kinetic force upon impact, but also reducing the time to target and thus the amount of drift possible during transit...which meant slightly improved accuracy. After the ship's entire arsenal was depleted, Paul switched viewing angles and watched from 'above' as the rounds traveled the distance between ship and station.

Three of the rounds missed the station cleanly, four others clipped the edges and ricocheted off at odd angles while putting deep furrows in the armor plates, but the other 13 that hit squarely against the station broke through the 5 meters of armor and into the station interior, clawing out much larger holes as the metallic rounds deformed on impact. Using his 'omniscient' camera view, he studied the damage to the station, curious as to how much damage he'd inflicted.

While the holes were aesthetic eyesores and decompression hazards, the damage was minimal to the overall structure. Had there been people inside, many would have died in the affected compartments, and Paul did note that several weapons batteries had gone offline, ostensibly because their power feeds had been cut, so that was an added bonus there, but it really didn't matter.

The rail gun attack had been nothing more than an experiment of Paul's, for the more he delved into the possibilities of space naval warfare, the greater concern he had with finding a way to protect their own ships. The kinetic velocities of attack weren't limited like they were in atmosphere, and even with putting meters of armor plating over their hull, an attack such as he'd just launched would punch right through. There had to be a better way, he knew, but so far Star Force hadn't developed an armor strong enough to stand up to physics involved, nor had they developed any other effective countermeasure.

Paul did know of a countermeasure to the second part of his attack, though apparently the trainers didn't...it was the old school defense screen, that had mobile ships deployed at distance around static targets to intercept enemies before they could do things like this...

Paul smiled as his navigational prowess shown true and his racing ship slammed into the approximate center of the station traveling several kilometers per second. Its armored nose cone punched through the armored hull, then the station exploded in a shower of debris with both large chunks and small specs of dust expanding outwards erratically. Even on slow-mo replay there wasn't much to see, the collision having occurred so fast, but Paul did give the designers of the basic physics engine in the simulators credit, for the program didn't glitch up and it provided quite the view as both the station and ship disintegrated in a mathematical fireworks display.

The challenge end symbol soon appeared on the screen along with an insanely high points score, given the fact that he'd only used a single ship to utterly destroy the entire station.

Paul popped open the hatch and left the simulator pod well ahead of schedule, planning on using the extra hour plus to get in some additional training time with the 'mongoose' four wheelers prior to their team challenge the following week. As he walked through the empty room he tossed a brief salute up at the one-way window where he knew the trainers were watching, underscoring the fact that he knew just how much egg he'd thrown in their faces.

Wilson, who'd made it a habit to be in the control room every time Paul or the 2s underwent a naval challenge, shook his head in a mixture of disgust and respect. He glanced over at the other trainers and programmers in the room, making brief eye contact with each of them.

"We've got to find a way to beat that punk."

8

5 weeks later...

"Oh man," Dan said as the 2s walked into the southwestern aquatics bay and saw their fellow trainees motoring out the open door into the calm, sunlit ocean water, "5s beat us here."

"The 1s are out there too, along with a lot of challengers," the bay master said from the counter. "Looks like it's going to be a busy day. How long do you guys have?"

"Two hours on the schedule," Jason answered, "but this is the last session of the day so we can stay over as long as we want."

The bay master smiled. "I'll make sure the refuelers are fully stocked. Go put up some new high scores...the water's perfect for it."

"Will do, Hank," Jason said as he and the others hurriedly walked past the counter and onto the narrow walkway that stretched out into the shallow swimming pool that held over a hundred jet skis. Two other pools were present in the bay, on flanking sides holding larger craft, but the jet ski pool was the only one that was elevated.

A third of the personal water craft were multi-seaters, but the 2s went straight for the highly agile and fast singles with the activation keys already in the ignition. Jason hopped off the walkway and swung onto the seat of one of the 40 blue jet skis reserved for trainee use. The rest of the craft were available to the rest of the Atlantis personnel as both a means of training and recreation.

Jason's half inch thick padded wetsuit ended at the elbows and knees, doubling as a life vest and body pads. It also had a small tracking unit imbedded in the material that allowed each person in the field to be monitored by bay control, along with a panic button in the collar which, if pressed three times in succession, would call for a pickup crew with medics to be dispatched.

Security and safety precautions aside, Jason didn't bother to worry about such things. He rarely got tossed off his ride, though when he did he was more worried about getting eaten by the critters roaming the ocean than anything else. To date no one had experienced any problems in that regard, but every time he went out onto the ocean he was conscious of the fact that the Humans weren't the only ones in the water.

That wasn't on his mind at the moment as he activated his jet ski and backed away from the walkway prongs separating each of the craft. He spun about then slowly maneuvered through the various lanes until he came into the only open section of the pool directly in front of a smooth ramp leading down to the commons area where the three pools met in front of the massive bay doors.

Megan and Ivan beat him to the edge, ramping up their speed suddenly and sliding up and over the flexible ridge holding the pool's water in. They skidded over the 'dry' edge and slid down the white slip'in'slide into the ocean water below, then jetted on out of the bay.

Jason followed them over and down the extra long drop, thanks to the current low tide, and accelerated through the short tunnel connecting the bay to the exterior of the city. He emerged into the bright sunlight and blinked away the glare as he followed the others towards the rightmost of three small 'islands' in the distance while the rest of the 2s split up to go their separate ways.

Emily and Brian met up with them at the obstacle course start pad, bumping up and over the soft edge of the island and into the small raised lagoon where the control staff logged them in from an elevated control cabana on the far side. A group of 'civies,' as the trainees thought of them, were waiting for their turn while a group of staff reset the course, but they gave up their slots upon seeing the blue jet skis arrive, as was standard procedure. They looked a bit bummed to have to wait longer, but also a bit eager to see the rock stars in action.

The five civies were familiar to the 2s and were regulars out on the water, having crossed paths with the trainees on multiple occasions.

"We're getting your record today, Mathis," Jason taunted as they swapped places.

"Go for it," the off duty aquatics bay worker responded pithily as Jason slid his jet ski up onto the release ramp. "We'll beat whatever you put up."

"With this crew?" Megan teased, gesturing to the others. "Overly optimistic, I'd say."

"New blood, new opportunities," Mathis replied as the controller in the booth signaled that the course was set. "Give us something decent to shoot for, will ya?"

"Happy to," Jason said, gripping the handlebars as he looked back over his shoulder and nodded at the controller. A countdown tone sounded, and on the third electronic bleat the narrow ramps underneath the five jet skis fell out and dropped them down at an angle into the ocean, where they immediately jetted off, water spraying in their wakes.

Large display screens on the walls of the cabana showed a diagram of the course with moving dots indicating the placement of the 5 teammates, along with a clock which would be the measure of their final score. The civies watched both the screens and the water as the group of trainees split up and headed for the various inflated obstacles tethered to the distant ocean floor below.

Jason let the others veer off left and right while he continued straight on ahead towards a neon yellow ring on a breakaway cord suspended between two inflatable pylons, equally as yellow and standing five meters high above the almost perfectly calm ocean water. With the lack of waves to buffet his craft around, Jason raced towards the target at high speed, literally feeling the seconds peeling off the clock. They hadn't had a day this calm since the aquatic bonus challenges had been added six months ago, and the past week had been so turbulent that none of the trainees had been able to get out on the water.

The 2s' team challenges had been winding down, now that they were approaching the final stage of their training, and given the fact that they were way ahead on their naval challenges and had just completed the last of their vehicular ones, they'd started using their extra daily team challenge time to double up on the remaining ones, as well as go back and try for higher scores on those that allowed repeats after completion.

They also had begun spending more and more of their time going after bonus points in the voluntary challenges, such as this water course. If they finished under par time, they'd receive a small amount of bonus points, enhanced through time brackets, but even if they totally rocked the course there wasn't a lot to be gained, but they were eager to grab whatever they could to pad their points lead, especially with so few big point scoring opportunities left.

Jason slowed to half speed as he approached the inflatable gate and reached up with his right arm and grabbed the bottom of the ring, yanking it off its tether and collecting it over his shoulder as he turned hard to port and accelerated towards the next gate. Once he straightened out his line he reached back and attached the ring to a small clipped hook behind his seat, freeing his hand and arm from his bounty.

His teammates were likewise collecting rings from dozens of gates along the first segment of the course. The yellow ring Jason had collected was considered an easy grab, and therefore only 1 gate point. The red gate he was headed towards now was a medium one and had its ring suspended higher above the water…too high to reach up and grab.

It did however have a small ramp on the north side of the gate, which Jason had to swing a bit left to get in front of, then pulled a hard right turn to line himself up properly. A few hard seconds of charging later and he was to the ramp, decelerating just before he hit it so he could have a smooth jump.

He didn't slow down enough though and overshot his mark, catching the red ring on the front nose of his jet ski and pulling it off as he flew through the air and started to head nose first into the water.

Jason stood up, pressing the rear of the craft down with his legs and managed a half decent landing, but he had to brake hard and then reverse a meter or so to get the ring off the nose. It floated up on the water in front of him where he quickly picked it up, leaning way over the side as he motored by and sped off across the water.

He met up with the other 2s at a primary gate…which was actually a 'gate' gate. Two pylons, each twice as large as their smaller cousins, were connected by a solid wall of green padding blocking access to the other side. Each pylon had a hook near water level, which the 2s quickly deposited their captured rings on. Tiny chips imbedded in each ring were scanned on the hooks, determining their point value and number, and after a sufficient amount of points had been deposited the main gate raised up, allowing the 2s to cross into the second section of the course.

Here there were less yellow gates, along with a few blue ones, indicating the hardest to capture and worth 3 points each. Jason immediately roared ahead while the others fanned out again, as was their agreed upon plan to keep them slip apart and not headed towards the same targets and wasting valuable time.

The nearest gate to Jason was a red, but this one didn't have a jump. Instead, it had a mount suspended above water with a ring half imbedded into its surface. He decelerated heavily as he approached and slid his jet ski up the short ramp, hoping not to overshoot or cut it short, which would leave him sliding back down into the water.

Fortunately this time he did neither, sliding up the ramp and coming to a halt on the flat top next to the ring. He had to get off his seat and take a large step to his right to grab it, stretching out his safety cord, but otherwise he had timed the ramp perfectly. Hooking the ring on the back of his jet ski, Jason gave the watercraft a strong shove then ran and jumped back up on before it could pass all the way over the edge.

He bounced around on the seat awkwardly until it slid back into the water, then righted himself on the pommel and raced off again to collect more rings and more points for the next big gate, which required twice the points of the first to pass through.

Jason eventually arrived at the gate with four reds and a yellow, but saved one of the reds when the green padded barrier opened before all the rings had been placed on the hook, meaning they'd grabbed more than they needed, but that was ok because they could use the spares on the last gate, which required four times the points of the first.

When they moved through and fanned out again there were no yellow inflatable markers visible, only a spattering of reds and a lot of blues...

Jason snagged another red, having to maneuver through a marsh of poles that required precise movements, then headed towards one of the blue gates with its two inflatable pillars showing, but without a ring in between them.

"Here goes," Jason said to himself as he slowed to a crawl and positioned himself carefully before ramping up the engine and yanking on the handlebars to launch him into the air...where he pulled some impressive aerobatics to get the jet ski to come down nose first and penetrate the water. Both he and the craft disappeared below the surface for a few seconds, then reappeared on the other side of the gate, bursting up out of the water with a blue ring in hand.

Jason coughed some water out of his mouth and nose as he slowly turned about and got his bearings, adding the three point ring to his stash. In the distance he saw Megan fly off an angled ramp doing a corkscrew, rotating an entire 360 degrees and managing to grab the suspended blue ring just before she hit the water.

Her hand hit the ring and knocked it off, but she couldn't keep hold of it, nor the jet ski as it landed at an twisted angle. She flew off the seat, pulling the activation key out with the long bungie attached to her left wrist, and hit the water hard. Jason, still coughing up a bit of water, motored over to her position.

"You ok?" he said when he got to her several seconds later.

"Peachy," she said, grabbing the edge of his craft. "Grab my ring."

Jason dragged her through the water and over to her jet ski before circling back around and grabbing the blue ring out of the water. Before he could give it back to her, Megan zoomed off towards the next gate, intent on not wasting any more time.

Jason smiled and attached it to his stack, then raced off towards the next gate, grabbing another red ring before spinning around and making a direct line to the last giant green gate. He met up with Emily there and deposited all of his rings, then spotted a nearby blue gate that hadn't yet been plucked and went for it while the other three were still a good distance away.

It was another submersed blue ring, but Jason didn't come up with it when he emerged from the water this time.

He coughed his lungs clear and spun around, setting up for a second dive attempt when he heard Emily yell at him.

Grateful, he let the gate go and sped back over to the others as they were putting their captured rings on, meeting the required amount with a red to spare. The gate pulled up and revealed a set of navigational buoys that they raced through in a giant turn that sent them back towards the start area at full speed, thanks to the calm water.

The five of them zipped past the finish line in close formation, stopping the clock at 14:32.

"Son of a bitch," Mathis muttered, seeing his team record smashed by 54 seconds.

"They really ate up that calm water," one of the staff in the cabana noted.

One of the others in the control booth glanced over at him. "Yeah, the water. Right."

"Alright boys, there it is," Mathis said, pointing at the stopped clock. "That's what we're beating today, so get yourselves psyched. It's going to be one wild ride…"

9

When Paul left the aquatics bay with the others he headed for the middle 'island' far out away from the city, which stood like a gigantic metal mountain behind them, rising up dozens of stories above the water with a mass of tiny towers on top. The outer face was almost sheer, with just a bit of an angle going straight up, with a relatively small hole at the base that was the tunnel back into the aquatics bay.

Jack pulled up and paced beside Paul as they made the long haul out to the group of race courses facilitated by the artificial island more than a mile away, keeping between the navigational markers to avoid drifting into any of the competition zones. Everywhere around them were moving craft and thousands of inflatable markers, making for an amusement park feel to this part of the ocean surrounding Atlantis.

There were eight aquatics bays in total, but this one was reserved for Star Force personnel only, while some of the others would be made available to the public on a limited basis once the tourists started to arrive en mass. For now though, all those out on the water had legitimate business zooming about as they honed their skills for their occupations or just for the challenge of it.

When Paul and Jack got out to the island there were several dozen other jet skis and riders milling about in the raised lagoon, but this island was far larger than the one servicing the obstacle courses. There were six cabanas overseeing the race courses along with a few other buildings to service the riders given how far out they were from the city, along with gigantic display screens showing live images of racers currently out on the courses.

Paul ramped his jet ski up into the lagoon and motored through the shallow water to where some of the 1s and 5s were milling about as they watched the screens. "Anyone gone yet?"

"Sara's on course 2 right now," Zak answered, pointing to one of the screens on the left.

"How's the water running?" Jack asked.

"Smooth as silk," Aaron said. "The civies have even broke a few of our records."

"Which ones?" Paul asked as Zak and Erin moved up towards the starting blocks as some of the courses cleared.

"Yours, Jason's, and Morgan's," Aaron told him.

Paul frowned. "All of Morgan's?"

"No, just course 6."

"Who's the culprit?" Jack asked, curious.

"Some new guys, just arrived a couple weeks ago for the opening ceremonies."

"Where are they?" Paul asked, wanting to see who'd broken their records.

"Umm...I think one of them is still out here. Yeah, course 3. Looks like he's going to be close to Kerrie's mark."

"Not for long," she said, waiting in line a few meters over.

"Looks like we've got some work to do," Paul noted, looking at all of the starting blocks. Most had two or three people waiting in line, but there were a pair that stood empty.

Jack and Paul exchanged glances. "Wanna try?"

"Why not?" Jack said, trolling over to the open slots. "Consider it a warmup."

"I'll take 12," Paul said, heading over and ramping up into the starting block. He gripped the handlebars tightly and stood up a few inches over his seat, then signaled to the nearest cabana. A moment later his countdown tone started.

"Here goes…" he said, feeling the ramp fall out from under him.

As soon as he hit the water he jetted off at maximum acceleration, then took a hard right/left S-curve around some boulder-sized spherical buoys before hitting the first obstacle on the Mario Kart-like course…a small ramp set between gate markers that he had to pass through. He backed off on his speed just before contact to diminish the amount of air he'd get, for as soon as he landed he had to make a hard left turn and begin zigzagging between several dozen 'posts' sticking out of the water like street lights.

Usually Paul preferred to stick to the flat water courses and had some of the best times there, but at the moment he felt like racing instead of sitting around and waiting, so he might as well play a bit on the 'interesting' ones…which had a habit of knocking off their riders. He really didn't feel like tasting salt water again, but it was worth the risk just to get some racing in right away.

After passing through the posts, Paul approached a gauntlet of water cannons spraying laterally in a specific pattern. If he timed it right he wouldn't get hit, so he slowed down and began mentally counting. When the moment came he ramped up the jet ski's engine and darted headlong into the long stretch of water between two floating walls, seeing nothing but water jets crisscrossing in front of him.

Just before he hit the first one it cut off, right on time, and he cut back on the throttle. If he exceeded 80% then he'd outrun the gap and hit the water jets ahead of him, which he'd learned from watching Jason on previous days. Patience and precision were the key, though a lot of riders just tried to blast their way through, with about 2/3rds of those getting knocked off in the process.

Paul came through cleanly then hit another small ramp at the exit, coming down at a bad angle and bouncing him off his seat, but he held on and quickly righted himself as he entered a stretch of flat water racing that reminded him of going through the double corners of Indy...in video games anyway. He'd never actually driven on the gigantic motor speedway.

Cutting close to the buoys, Paul ran through that section of the course as quickly as possible, enjoying the waveless water and knowing he was making excellent time as he came to a section of 'moguls' and hit the tiny ramps at half speed, bouncing up and down in sequence to avoid bubble-like inflatables blocking the clear water in between. This also caused him to have to weave left and right, for the ramps weren't set in a single line, and hitting them from an angle made the jet ski wobble a bit on landing, from which he'd have to execute another quick turn in the opposite direction.

Paul lost half his speed in the process, but maintained a semblance of rhythm and got through the washboard-like moguls without tipping over...which was no small victory. He proceeded to go through three more small obstacles then another flat water section leading up to the final jump on the course, and the biggest of them all, which was the primary reason no one had been waiting in line.

Paul caught his breath on the flat water and lined up his approach, which was easy without the waves buffeting him around. He accelerated up to 75% speed and hit the 5m high ramp dead on, launching him way up into the air, giving him a clear view over the top of the cabanas and down into the lagoon just off to his left.

Paul stood up on the jet ski and braced for the impact, using his body to reposition the craft beneath him as flat as possible, but it still hit a bit nose down, cutting into the water and dragging him under. He ducked his face down into the side of his arm just before the wall of water washed over him and he disappeared beneath the ocean's surface.

With his eyes closed and his head disoriented, he used the hand controls and accelerated forward underneath the water, pushing his legs down and with them the back of the jet ski which began to rise nose up towards the surface.

Paul popped out of the water, gaining a bit of airtime in the process, then splashed back down, banging his butt on the seat as he coughed out some water that had, as usual, gone straight up his nose. He shook more water out of his hair and eyes and spied the finish line just ahead of him, so he ramped up the engine again and jetted forward, only able to half see where he was going. When he crossed the finish line's motion sensor a loud tone sounded, along with a triumphant musical blast that he recognized as the audible signal of a new course record.

Paul spit out the last of the salt water from his mouth and slowly moved back over to the lagoon, gently ramping back up and over the lip that separated the elevated pond from the rest of the ocean and motored back over to the clump of trainees that now included a couple of the 8s who had just arrived.

"I can't believe you just beat the nut cracker!" Sara yelled at him as he pulled up, using the name for the course given to it by some of the male staffers who worked the control cabanas.

"That was me?" he asked, half thinking that the sound had been for one of the other courses. He hadn't expected to be anywhere close to the leaders.

Sara pointed up at the scoreboard, listing the top 25 times for each of the courses. Paul's name now held the top spot, a good 4 seconds better than the previous record, held by Morgan no less.

"Wow," he said, realizing what he'd just done. "That calm water works wonders."

"Morgan's going to be pissed," Rafa said, laughing slightly. "I don't think the 6s are going to get out here today."

"Really?" Paul said sarcastically, with a smirk forming on his face. "That's a shame," he said as a jet flew by overhead.

Air traffic wasn't uncommon over Atlantis, with planes coming and going at all hours of the day now that the final construction had been finished, but this jet was lower than normal and not a transport...it was military.

"That's an F-35," Sara pointed out as it circled around the city. Another identical one was visible in the distance, also circling. "What's it doing here?"

"Guarding that," Paul said, pointing up into the sky as a large jet was making a landing approach to Atlantis...with two more of the fighters flying in escort formation around it. "I'm pretty sure that's Air Force One."

"Guess the big wigs are starting to arrive for the grand opening," Rafa noted as the American President's plane disappeared over the mountainous edge of the city. "I hear Davis is hosting one hell of a party."

"With heads of state?" Sara asked indignantly. "Bet that'll be *loads* of fun."

"I was referring to the festival," Rafa clarified. "It's supposed to last more than a month and draw in over 2 million tourists."

"As long as they stay out of our way," Paul said, looking at the waiting lines. He wanted to get back out on the water as soon as possible.

"You don't need to worry about that," Sara told him. "Our sectors in the city are fully secured. We're ghosts here as far as the public is concerned."

"Hope it stays that way," Rafa said, wheeling his jet ski around. "I don't want to share the water with a bunch of bratty kids on vacation."

"Speaking of which," Paul said, seeing course 4's line drop down to 1 person. "Let's make sure we get our records back from the civies before the day's over. We might not get this good of weather again for months."

"I already got one back," Sara boasted, moving off towards the lines with Paul. "Looks like they've still got four others."

Paul looked up at the score board and frowned. Sara now had the record on his best course.

"You know, I *am* going to have to take that one back from you..."

"Feel free to try," she challenged with a smile, darting ahead of him towards the waiting lines.

10

Four days later...

"I'd like to welcome all of you to this pre-festivities summit," Davis said congenially as he looked out at the national leaders and representatives filling the medium-sized amphitheatre set beneath a dome of semi-transparent glass in one of Atlantis's many towers, "and I apologize for the lack of media access, but given the matters I will be disclosing, I felt it best that we keep things behind closed doors until you have a chance to consider all of your options."

A subtle murmur swept through the crowd. Davis had extended invites to thousands of celebrities, making the next day's opening ceremonies the social hot spot for the planet, with many more unsolicited requests for VIP status flowing in over the past 12 months in addition to the hundreds of thousands of tourists already present in the city, with many times that scheduled to fly in over the next week.

A second, more subtle invite had been extended to each nation on the planet, along with a summons to the heads of the prominent corporate entities that typically did business with Star Force, stating that he would be making an announcement concerning matters of national security and the future colonization of space. Follow up requests for more detail had been denied, reemphasizing the need for each invitee to be represented in person. Given that level of secrecy, and the profitability that Star Force afforded the planet, none of the invitations had been declined and many heads of state who were here for the opening ceremonies were also in attendance.

"It has always been Star Force's mission to facilitate the colonization of space. To make it affordable, productive, efficient, reliable, and above all else...viable. A few decades ago, many people considered space exploration to be a waste of time and a capital black hole. I believe we've allayed those fears by now, but in truth we've barely scratched the surface of potential colonization. Today, with the opening of Atlantis to the public, I'm proud to announce that Star Force is taking the next step forward."

Using a number of large, wall-mounted viewscreens placed above and behind him, Davis brought up a series of schematics and images of spacecraft and space stations.

"To date, Star Force has allowed your countries and corporations access to leases of portions or entire space stations, as well as transit contracts for both personnel and cargo using our fleet of dropships and starships. I believe most of you have found the arrangement to be mutually profitable, especially the smaller nations and companies who could otherwise not have fielded any space infrastructure on their own. I don't believe it is an exaggeration on my part to say that Star Force has succeeded in granting virtually everyone access to the orbital economy."

A soft, but widespread round of applause followed his statement, and he paused a moment to let it die out.

"Many of you, however, have requested more autonomy for your space programs, wishing to purchase craft and stations for your exclusive use. We have, categorically, denied such requests, insisting that if you wished to pursue that endeavor you would have to build such infrastructure and transportation yourselves. A few other startup space enterprises have offered you limited services in that department, but the truth is they are not sufficient to the task, nor are any of you capable of producing both the numbers and quality of equipment that Star Force currently fields."

"There are two announcements that I have to make today. The first of which is the privilege of informing you that Star Force has grown to sufficient size that we now have adequate orbital construction capability to build our own equipment along with servicing external orders."

Davis pointed up at the images behind him.

"These models we are now making available for purchase. They will be built on demand and delivered to a location of your choosing for your exclusive use. Star Force will not require any oversight or control of said ships and stations. They will be yours upon purchase, to use as you see fit."

A much louder round of applause broke out, following by a standing cheer from all those assembled. This move by Star Force had been long overdue, so they attested, and had been lobbied for heavily. That lobbying had met a solid wall, angering many who resented Star Force's resistance to corruption and the usual back door deals/arm twisting that planetary politics was plagued with.

Davis waved off the applause so he could continue. "Orders will be met as resources are available, and I imagine a backlog will develop quickly. I've designated one of our primary shipyards to handle your orders, so I promise you won't have to wait an inordinate amount of time. Also, as we continue to expand our orbital infrastructure more shipyards will be coming online to handle the increased demand. We project our construction capabilities to triple over the next five years, which is why we're now opening up our manufacturing division to outside orders. Until now, there was simply no way we could have kept up with the demand."

"Now, as to who's orders get filled first...that's up to the construction schedule, though we will give some level of priority to first time orders so that you can establish an orbital foothold as soon as possible. Meanwhile, our leasing program will continue as it has been. If you wish to continue with that route of colonization, the choice is yours. Star Force maintains that we will provide you with options...the path you choose is your own to decide."

"As you can see, there are several models of dropships, starships, and stations available. These have all been field tested to the extreme, with the new models of Star Force equipment not on the list as we work out the kinks on our own time. From now and into the indefinite future, all equipment offered up for sale will be established designs. Experimentals we will keep to ourselves, along with the risk inherent in them. All production models will have operational history and safety assessments attached to the brochure for you to review."

"We urge you to take your time in choosing the proper craft for your needs, for while the costs are reasonable, they are definitely not cheap, and you will undoubtedly want to maximize your expenditures. We will assist you with planning if you inquire. We are, after all, interested in the successful colonization of space, and helping you helps us accomplish our mandate."

Davis paused as he let all that sink in...then he blanked the viewscreens.

"The second announcement I have to make is the more important. Many of you may not like what I am about to say, and if that is the case I apologize, but it is not up for discussion. It is often said that those who do not study history are doomed to repeat it, and in studying the history of colonization on our planet it is evident that your countries cannot be trusted."

He let that hang in the air for a moment, then continued.

"Back when Columbus first discovered the Americas there was an extraordinary amount of potential in exploring and colonizing the new lands. In fact, many of the nations present here today are a result of that discovery...but the way in which events took place in the following centuries was abhorrent. The possibilities afforded to your nations were squandered through petty bickering, a lack of cooperation, and numerous misdeeds."

"Wars were fought out of greed and the ambitions of evil men. This history is not one that we can allow to repeat itself. One would like to think that Humanity has progressed since that era...but present day events seem to suggest otherwise. You look now at the condition of certain regions of this planet and you will see how unenlightened that you are. Many of you cannot be trusted...others simply do not know what to do, and out of ignorance make many mistakes, some of which turn out to be fatal."

"Then again, some of you offer a glimmer of hope. With our assistance you have accomplished significant feats, and we intend to further those relationships. To the rest, I have a warning to give you. Star Force will not tolerate your misdeeds transitioning into space. We do not, in any way, condone what is happening and has happened on the surface of Earth, but we will be judging you by your actions above it."

"Any nation, corporation, or individual violating Star Force's standard code of conduct...which we are now expanding well beyond the document that currently outlines your expected behavior onboard our installations...will be hence forth barred from any form of commerce with Star Force for a duration of our choosing, but two primary points I will tell you now. If any of you instigate warfare in space, you will be banned from Star Force services for a minimum of 10 years. If any of you should attack Star Force property or personnel, you will suffer a PERMANENT ban...and no governmental restructuring will circumvent it."

"Let me make this crystal clear," Davis said in a growl, almost berating the assembled representatives. "We will not tolerate bad behavior of any kind, and we will hold you accountable for it. Some of you may not take me at my word and be forced to learn through example...so be it. I am serious about this, as is the rest of Star Force. If we allow even a sliver of the problems on the surface of Earth to rise above the atmosphere, we will be killing our future."

"It is your responsibility," he said, pointing out at the leaders, "to solve the problems on our planet...Star Force will take care of space. And no, we do not need a UN resolution to sanction that position. We are the dominant force in the orbital economy. You all know it...you may not like it, but you recognize that fact, and today Star Force is asserting its latent authority to circumvent a potential powder keg on the horizon."

"Before I get to that, let me reemphasize a point. Star Force unequivocally stands by the premise that all nations should have access to space travel. We will never use our influence to suppress one of you, regardless of whether you choose to do business with us or not. If you wish to go it alone and develop all your own craft, we welcome the company so long as you behave yourselves. What I am about to do is not an ego move by Star Force...it is a move designed to ensure global access to space colonization for all concerned. We are the arbiters...not the rulers."

Davis hit a button on his podium and a large picture of Luna appeared behind him.

"To date, three nations have outposts on the Moon. The United States, China, and Russia. Star Force hereby recognizes the prior claims to these locations," he said, highlighting the three spots on the rotating picture, "while we hereby lay claim to these territories."

The three tiny red hexagons on top of the outposts were suddenly engulfed in a mass of green covering 2/3rds of the planetoid.

An uproar from the representatives followed...as expected...and Davis waited it out, staring down at the politicians and corporate execs but saying nothing. A few minutes later their protests died out and returned to their seats as Davis continued to stare them down, but they were still on the brink of another outburst.

"That's better," he continued calmly. "You will note the remaining third of the planet we are not laying claim to. As I've said, Star Force has no intention to rule space, merely to lead the way and arbitrate between the rest of you. These regions," he said, highlighting them blue, "will be divvied up between the nations of this planet over the next thirty years...but you will have to prove yourselves worthy. You get nothing simply for existing, as many of you will probably argue later. Our decision is final, and this is how things are going to play out."

"If you wish to establish and operate a colony on the Moon independent of Star Force, so be it, but in order to lay claim to territory there, you must get there on your own. We will provide you with a specialized beacon, approximately the size of a car, that you will be required to transport from the Earth's surface to the surface of the Moon intact...using no Star Force technology."

The crowd couldn't contain its fury anymore and another outburst followed, but it was quickly stifled by the Russian delegation, who vocally berated the others demanding silence...with about half of them submitting. The rest remained vocal for a few moments longer, then eventually settled down after Davis hit a noise pulse button on his dais. The resulting screech/siren blanked out all conversation for a couple of seconds.

"Please proceed," one of the Russian representatives said as he glared at the other delegates.

Davis nodded his thanks. "You will have exactly 10 years from today to successfully deliver and activate the beacon on the surface of the Moon, which must be accomplished by hand, meaning you have to send a manned mission and not just a delivery probe. All those nations, or conglomerates, accomplishing this task prior to the deadline will be included in the division of one third of the available territories, after which a second 10 year period will begin. Any nations added into the mix during this period will take part in the second allotment, followed by a third and final opportunity, at the conclusion of which the last remaining Lunar territories will be assigned."

"Now, those of you who do not wish to attempt an independent Lunar landing but still wish to establish a foothold on the Moon will be able to do so within Star Force's territory...under lease, similar to the system we are currently using for our space stations. Furthermore, any nation attaining possession of their own Lunar territory can supplement that with leases as well. This is not an either/or proposition. You can proceed as you choose...we are merely affording you options."

The US President stood up while casually waving a hand to get Davis's attention, then yelled loud enough to be heard from his position near the back row of seats. "Am I correct in assuming that our Lunar base already qualifies us for this first draw, along with Russia and China?"

"You are correct," Davis confirmed. "You have already sent a man to the moon, and because you have done so prior to Star Force's arrival, the territory you already have inhabited will be recognized as yours in *addition* to the first allotment."

"What about our Martian colony? I'm assuming that at some point you'll be wanting to divide that planet up as well."

"You currently do not have a colony on Mars," Davis reminded him, "but your landing there will most likely be accredited when we get to that point. Currently, Star Force has no interest or intention of traveling to Mars until we get our infrastructure in the immediate area of space established, though you can expect a similar allotment procedure to be employed down the road."

"How dare you!" one of the execs bellowed from the front row, seated just below where Davis was standing. "Star

Force hasn't landed on Mars or the Moon! Yet you want to dictate to us what we can and can't do there. You have no rights whatsoever to order us around!"

"But we can choose who to do business with, Mr. Arcardo," Davis said, looking down at the head of one of Star Force's 'major' competitors in the field of space tech. "And anyone who wants to fight us on this will no longer have access to our services."

"That's blackmail!"

"Sit down!" the American Secretary of Defense said from behind. Arcardo turned around indignant, then reluctantly bowed to the wishes of his number one customer. "I see now why you didn't want the media present," he added to soften the now tense tone of the summit.

"I don't expect all of you to like this arrangement," Davis acknowledged, "but after you leave this room and think the logistics through, you will find that it is a mutually beneficial arrangement...unless you prefer starting World War III to decide who has claim and who doesn't."

"That should be up to the UN!" someone else shouted.

Davis fervently shook his head. "You are the UN, and you could never come to an agreement...and even if you did, it would not be a fair one. Star Force holds all nations as equals, with equal access to our technology and an equal chance to gain Lunar territory. You won't find a better deal...nor are we giving you a choice."

"As for Mr. Arcardo's claims that Star Force has never been to the Moon or Mars, I would like to point out that we are currently constructing a starport in orbit around the Moon to facilitate the transfer of cargo and personnel to the surface. Once completed, it will link to our Earth orbiting starports via a number of dedicated starship ferries, expanding the conduit to space into a larger transportation network."

"Once constructed, the Lunar starport will connect to the surface via specially designed dropships, due to the planetoid's reduced gravity and lack of atmosphere. They will shuttle down the supplies and crews necessary to establish a proper spaceport, from which we will begin spreading out across our territories, prepping them for lease."

"As for Mars...a number of our starships are capable of traveling there and back if we so wished, but at this point we see no value in it. We will go when we are ready to extend our transit network there, not before. But make no mistake, we can plant a flag there easier than any of you can."

Davis turned his attention back to the group as a whole. "Over the coming weeks, you will see this city swell with a population ready and eager to reach out towards the stars. Consider wisely how best to proceed, both for yourselves, your nations, and for the collective good of this planet...and in the end, I believe you will come to realize that this is the only realistic way we can move forward."

"Take your time, consider your options, enjoy the festivities...you have ten years before the first allotment, so there's no rush."

He deactivated the territorial map behind him, with several realtime images of the sunlit city coming up as screensavers as he brought the briefing to a close.

"And of course," Davis added a bit tongue in cheek, "welcome to Atlantis."

www.aerkijyr.com

Made in the USA
Middletown, DE
17 January 2020